A NO1

ROUGH AND ROWDY

rough

AND

rowdy

Harper ~

Are you ready
to get Rowdy?

Jaime

HAYLEY FAIMAN

Rough & Rowdy
Copyright © 2016 by Hayley Faiman

ISBN-13: 978-1523662395
ISBN-10: 1523662395

Editor: RC Martin, Another Pair
Cover: Cassy Roop, Pink Ink Designs
Formatting: Champagne Formats

Tanisha Elizabeth — Nisha— Auntie Sheehsa — Boo Bear —
My sister from another mister —
My first really bad boy had to be dedicated to you. I hope you enjoy.
Thank you for the years of friendship. Thanks for always being there.
Thanks for always being goofy with me.
That's Yo Man. Save yourself.
And about a million other inside jokes.

Every man has a wild beast within him.
-Frederick the Great

chapter one

Kentlee

I sigh out a frustrated puff of air as I stand in front of the boutique. I don't want to go inside. I know what lies ahead, and none of it is good for me. It isn't good for my sanity, my self-confidence—and it certainly won't be good later tonight when I will, undoubtedly, be crying into a pint of chocolate fudge brownie *FroYo*.

Nevertheless, it is something I have to do. For Brentlee, my one and only sister. My *little* sister. Four years younger than me, only nineteen years old, and she's getting married. I feel like the spinster-sister standing next to her, even though I am only twenty-three.

I suck in a breath and open the heavy boutique door—plastering on my sweetest smile. I notice immediately that all of the witches are present and accounted for.

"You're late," my mother scolds as soon as I walk inside. Well, I have *one* foot inside.

"We've been waiting around *forever*. Brentlee insisted we wait for *you*," Missy, my sister's best friend and future sister-in-law, points out. She crosses her arms over her chest.

"I was working," I offer with a smile that looks somewhat apologetic. Though, I'm not in the slightest.

They knew I had to work today. I am lucky to even be off this early. I had to beg for my early release from the menial job I hold.

I am a receptionist and gofer at a local real estate office. I am always given the assignments that nobody else wants—showing rentals. They are appointments that provide income for the company, but no commission for the agents. Therefore, I show them for my regular hourly wage, at night and on weekends.

"*Work*? You need a man." My mother waves her hand in the air, and inwardly I roll my eyes.

"I'm never going to work. It's pointless. I want a husband who can take care of me the way I deserve," Missy pipes up.

My mother pats her thigh with a smile.

If Missy were to meet a man to treat her the way she deserved, she'd be living in a box down by the river.

My mother married my father, *a doctor*, and quit her job the next day. Then she produced my brother, approximately nine months later, me, four years after that, and then my sister, four years after *that* — securing her role as the doting stay-at-home mother and wife.

By the time we were all in school, I don't think my father could function without her taking care of *everything*—including *him.* He never mentioned her working outside of the home again. My sister and I were expected to do the same, and marry a man to take care of us. My brother is already in his residency to become a doctor—just like our dad.

Truth be told, I wouldn't mind being a stay-at-home mother, if the opportunity presented itself; but I'm not going to date dollar signs just to accomplish that dream. I want to meet someone, *fall in love*, and then get married.

Too bad I am too much of a homebody to ever actually *meet* anybody. My previous two relationships were failures— *in a huge way.* I am still licking my wounds from the last one. I closed myself off from most of the dating world after him.

"Jason and I just broke up, mom," I whine.

She shakes her head. "That was months ago, and he was a loser. You need to see if Scotty has any cousins for you," she says with a wink. I scrunch my nose.

"Our family is chalk full of successful businessmen. Honestly, I don't know if you're any of their type," Missy sneers.

My mother pretends not to hear her.

Scotty is my sister's fiancé, and he makes me gag. At first glance, he is just *too* perfect—his hair, his smile, his manners, and the fact that he is preparing to take the *BAR* exam to become an attorney.

In reality, Scotty only *seems* perfect. He lingers too long when he gives me a hug, he stares at my breasts, and he's always – *always* – putting Brentlee down in such a way that she'll strive to be even better than she was before. He has given me the creeps from day one. He's manipulative and, frankly, a tool.

Scotty is also nine years older than her; not that the age thing bothers me. It's just that Brentlee is young and beautiful and should be having fun instead of settling for such a giant douche. Brentlee, to me, is perfection personified. Together, they *look* like perfect robots, designed in a lab or something. It just feels all wrong. *Always has.*

"Dress number one." Brentee's voice floats through the boutique and we all turn around to watch her come through the fitting room with a wedding gown on her slim lithe body.

"It's so gorgeous," everybody gushes.

I have to admit, it is very pretty. Long lace sleeves, a sweetheart bodice with lace coming up into a high collar. It is A-line and very Princess Kate like. It is perfect and demur—nothing like my flashy sister.

"Kentlee, what do you think?" she asks looking up through her long, chocolate brown lashes.

Brentlee and I are night and day in the looks department. Brentlee has long dark hair. She's tall and thin, her skin almost olive in complexion, and she has chocolaty brown eyes. She looks so much like our dad, with his Italian roots.

I, however, am short and curvy with ass and tits that I think are just *too much.* Unfortunately, I can't lay off of the *FroYo* to save myself, so the ass and tits are probably forever going to stay. I keep my hair long, past my elbows, and am naturally blonde, like our mom, with pale skin. My eyes are a deep blue, almost black.

Most people don't even believe we are related, let alone sisters.

"I think you look really elegant, Brent. It's beautiful," I admit.

I am telling the truth, but she could wear a trash bag and still look gorgeous. I wish that she would sex it up. She always dresses super sexy, and I don't think her wedding day should be any different. But it isn't my place to say anything—so I don't.

"This is it. Scotty is just going to love it," she gushes.

My mother and Missy gush as well. I smile politely and wait until I can leave. I don't gush; it isn't in me. The gushing is *too* much. I am totally not that jumping-up-and-down-with-excitement kind of girl.

"Okay, Kent, don't forget—*Saturday* is the bachelorette pre-party. Just a little bridesmaid's get together, dancing and cocktails. We'll start planning the bachelor and bachelorette parties. Then we can talk about my bridal shower. *Squee*."

She actually says the word *squee*. I try so hard to keep from rolling my eyes.

I deserve a fucking medal right now.

"Saturday night, yeah. I'll be there," I nod, tapping it into my phone's calendar. Though, I'm not quite sure why. It isn't like I really have much of a social life these days.

"Try not to look homeless, *please*," Missy snaps.

I pray to Jesus to give me patience before I slap the shit out of this little bitch.

"Cool," Brentlee grins, ignoring her asshole of a friend. I smile back at her.

Once she changes out of the white gown, she comes right for me and starts to speak in a low tone.

"You're really okay not being my Maid-of-Honor?" she asks me for the fifteenth time.

Truthfully, Brentlee *had* surprised me when she *broke the news* that I wasn't to be her Maid-of-Honor, and that it would be Scotty's sister, instead. It had hurt my feelings that she didn't want me right next to her, helping to plan her showers and parties. I understand it, though. Missy is not only her best friend, but her future sister-in-law, too.

Brentlee and I used to be best friends. Somewhere around high school, she blossomed into one of the popular girls and had a whole gaggle of girlfriends, whereas I stayed more of a loner. I dated and I had friends, but I was definitely never in the *it* crowd. Brentlee was their damn leader, even as a freshman. Scotty's sister had been her sidekick from the age of fourteen, so I wasn't really shocked that she wanted her to take the coveted title of Maid-of-Honor. It stung, nonetheless.

"You've been friends with Missy since you were fourteen years old, and you're marrying her brother. It's cool, Brent," I say, plastering on my fake smile. She smiles back—genuinely, I'm sure.

After an hour of wedding talk and harping from my mother, I am finally free. I almost skip down the street toward my car, I am so excited. But I am dressed in my work clothes, a black pencil skirt and satin camisole with five inch, black high heels, so I decide against it.

I hear a rumble from a distance. Then, suddenly, it feels as though a million bumble bees are surrounding me. I let out a gasp, my eyes widen, and my step falters as I watch the group of motorcycles pull up next to my sporty little black, convertible Camaro.

My Camaro is the reason I work weekends for a real estate company, as well as several evenings a week, showing rentals to perspective clients of my boss. He hates showing rentals and I want to be able to afford a cute convertible. It works out for both of us in the end.

"Nice ride." A deep baritone voice rumbles next to me as I try to open the door quickly and slide into my car without being noticed.

"Thanks," I mutter, looking up and simultaneously losing my breath.

The man behind the sexy voice is... *well*... the sexiest man I have ever seen. He is tall. His arms are crossed over his chest, and the sheer size of his biceps makes me whimper. They are the biggest I have ever come across—*in real life.*

My eyes travel down to his middle and I almost purr. He has a firm, thick torso, with jeans that hang low on his hips. And his thighs? *Tree trunks.* He is big everywhere I can see; and probably everywhere I can't see, too.

The sexy stranger clears his throat, and when I look up into his handsome face, mine turns bright red. He caught me ogling him, and a shit-eating grin curls his mouth. He has messy dirty blonde hair and light gray eyes—his jaw strong and chiseled. I know by the smirk on his lips that he thinks he's every bit as sexy as I do.

Cocky bastard.

"What's your name, sugar," he whispers, deep and husky. I shiver and his lips quirk even more.

"Kentlee," I say as I slide into the driver seat of my car.

I try to close the door but his hand shoots out to stop me. He quickly crouches down between the door and my seat. He is almost eye level to me, he is so long.

"Pretty name for a pretty girl," he grins. Then his hand comes out again, wrapping around the back of my neck.

"Why don't you come down to the clubhouse and party with me tonight, babe?"

I blink at him.

I know what he is.

He is a *Notorious Devil.*

They are legends around our town.

7

HAYLEY FAIMAN

The local outlaws.

Parents tell stories to their children to scare them away from the group, and rumors about them always run rampant in adult circles—about their women *and* about their parties.

No way in hell am I going to be some innocent girl, lured into the lion's den, so they can pull a train on me.

I have read and heard enough about them, and other MC's, to know the things they do.

No way. Not this girl.

"I don't think that would be a good idea," I say quietly, trying not to rile him up.

Just last week, three of the members were arrested in a bar brawl. Billy Smith, a guy I know from school, went to the hospital.

Granted, Billy is a giant dick and he most likely deserved it—but still.

"Why not, sugar?" he asks.

The hand behind my neck starts to massage me lightly. I almost moan at the contact. His strong fingers digging into my neck, combined with the smell of grease, oil, and *man* is sending me over the edge.

I haven't had sex in almost a year, and I am horny as hell as it is.

"I'm not… I'm just not the kind of girl that should be at one of those parties," I murmur, trying so hard not to offend him as I simultaneously try not to wrap my thighs around him and beg him to fuck me, right here—*right now.*

"What kind of girls are at our parties, babe?" he asks.

I can sense an edge to his tone forming. My wide eyes lock with his and I tell him the truth.

"I'm a good girl. I don't smoke, I don't drink much, and I

8

don't sleep around… like ever," I confess, my cheeks turning bright red and heated.

"Could tell you weren't a bad bitch, honey. Still, you look smokin' in that sexy secretary getup and I want to see more," he grins.

Panties. Fucking. Melted.

I open my mouth to answer him, though I don't know what I am going to tell him, when another man steps up behind him and halts my voice. He is huge—round belly, long hair in a braid—and he is glaring at me with what I can only guess is hatred.

What I ever did to him, I do not know.

"Prez, we gotta get movin'," the burly man growls.

I shrink back a bit at his tone. The man's hand around my neck squeezes gently before he releases me, ignoring the angry giant behind him.

"You want to come on out, you just come on out, sugar. You'll be perfectly safe with me. Just tell the man at the door that *Fury* sent you, okay?"

I nod, even though I know there is no way in hell I am going to this man's clubhouse.

I have seen most of the men around town, but this guy, he's new—*different.* He looks to be around ten years older than me, but I have never seen him before.

Our town is fairly small and you tend to run into people. I even spot a few guys from high school standing by their bikes, part of the club now. But this man, he is a complete stranger.

Once he turns to talk to the big man behind him, I hurry and skedaddle the heck outta there. I have *FroYo* to eat, and I need to freak out—*alone*—in my little one-bedroom rental house.

When I am in inside my home, I lock the door and grab my coveted ice cream. Sitting down on the sofa, I realize I'm in complete shock. I look around the room as I shovel the chocolate into my mouth, trying to forget about what happened just minutes ago.

Long gone are the memories of my sister's bridal dress shopping moment. My brain is now flooded with the strange and sexy biker.

Holy shit, he was hot.

I wish that I had some slut in me, because I want nothing more than to end the dry spell I am currently in and walk on the wild side of life.

I figure a man like Fury would know exactly what to do with what God gave him.

I imagine he would throw me against the wall and just take what he wants. I shiver from the thought. Jason didn't know a clit from a nipple, and he fumbled and bumbled through every single sexual experience we had together.

If that wasn't bad enough, he was a habitual cheater. How he found so many other women to screw, I don't know. The man was horrible. At least, I hope he was horrible. He was my only experience, and if it's that way with every man, I am going to become a spinster, cat lady for sure.

chapter two

Fury

I wanted to throttle Buck. I had that sweet girl in the palm of my hand. She was hot as fuck in her little skirt and high heels, too. *Sweet looking.* I don't come across sweet too often in my life. I want sweet.

I'm tired of all the whores.

I am determined, after the takeover of this club, to find a sweet piece to sink myself into night after night. Probably won't ever claim her or anyone else as my Old Lady, but it'd be nice to have some sweet pussy on the side when club life becomes too much. As the new President, I'm sure it often will.

"You gotta look somewhere else, brother," Torch says, throwing his cigarette on the ground.

"What?" I bark, already irritated.

We are going to scout out an empty space for a new titty bar down the street. I brought the voting brothers along to look at the space at the end of the downtown strip. Torch is my Sergeant-at-Arms— my weapons and security officer.

"Kentlee Johnson. That bitch's cunt is locked up tighter than Fort Knox, brother," he says with a laugh. I am seconds from beating the fuck out of him, but I stop myself.

He knows the girl.

"How do you know her?" I ask.

"Went to high school with her, man. Graduated with me. Trust me, we all tried to get in those panties back in the day. She was so quiet though, she gave *no one* a chance. Dated one guy for about a year and I don't even think he got tit." Torch chuckles then he leans in close. "Her little sister, *Brentlee*—now that's a bitch that'll spread for you, man." Torch wags his eyebrows and I consider punching him again, just because he's an idiot.

"Let's meet with this real estate asshole," I bark before I start walking toward the empty building at the end of the street.

The men will follow.

They will always follow.

The second they watched me slit their president's throat for being a traitorous bastard, I knew they would fall in line. I never planned on becoming the president of a charter. I was happy being in the original charter, where my dad is the President; where I could fuck around and never really commit to anything in general. That was until we found out money was missing and morale was shit at this club.

My dad sent me down here to figure it out, because he knew I wouldn't stop until I found out the fucking truth. I did, and I took care of the problem; but something else happened. I discovered I like it here. I like most of the guys, and they respect me.

I'm not just the President's snot nosed kid here. At thirty-five, I'm older than most, and they fuckin' look up to me. So a year ago, I cleaned the shit hole up and I stayed.

"Tommy Walker," the man standing at the storefront introduces himself. He's in a cheap suit with a slimy grin on his face.

"Fury," I grunt. He just keeps on smiling.

"Rent's reasonable. Bar is in good shape. Stage would be good for live music," he prattles on as we walk inside. I chuckle.

"No live music, man. Live *girls.* Titty bar," I explain, watching him smile widely.

"Old bitties in this town won't like that, but can't say it wouldn't be nice to have a place to go after hours," he confesses.

I nod, as if his opinion means dick to me.

It doesn't.

My brothers walk around, checking shit out. I trust them, and they would be straight with me if the place sucked. I don't think it does, though. I have a feeling this is going to be a great, little, *legit* money maker. The boys all nod, one by one, giving me their final vote. I turn to Tommy and pull him to the side.

"We'll take it. Ten-year lease with an option to buy after five years," I offer. I then watch as dollar signs practically appear in his greedy eyes.

"Sounds great. I'll have the paperwork drawn up and leave it with my secretary Monday morning. Come in anytime at all and sign it," he explains eagerly, shaking my hand.

I signal to my brothers and we leave, riding to the club-house.

It isn't anything fancy—a big brick building with a metal building off to the side. We live in the back of the brick structure. The front is a bar, complete with a few pool tables and room for dancing. I walk straight behind the bar and grab a cold beer before making my way toward my private room.

The rooms aren't much, just enough space for a small bed, dresser, and nightstand. I am the only one with my own private bath; the other guys have to share communal showers and toilets. It is the one luxury afforded the president, and for that I am fuckin' grateful.

I never was any good at sharing, and I like my shit clean and orderly. My mother, what I remember of her, was OCD. Our house fucking sparkled. I never could live in filth.

"Hey, baby, need some company?" Kitty asks, leaning against my bedroom door.

Kitty is cute—in a trailer trash, rode hard, put away wet kinda way. I know she's young, but you can't tell by looking at her. Her face is caked with makeup, making her look older; and her hair is fuckin' fried from dieting and bleaching. Her body is solid, with a big fake rack, but she gives good head, spreading whatever part of her body I tell her to.

I start to tell her to go ahead inside, but an image flashes in my mind. *Kentlee*. With her pretty, natural, long blonde hair, and her luscious curves, I can't imagine fucking the bag of bones in front of me anymore. But I need relief.

"You can blow me right here, Kit," I order. I roll my eyes when she greedily drops to her knees.

I imagine its Kentlee on her knees for me. *How fuckin'*

14

sick am I?

Kitty pulls my cock out and strokes me until I go from semi-hard to fully erect. She licks the head of my dick and then takes me fully into her mouth. She's an expert. *Too* good for my taste.

I like a girl to be a bit intimidated, nervous, and even a little shy. It is a turn on to know the girl I'm fuckin' isn't a damn pro. Kitty is a club-whore; she's seen more cock in her young years than a urologist.

I grab onto her straw-like hair and fuck that mouth of hers until I come down her throat. Kitty looks up at me, her eyes rounded in feigned innocence as she smiles coyly. I watch while she licks her lips. It might be hot, if she weren't such a fuckin' train wreck.

"What about me?" she asks when I step around her and unlock my door, ready for her to leave.

"What about you?" I arch a brow. I know what she wants, but she isn't getting it—at least not from me.

"Aren't you going to return the favor? At least make me come?" she pouts. I shake my head.

"Don't recall it being my job to *service you,* Kitty," I grunt.

Her face forms a look of surprise before I go inside of my room and slam my door closed — locking it behind me.

I need to finish my beer and take a fuckin' nap.

I need to think about how I am going to get sweet little Kentlee in my bed, on her knees, and addicted to me, so that I can have her whenever I want.

I'm the kind of man that always gets what he wants, and what I want is all that sweet innocence Kentlee Johnson could provide.

A sweet place to slide my cock inside, and forget the

roughness of this world I live in.

Kentlee

I stay inside my house all day Sunday. By Monday morning, I am no less on edge than I had been after running into Fury.

What kind of name is *Fury,* anyway?

Maybe I do need to get out more.

I dress for work in a pair of light gray skinny slacks and a white, button down top, pairing it with my black high heels. I keep the top up on my car, even though it's a gorgeous morning, so that my hair doesn't look like I walked out of a *White Snake* video after my drive to the office.

"I have a client coming in later to sign these. Make sure you give him a copy, too, once he's signed. I'll be out of the office all day, since I had to do your job on Saturday," Tommy Walker — my boss — announces.

I watch him step outside and turn right toward the parking lot. Not even in the office for thirty minutes before he's gone for, most likely, the entire day.

"He's just bitter because he never gets laid," Marcy, one of the real estate agents, giggles.

I situate myself and gather the contract Tommy left for me, setting it to the side.

"I don't want to know about all that," I cringe, powering on my computer.

"His wife and I are friends. I know the truth, girlfriend," she sings. I just shake my head.

Tommy is attractive, for a man in his mid-forties, and his

wife is beautiful. They have three small children though, born back-to-back. I know the poor woman has to be exhausted, especially since Tommy stays late at the office every single night of the week... *working*.

I'm not sure what he actually does, and I suspect he's having an affair, but I stay out of his business. He pays me, and until I see something concrete, my lips are sealed.

I know what it feels like to be the one being cheated on, and I wouldn't wish it for anybody. I also know that if you don't have concrete evidence — the victim wouldn't ever believe it. I didn't believe it, not when Brentlee informed me that Jason was a douche and I should leave him. I didn't believe anything until I saw it for myself. He was in a bar down the street from my office when he was supposed to be home helping his sick mother with his little sister. *I believed him because I was a trusting fool.*

I roll my eyes and chastise myself for even thinking of Jason. I didn't love him, but the betrayal still stung, even months later. I hear the bell ring above the door. I close my *Facebook* newsfeed on my computer before I lift my eyes to greet the new customer.

Then my face pales and my breath hitches.

"Well, if it isn't little Kentlee Johnson," the rough voice drawls. I stare up at him in shock and awe.

I watch him walk toward me, like a dieting woman watches a waitress walk toward her with a mile-high chocolate cake. *Hungry.*

No, *Hangry.*

Starved.

"How... how did you find me?" I stammer. He grins before he winks.

"I'm here to sign some papers. You, *sugar*, are just a happy coincidence," he chuckles. I grab the papers Tommy left me, scanning them for a name.

"You're Pierce Duhart?" I ask in surprise. He nods.

"Don't tell anyone my real name," he grunts, taking the papers from me as he begins to read through them.

"Why? Would it ruin your street cred?" I ask innocently.

He pauses, looks at me, and laughs. A full on belly laugh. It's so deep, sexy, and beautiful. I stare at him, my mouth slightly agape.

"Somethin' like that, darlin'." He smiles as he continues to read through the document before he signs it.

"All done. Anything else?" he asks. I smile back, taking the papers from him.

"I just need to make a copy. I'll be right back," I stand and hurry over to the copier, feeding the papers through and trying to gather my breath.

I try to compose myself before I take them back to him; but it's difficult when the roughest, most handsome man you have ever seen is looking right at you, totally focused on you and nothing else.

"You didn't show Saturday," he almost whispers as his hand wraps around mine.

I am trying to give him his papers, but he is suddenly pulling me toward him. In the blink of an eye, his other hand is wrapped around my lower back and my breasts are pressed against his chest—his rock-hard chest.

It is a sneak attack, and I am completely dazed and confused by his moves. I'm also so turned on that I'm half tempted to tackle him *right here — right now*.

"I… I was busy?" I say.

It comes out as more of a question than a response, totally ruining my excuse.

"You were scared shitless, babe," he murmurs, his gray eyes dancing. *So sexy.*

"Well… *yeah*," I admit.

He smiles even wider as he dips his head down. For a second, I think he's going to kiss me, but his lips go to my ear instead, lightly brushing against my skin and sending chills throughout my body.

"I want you, Kentlee," he whispers in my ear.

I practically melt *right then and there*. He lets me go, takes the papers, turns, and walks out without looking back.

I stay rooted to my spot, dazed and *freaking* confused all over again, watching his perfect, sculpted ass walk through the front door. I stare at the path he made, my lips in an O shape, surprised, turned on, and completely shocked by what had just happened.

"He was hot as hell. What's going on with you two?" Marcy asks from her office.

"He wants me," I whisper in awe.

"He'll eat you alive, baby," she laughs, leaving me discombobulated.

I try to work throughout the day, but I can't concentrate. I can only think about his hand on my lower back, and the way he felt pressed up to me. The phone rings and I don't make a move to answer it. Luckily, Tommy isn't in the office and Marcy takes up my slack. My mind is only on Fury.

How he makes me feel.

How I want more.

How I shouldn't.

How I don't care.

On my way home, I continue thinking about him. His words echo in my head — *I want you, Kentlee* —they play on a constant loop. I have never had a man tell me that he wants me, not like Fury did. It makes me want him even more.

It makes me want to go to him and beg him to take me, to use me, if only even for a night. I have never been that kind of girl, but I want to be for Fury—just once.

The rest of the week is rather boring. *It is like every other week.* I show a few apartments and a few houses at night, and by the time Saturday evening rolls around, the last thing I want to do is go with Brentlee and her besties to a club.

In all honesty, all I want to do is crawl beneath my sheets and pass out. I want to dream about Fury, about his whispered words, and pretend they are real. I haven't seen him again, so it must have been bullshit; but damn, it felt nice to feel wanted.

Once I've taken a shower and am starting to get ready, there is a knock on my door. I am surprised to see Brentlee *and her friends* standing on my porch. They look like quadruplets. Their hair is all long, brown, and straight. Their makeup is caked on, to make them appear older, and their barely-there mini dresses are all *red*.

I must have missed the memo on the matching outfits.

I open the door widely so they can all walk inside, allowing the bitch crew into my tiny house—even Missy.

"Don't tell me you forgot?" Brentlee asks, gliding past me.

"No. I just got out of the shower. I'll be ready in ten minutes," I murmur. Missy, gasps.

"Ten minutes? How can you get ready in ten minutes?" she asks, gaping at me.

"I'm quick," I shrug.

"You're going to go out with us looking homeless, aren't you? I knew it, Brent. I fucking told you," she screeches.

I have to dig my fingernails into the palms of my hands in order to keep my cool and not punch her in her anorexic face. Instead, I turn on the music channel for the girls to listen to while I change. Brentlee follows me and starts rifling through my closet.

"I knew you'd have nothing suitable," she murmurs, almost to herself, as I loosely curl my blonde hair.

"I was going to wear the black dress," I announce, finishing my hair.

"You should wear this one," Brentlee says, shoving a wad of material at me. I don't recognize it at all. I take the flimsy material in my hand and hold it up before gasping.

The fabric is a stretchy, clingy, royal blue, and it looks like it's short enough to be a top. It is in no way, whatsoever, meant to be a dress. It also appears to be backless, and the front sweetheart neckline looks suspiciously flimsy. The whole damn dress is nothing more than stretchy spandex, and it's almost see-through. I shake my head once, but Brentlee just holds her hand up, effectively silencing me.

"Do it for me, *please*? The other girls all wanted to wear red, but I know you hate red. This was a compromise. Come on, it'll be fun," she pouts. I sigh before pulling on the skin tight dress.

The only person I would ever stuff myself into a *too tight, way too clingy dress for*, is my sister. I instantly hate it. I feel like I can see every single bump and bulge I have going on, and then there's the simple fact that I cannot even wear a bra.

I'm twenty-three, so the girls aren't sagging *too* low yet, but they're large and they're real, so they sag a little. I like the lift and support a bra gives me, and I feel uncomfortable setting my girls free in public.

"I love it. You look so awesome, Kent. I wish I had your ass," she giggles. I turn around to look at my barely covered booty.

I can't believe I am going out in public this *uncovered*. I am by no means a prude when it comes to dressing, but I don't like to show too much, either. I don't want the creepy attention it can bring.

"Let's just get this over with," I grumble, snatching up my purse and slipping into my sliver high heels.

I should have taken my own car, I think to myself as we drive to the only club in town.

The girls beside me are singing and dancing to what has to be the most obnoxious pop music on earth. I love music, but this is total trash. I actually think my ears might start to bleed by the time we get to the club. It isn't really a club like in the big city; it's a bar that has music pumped in through the speakers from the bartender's iPod.

I walk in and go straight to the bar. I need a cocktail and I need it fast. The bartender's name is Anthony, and I've known him since we were six years old. We went through school together, so when he winks at me as he hands me my vodka and sprite—I cringe.

Anthony is nice, but when you watch somebody go through childhood and into adulthood, it can make seeing them as anything other than a friend *awkward*.

"Beautiful as always, Kentlee. Your sister's getting married, huh?" he asks, nodding his head toward Brentlee. She is doing a shot with Missy and swaying her hips in her teeny, tiny little dress. *I'm sure Scotty has no idea she's wearing it.*

"Uh, yeah. How did she get liquor? She isn't twenty-one," I point out. Anthony shrugs.

"Brent is special, you know that. Besides, she's going to be a married woman. She can let loose a bit," he says. I narrow my eyes at him suspiciously.

Before I can ask him why Brent is so *special,* I feel a hot hand squeeze my ass. I spin around and come face-to-face with a stranger. He's around my age, taller than me, but not by much, and he's so drunk, he can hardly stand.

"Fuck, you got a fat ass, baby. How about you come into the bathroom and show it to me?" he slurs. My eyes widen.

"How about you get the fuck outta here, asshole?" the gravelly voice I have been dreaming about demands.

Standing just to the right of *Mr. Handsy* is Fury, and now I understand how he got his little nickname. He seems bigger than he had a few days ago. His chest is puffed out a bit, and his knuckles are clenched and turning white. His jaw is also tight, and I notice he has some serious scruff going on.

It's hot as hell.

Hotter than I ever imagined. I didn't think he could even *get* hotter. His face, it's bright red with anger and he looks like he's about to explode.

"What's it to you, man? She's standing here, that big ass hangin' out, what am I supposed to do?" the drunk ass asks, wobbling a bit.

Before I even realize what's happening, *Mr. Handsy* falls flat on his back. I look down at him and then back up at Fury, whose face has gone from bright red, to deep red with anger.

"You hit him," I announce. Fury nods once, his eyes flying from the asshole to mine. "Thank you," I murmur.

I'm afraid to look away from his gray eyes of steel. He

blinks once before his lip twitches. His hand shoots out, *lightning fast*, pulling me into his chest.

"What in the fuck are you doing in here, and wearing *this*?" he groans as his fingers dig into my lower back, just above my ass. His touch makes me shiver.

"My sister's pre-bachelorette party. She forced me in the dress," I say, barely above a whisper, my eyes unable to disconnect from his.

Fury's eyes have captivated me—along with his short bearded jaw. Just the thought of that scruff anywhere near me sends jolt of awareness throughout my body.

I want him.

I want that scruff to scratch my skin.

I watch as he turns his head to look toward my sister and her friends for a beat before his eyes come back to me. I halfway expect him to let go of me and stalk after the quadruplets, because they are all taller, skinnier, and younger than me—not to mention fucking *perfect.*

"Good *god,* one of those little girls is getting married?" he murmurs. I laugh softly.

"The tallest. She's my sister. Nineteen," I explain. He nods once before his nose skims my jaw, and then his lips travel to my ear.

"Ditch the bitches and hang out with me and my boys tonight," he whispers, his warm breath fanning over my ear. I gulp.

I look over at my sister's table. They don't even realize I'm not there. They're giggling and laughing, throwing back shots. I know she invited me just to keep me in the loop. We really don't have anything in common.

I love her, but she's immersed in her wedding and all

things Scotty. There isn't much room for me right now; and Fury, he makes me *feel*. I shouldn't want to be around him. I know he'll most likely use me and lose me, but something inside is screaming to give those steel eyes and those kissable lips a shot.

"Yeah, okay," I mutter. His lips tip into a small smile as he takes a step back, his hand still wrapped around my lower back.

I turn to look at my sister's table and shrug when her eyes widen at the sight of Fury's arm wrapped around me. She grins like a crazy woman, giving me a thumbs up. I roll my eyes at her. Of course she would understand me ditching the group for a guy. It's something she's done a million times. When she was young with her first boyfriend, and then countless times with nameless boys after him.

I should care that I'm ditching my sister, but I don't.

Fury's presence makes me feel things I've never felt before. I'm too curious about him to care about much else right now. He's dangerous and older and sexy as shit.

I want to throw caution to the wind and follow my desire.

I want to turn off my brain and just go.

chapter three

Kentlee

Fury walks me to the back of the bar. I notice his entire group from the other day is there, along with a few new guys and some girls dressed scarily like I am — in barely there dresses.

Fury doesn't say anything as he leads me to an empty chair and sits down, pulling me onto his lap. I feel awkward and try to keep most of my weight off of his thick thigh. But after a moment, he pulls me even farther down his leg. With my hip nestled with his crotch, he wraps his hand around my waist, holding me still.

"I'm too heavy," I murmur. He smiles before squeezing my side.

"You're fuckin' perfect, Kentlee," he grunts, nipping my

earlobe.

I start to relax in his hold.

Fuckin' perfect.

No one has ever said that to me before, and I like it.

"Hey, Kentlee. Your sister really getting married?" a guy I remember from school asks me.

I can't remember his name because we weren't in the same social circle. He was a popular boy, though. I remember that much—hung out with Brentlee's friends.

"Yeah, in six months," I say with a smile.

"Huh. Never would have thought she'd settle down," he says with a shrug. He then turns to a woman wearing what appears to be a bralette as a top with a miniskirt.

"You ready to settle down like your sister?" Fury asks as his thumb makes firm circles on my hip.

"I'd actually have to date to settle down," I practically snort. He chuckles behind me, his hot breath fanning over my sensitive skin.

"I bet guys are constantly falling all over you," he whispers, placing a gentle kiss on my neck. His scruff gently brushes my skin and I love it.

"No, they're not," I murmur.

"Let me take you home tonight. Show you exactly how I feel about you," he murmurs against my neck. His lips trail down my neck, then my shoulder.

I should say no. I really, *really* should. I have never had a one-night stand, and I never thought I would — in my life… but Fury makes me want to be *bad*. He's sexy and he wants me. He's told me, and now he's showing me.

No man has ever acted this way toward me before—touchy and feely, kissing in front of his guys—and it is beyond flattering. I shouldn't be flattered. Odds are, it's just a game, a way to get in my panties—but I want it and I want him.

I want to be bad, just once. I want to *feel* desired by a man. I try to talk myself out of allowing him to take me home for about a second. I don't know him. He's part of a dangerous motorcycle club.

He's bad, so very bad.

Yet, I want him, all of him — anyway I can have him.

"Yeah," I shakily agree.

Fury doesn't waste a second before he's standing and giving chin lifts to all of his friends. A few of them wink, and the couple boys I knew from school look at him in complete shock as we walk together toward the door.

I catch my sister's eye on our way out, and I watch her sway and smile toward me with a thumbs up. She's drunk and obviously happy I'm getting laid.

Once we're outside, Fury walks over to a motorcycle and throws one of his strong, thick thighs over the seat, straddling it. I stare at the motorcycle in horror. How the hell am I going to ride on the back of this thing in my skin tight dress and high heels?

Uh-nuh. No way — no how.

"You okay, babe?" he asks, his eyes narrowing on me.

"No. I can't ride on this thing. And don't we need helmets?" I ask as he smiles.

"No helmet laws in Idaho. Hop on. Put your feet on the pegs and hold the fuck on, sugar," he smiles.

I decide right then and there, I'll do anything he wants if he'll smile.

It's *that* beautiful.

I do as I'm instructed, trying to keep my ass from falling

out of my dress while placing my feet on the pegs of the bike. Then I give him directions to my house before we take off down the road.

I know I am clinging to his muscled waist as if I'm going to fly off at any second, but I can't help myself. It's scary as hell being wrapped around him in the open air.

It's also exhilarating and exciting.

His stomach has hard ridges—muscle packed onto muscle—and my thighs clench around him in anticipation of seeing all of that bare.

Too soon, we are pulling into my little driveway next to my Camaro. I quickly scramble off of his motorcycle and try to pull down my dress.

"You have fun?" he asks, quirking a brow.

"I did." I smile widely as he wraps his hand around my waist, pulling me toward his still seated body.

"You felt good back there, baby girl," he murmurs, his face serious and his eyes focused on me.

The nickname sends something warm through me, settling in my belly. I turn bright red and smile, unsure of what to say.

"Come on inside," I finally say softly.

He nods before swinging his long, thick leg over his bike, following behind me.

"Cute little place you got here, babe," he remarks, closing the door and then flipping the lock.

"I've never done this before," I blurt out. He blinks once before studying me.

"Have sex?" he asks, cocking his head to the side.

"No, I mean I've had sex. But never with someone I hardly know—only in a relationship. And it was only one guy, and

I'm pretty sure he was really bad, because I never liked it," I admit, unable to stop my blabbering.

Fury doesn't say anything. Instead, he takes two steps toward me, crowding me, and then his hands slide to my neck as his lips descend down onto mine. They are soft, warm, and firm all at the same time. After a second, I begin to melt into him.

When his tongue slides between the seam of my lips, I moan, opening my mouth for him as I move my hands to his chest, grabbing onto the soft cotton of his shirt.

Not wasting a moment, Fury glides one of his hands down to cup my ass as his tongue plunges deep inside of me. I moan again as I rub my aching breasts against his chest. I know he has to be able to feel my hard nipples, but I don't care. I need relief. I need *him*.

I have never *needed* like I do right now.

Fury moans and moves his hand to wrap around the back of my thigh as he rips his lips from mine.

"Fucking hell," he says in disbelief.

"Please," I whisper, my lips swollen from his kiss and my body aching to be touched, to feel relief.

Fury looks down on me and it is as if something snaps inside of him.

Wordlessly, his hands wrap around my thighs and he picks me up — *Picks. Me. Up.*

I gasp in surprise, too shocked to tell him to stop or to put me down. My eyes don't leave his. All I see is hunger in them, *pure hunger*. I shiver as my hand wraps around his neck for stability.

"Bedroom," he grunts. I point toward the closed door in the back of the house.

Fury walks toward my bedroom, kicking the door closed with his boot, and then he sits me down on the edge of the bed before taking one step back from me.

I bite the corner of my lip nervously. Fury's thumb pulls my lip away from my teeth and traces it with the pad of his finger.

"This mouth is fucking heaven, Kent," he murmurs, his eyes solely focused on my lips. "Want your mouth on my cock, baby. That gonna be a problem for you?"

My eyes widen at his words and I look up into his face.

"I... I... I've never..." I stutter, letting the words trail off.

"Then we wait until you trust me." He shrugs and I stare at him in shock.

I can't believe he isn't trying to talk me into it. Lord knows Jason tried enough, but I just couldn't do it. It didn't feel right. Somehow, I think with Fury, it wouldn't be so scary. Maybe he'd take care of me and he'd be patient.

"Want you, Kentlee, but I ain't gonna scare you. Let me show you how good we'll be together," he rasps slowly, crouching down before finally resting on his knees.

I nod.

I'm unable to speak as his hands rest on the insides of my knees, gently pulling my legs apart. I jump when I feel his short beard tickle my thigh as his lips touch my skin.

I sigh when his shoulders dip and spread my legs even farther apart. I moan when one of his hands presses against my belly and pushes me down. I feel his hot breath against the lace at my core, and then I gasp when his mouth is there. He sucks on me through my panties.

"Fuckin' perfect," he groans before wrenching my panties to the side, sliding his tongue through my pussy.

31

"Fury," I gasp, closing my eyes tightly.

"Sweet. So fuckin' sweet, *sugar*," he grunts. I whimper at his slurred words—he sounds drunk.

I feel his warm tongue circle my clit before he flicks it and pulls it between his lips. *Phenomenal.* He flicks my clit one more time before he slides his tongue inside of me, nuzzling my clit with his nose.

The scratchiness of his beard against my sensitive skin makes my legs quiver.

Nothing has ever *felt* this good before.

Nobody has ever *made* me feel this good before.

I arch my back, pushing myself closer to him, needing more, wanting more, so close to my release.

"I want you coming on my cock the first time," he announces, pulling away from my aching core.

I open my eyes and watch him slowly remove his leather vest thing, placing it on my reading chair in the corner. I widen my eyes as he takes two guns out of his shoulder-holsters, placing them on my nightstand, along with a huge knife. The man is packing some serious weaponry. I open my mouth to say something about it, but all thoughts leave my brain as he sheds his clothes, leaving them in a pile on the floor.

I groan at the sight of him.

I was right.

He's big *everywhere*.

His chest is wide and his biceps are easily the size of my thick thighs. The part of him that has me shaking, though, is his cock — *holy shit*. He's long and thick and *long*.

My eyes snap up to his and he smirks, having caught me eyeing his dick. He's obviously proud — as he should be. He's got Jason beat by inches.

"Take that dress off," he orders.

I quickly sit up, sliding the dress up and over my head before throwing it somewhere behind me, happy to obey at this exact moment.

"Panties and shoes, too," he chuckles.

I kick my heels off before rising to my knees on the bed and shimmy out of my now *wet,* lacy panties. I've never moved so fast in all of my life. I can't wait to feel his body pressed against mine, and to have that giant cock of his moving inside of me.

I think I'm *dick drunk* at the sight of all that is *Fury.*

"Fuckin' hell, woman," he hisses before closing the distance between us.

I feel his warm hand wrap around my waist. *He makes me feel small next to him, and I love it.*

"Fury," I breathe, unable to say anything else.

"Gonna take this sweet cunt, baby. Gonna make you scream for my cock. Gonna make you addicted to me," he promises. His head dips down, and he captures one of my hard nipples between his lips.

Fury sucks my breast deep into his mouth. My hands fly to his hair, pulling him closer to my body as I arch my back toward him, loving the rough way he's handling me as he lies me down on the bed.

I cry out when I feel his hard length slam inside of me. It burns as he stretches me, filling me, taking me.

"Fuck, so tight," he groans from above me, his hands shifting from beside my head to tangle in my hair — pulling it tightly in his grip.

"More," I plead.

My pleading word is like waving red in front of a rag-

33

ing bull. Fury slowly glides out of me completely before he slams back inside. His hands in my hair are pulling my head back so far, my neck is arched toward him and my breasts are smashed against his strong chest.

I'm completely paralyzed—frozen by his weight pressing against me.

I love the way he has control. I should be scared, but I'm not. It feels too good, and I feel too safe in his arms to be anything but turned on.

"Cunt's so good, sugar," he moans as he continues to roughly piston his cock in and out of me.

He's rough and rowdy.

The pain and pleasure are amplified with each thrust of his strong hips, bringing me higher and higher toward my climax.

"Please, Fury, *please*," I beg as my body climbs, so close to my release.

"Soon," he growls as he slides to his knees, one of his hands leaving my hair to wrap tightly around my hip. "Baby, love watching those fat tits bounce," he mumbles, his eyes focused on my breasts as they sway with each plunge of his cock.

I gasp when he pulls completely out of me and flips me onto my stomach. I try to move to my hands and knees, but Fury's hand wraps around the back of my neck and pins me to the bed. His other hand wraps around my hip, pulling my bottom half in the air. His hand slides around my hip, and I feel his fingers press against my clit before he slams back inside of me from behind.

I close my eyes in sweet relief, knowing that soon, *soon … I'll explode.*

His hold on my neck is firm, pinning me into place as I accept everything he's giving me. It's the first time I have ever been pinned down, held down, and roughly fucked.

My pussy throbs from his relentless thrusts.

I hear his soft grunts from behind me and feel his fingers pressing against my clit. I inhale and accept —*everything.*

I have never felt so desired or so beautiful in my entire life.

My breath hitches before I involuntarily scream, my climax rushing through me like a freight train. I come long and I come hard, light bursting behind my eyes, my body shaking beneath him.

A second later, I hear Fury roar above me, and his cock twitches. I feel spurts of his release fill my body.

"Never want out of this cunt," Fury murmurs as he continues to lazily slide in and out of my body.

I feel his chest press against my back, his lips nuzzling and kissing the crook of my neck.

"Fury," I groan once he stops moving.

He stays planted inside of me, on top of my body.

"Babe," he responds.

"You didn't use anything," I mention, suddenly realizing that this could be bad.

This could be really bad.

My heart starts to race and I feel sweat beading up on my skin. I have no clue how many women this guy's been with, never mind the fact that he could have gotten me *pregnant.*

"You're clean. I'm clean. Never want to fuck you anyway but bareback," he grunts into my neck.

I try to move, but his big body still has me pinned to the mattress. I feel his hand slide from my clit to wrap around my waist as his other hand goes from around the back of my neck to fist in my hair. I gasp when he pulls my head back and turns it slightly, his eyes narrowing on me.

"The fuck?" he asks, looking pissed.

I fight everything inside of me not to melt at the beauty of his gray eyes and his gorgeous face, so close to mine.

"Get off of me," I grind out between clenched teeth.

"Not leavin' this cunt anytime soon, babe," he announces. I feel my face heat.

"I'm not on anything, you asshole," I snip.

Fury is looking at me like a beautiful, pissed off, god of a man. A beautiful, pissed off, god of a man that has no damn right to be pissed off – *at all*. He finally chooses to pull out of me and stands up. I roll over onto my back, grabbing my sheet and pulling it over my naked breasts.

"Then you'll get that pill they're always talking about, and then you'll get on *the* pill," he announces as he plants his fists on his hips.

I stare at him, jaw agape. *This asshole cannot be fucking serious with me right now.*

"I don't believe in the morning after pill," I say. He grunts before he responds.

"What's *not* to believe? You take it and it takes care of *it*," he mutters.

"You need to leave," I say quietly.

"The fuck?" he asks, looking genuinely confused.

If I wasn't so pissed, I might laugh at the look on his handsome face.

"You fucked me with no protection, and then you expect me to compromise my morals, because you fucked up? *Get out of my house*," I say, a bit firmer.

"Crazy bitch," he bites out, sliding his jeans up his hips.

"I'm not the one fucking girls with no protection, *asshole*," I grind out as I stand and walk over to his stupid leather vest thing.

I take it in my hand and shove it against his chest as soon as he slides his shirt over his head.

"Should have stayed with the club whores instead of trying to deal with a civilian, princess cunt," he grumbles.

I watch as he finishes getting dressed.

"Yeah, maybe you should be fucking whores—bitches who don't give a shit about silly little things like protection."

I've had it.

He takes a step toward me and tangles his fingers in my hair, wrenching my head back, arching my neck, and forcing my eyes to meet his.

"You're a crazy fuckin' bitch, you know that?" he mutters, his eyes focused on mine.

"I must be if I let you inside me," I retort childishly.

"Still want to fuck you, though," he murmurs as his lips crash down onto mine.

I struggle against him for a moment, but then succumb to his kiss. I refuse to open my mouth for him, though. He slides his tongue over my lips, but I resist — hardest resistance of my damn life.

"Get out or I'll call the police," I whisper once he breaks away from me. I have to give the warning. If I don't, if he doesn't leave, I'll lie back down and spread my legs for him again.

"*You're a Crazy fucking cunt*," he growls. He walks away from me, slamming my front door behind him.

I listen for his motorcycle's rumble before I sink to the floor of my room, in nothing but the sheet wrapped around my body.

I cry.

I am such an idiot. Such a fool. I slept with a stranger, a complete stranger. I talked myself into some kind of illusion that he was good, that he was safe. In reality, he was a fucking asshole, like every other man.

I didn't matter to him. Not really. Just my body. Why would I matter to him, anyway? I'm just some stupid girl who spread her legs as soon as he pointed those gorgeous gray eyes her way. He could have whoever he wanted, and for a night, he wanted me. He'll probably never think of me again, and I'll do nothing but regret the one time I decided to throw caution to the wind.

I am such a naïve idiot.

I cry myself to sleep on the floor, and that is where I stay until Monday morning rolls around.

The following week goes by in a haze. I half expect to have Fury barrel through my office or my home. But he doesn't. By the end of the week, I've given up on ever seeing him again. He got what he wanted and he didn't want anymore.

Just like Jason.

It's me. I'm not worth keeping around.

chapter four

Kentlee

It's been two weeks since I made Fury leave my home. I haven't heard a word from him. Every single time the front door opens at work, I look up, holding my breath in hopes that it's him.

Why do I still want him?

What is wrong with me that I want this rough man?

I want his lips on mine, and I want to hear his dirty words whispered in my ear. I want him to pin me down, immobilize me, and fuck me until i scream. *I'm so screwed up.*

"What's up with you, girl?" Marcy asks one day after coming back from her lunch.

"Nothing," I murmur as I pretend to be busy.

"You've been sulking for two weeks. Tell me," she urges. I

shake my head and plaster on a fake smile.

"I'm good, I swear," I say brightly.

"You're a shit liar," she chuckles, walking away from me.

I pick up my phone and contemplate calling Brentlee to tell her about my man troubles. It would be nice to have someone to talk to.

Marcy is friendly, but I don't know her well enough to know if she'd keep quiet or blab my problems around town.

I sigh and turn back to my work.

I need some girlfriends.

Fury

Another bottle of Jack and another blow job from Kitty.

My days are melting together.

I still want the little blonde secretary. I still want Kentlee. I close my eyes, relishing in the spinning feeling I have going on, and think about her.

It's been three weeks since I've laid eyes on her. Three weeks since I've been inside of her. Yet, my memory of her isn't fading, no matter how much I drink, or how many times Kitty sucks my cock dry. It's always Kentlee in my thoughts. Always Kentlee's face I see before I pass out. Just her.

How this bitch got under my skin after one fuck, I have no goddamned clue. The only think I know is that I want her under my body again, soon. I pass out thinking about how her skin tasted, wanting her again.

The next morning, I wake in a shitty mood, like I have every morning for the past three weeks.

"What's wrong with you, you surly bastard?" Dirty Johnny asks me with a frown.

"Nothin'," I grumble, pouring myself a cup of coffee. It probably tastes like fuckin' shit, but I need something for my pounding fuckin' head.

"That bitch get under your skin?" he chuckles. I narrow my eyes on him. "She's a hot piece, brother. I get it."

"You don't know shit," I grunt.

"Yeah, I don't know a fuckin' thing," he says before he flips me off and walks away.

Fuck that asshole. He doesn't know what he's talking about, even if he's semi-right. Kentlee is a hot piece and she's under my skin, but not just because of her hot, wet cunt. No, it's also because she took what I gave and fuckin' loved it. But then she got in my face when I pissed her off. Made me hard, then wounded my pride when she didn't immediately back down.

Kentlee is going to take effort. I'm not sure I want to put in that kind of work on a side bitch. I want soft and sweet, but I don't want to be questioned. Kentlee is going to question the fuck out of me and test my patience.

But I want her.

I want her to take me as I am. Take what I can give and not give me any shit.

I walk outside to my bike and straddle it. I need a long ride.

An hour later, I end up downtown, watching Kentlee's office. When she walks out for her lunch break, she takes my breath away. Her blonde hair is down and sleek, her skirt tight on her hips, encasing her thick ass and thighs. *Fuck, I want in there — right now.*

It takes everything inside of me not to march across the street and fuck her on the sidewalk for the world to see.

Instead, I watch her. I watch her ass sway as she goes into a little café and sits down with her phone in her hand.

Then, I leave.

She doesn't need me in her life, fuckin' shit up. But I'll probably do it anyway. I want her. I can't stop thinking about her and I've never not taken what I want. I'll leave her alone for now, but when she least expects it I'm taking her again.

Kentlee

I predicted it.

I knew this was what was going to happen.

No way a man that big, that burly, that fucking *manly* wouldn't have *super sperm*, too. Dr. Parker confirms it for me with a sad smile and a shake of his head. I should have gone to the free clinic or something, but I didn't feel like I could trust a free clinic with my body.

Dr. Parker has been my doctor since the day I turned eighteen. He is a kind, older man who is not only my doctor, but Brentlee and my mother's, as well. His wife is best friends with my mother, and I can only hope that he keeps his doctor-patient confidentiality just that, *confidential*— and that he doesn't tell his wife, or my mother.

"I want to see you back here in four weeks, Kentlee," he says softly, breaking me out of my mental freak out.

"Four weeks, okay," I shrug, agreeing.

My head is foggy and I feel both nauseous and dizzy all

at the same time.

"The father..." he begins. I shake my head.

"There isn't one," I confess. He smirks at me, his eyes still sad.

"So just like Mary, this was an immaculate conception? Shall we call the Pope then?" he says, trying to joke.

I can't joke right now — *nothing is funny.*

"It doesn't matter who the father is," I correct. He looks at me, disappointment clearly etched in his features.

"Every man deserves to know he's going to be a father, Kentlee. Let it be his choice if he wishes to be involved or not, but tell him about the child," he counsels.

I thank him and leave the room, making the next appointment before going straight home. It is well after five in the evening and I need to decompress. I need to think about my life and re-evaluate my entire situation.

Every man deserves to know he's going to be a father.

The words Dr. Parker said to me are on replay in my head.

I bite the side of my lip.

Dr. Parker is right.

Every man deserves to know if he is going to father a child.

I will let Fury decide what he wants to do with the information, but I am going to give him all of the information.

I think I pretty much know what his answer will be, based on the only real conversation we shared after the most amazing sex of my life. He will want me to *take care of it.*

There is no way in hell I could do that. It is unthinkable. I don't believe in abortion; and beyond that, I can't imagine killing anything, let alone an innocent child that I carry inside of my body.

43

I could put the baby up for adoption, I think to myself as I place my hand on my lower belly and gently caress my still flat stomach.

There is a living being inside of me and it's a part of me, and part of Fury. I don't think I could give away a life I created, either. I am twenty-three years old; I'm not a teenager anymore.

I'm an adult, and responsible adults take care of their lives, the mistakes they make, and whatever God throws at them. I can't move back home, but I can adjust my life. I can give up my sweet Camaro for something more practical and affordable.

Money will be tight, but as long as I budget, I could probably squeak by. I can do this. I will do this — with or without a man's help.

I decide to spend the evening trying to keep the baby and Fury off of my mind. Once I am home, I make a piece of toast and slather it with honey before I put a movie on. My distractions are fruitless. Not only does the sweet toast make me nauseous, but the movie does nothing to keep my mind off of the man and our baby.

Fury hasn't really left my thoughts since I saw him that first time after my sister's bridal dress shopping day. He's right there in my head—consuming my thoughts, he's wormed his way in and now, I'm afraid I'll never be free of him.

I shouldn't want to want him—at all.

But I do.

I want him so badly. It has nothing to do with the baby growing inside of me and everything to do with how I felt with him. Those few moments where he made me feel the most desired I have ever felt in my life and gave me the most

44

perfect orgasm I have ever had. Just thinking about it again sends a shiver up my spine.

After another movie and a ginger ale to settle my stomach, I can't handle it anymore. I need to tell him. I need to get it off of my chest.

I look over at the clock for the time — ten in the evening.

There is no better time than the present to tell *the man* the truth. I know that if I wait, I will never say the words to him. I'll chicken out.

I need to tell him now—not tomorrow and not next week. I just pray that he isn't cruel to me. I have been an emotionally unstable, crazy, hormonal person the past week, and I can't handle anymore insanity.

I take a deep breath and change into a pair of ripped up, old jeans that fit perfectly—for now—and a favorite V-neck, loose t-shirt. My long blonde hair is down and a bit wild, my makeup practically nonexistent, subtle and light.

This isn't a beauty contest

I'm not man hunting. I've had the man, and although he was wickedly delicious, he is an asshole of epic proportions. I don't plan on going back there with him. Ever. Even if he is my baby daddy. No matter how badly I want him. *Oh fuck, I'm so full of shit.* One look from his gray eyes and I'll probably melt into a puddle of mush on the floor.

I pull into the clubhouse's dirt lot and notice dozens of motorcycles parked in neat, straight lines. Everybody in town knows where the Notorious Devil's clubhouse is, but that doesn't mean that I have ever been inside of it before.

I walk up to the door and open it, surprised that they don't have a man standing guard. I would think a bunch of outlaws would have some guy on security duty, screening people who come inside.

The smell of smoke permeates the room, as does beer, sweat, and sex.

I scrunch up my nose at the latter.

My eyes roam over the space and I shudder.

There are men and women everywhere. The women are wearing either nothing, or next to nothing. The men are all decked out in jeans and leather. It is basically everything I had envisioned. Big men groping and screwing girls that look like they're one step away from the street corner.

"Kentlee? What the fuck you doin' here?" I swing around to see Jonathan Williams, a boy I went to school with, standing just a few inches from me.

"I'm looking for Fury," I explain wide-eyed.

I didn't even know Johnny Williams knew my name. He was one of the hottest guys in school, and now he's even hotter, covered in ink with lean muscles and a cigarette dangling from his lips. He grins and shakes his head before lifting his chin toward the bar.

"He don't know you're comin' does he?" Johnny asks. The answer dies on my tongue as soon as my eyes find Fury.

chapter five

Fury

I am fucked up. *I am a fuck up, too.* The Jack burns on its way down, but it doesn't replace the ache I feel inside of me. I knew the bitch for a matter of hours, but that doesn't mean I didn't already ache for her.

Kentlee Johnson.

That crazy fucking bitch wormed her way under my skin.

One look at her sweet innocent face, and I was fucking gone. One thrust inside of her tight cunt, and I was in another fucking, goddamned *hemisphere.*

When she came—her cunt squeezing my dick, her eyes so fucking bright, her face in awe—I was in another galaxy.

Then she had to act like a crazy bitch.

What kind of twenty-three year-old bitch ain't on birth

47

control?

I knew the answer—*a good girl.*

Kentlee is what I crave. A sweet innocent pussy to sink into night after night, and she welcomed me without question.

I am being a prideful asshole.

Mama always told me that my pride would be my downfall. She was right. I want Kentlee like I want air, but I can't bring myself to hunt her down and apologize – *fuck that.*

I never apologize. I've never needed to. I'll chase her down soon enough, but I won't apologize.

"Hey, baby, you need my mouth tonight?" Kitty asks, rubbing her hard, fake tits on my arm. She isn't even wearing a top. I scrub my hand over my face. *Fucking whore.*

"On your knees," I bark.

I watch as she happily sinks to her knees, in the middle of the bar. Kentlee would never do this, and I would never ask her to. No way in fuck would I want anyone to see her as anything other than *mine.*

Club whores are all the same. Ready and willing to spread any part of their body for a quick, fast fuck.

"Fuck, I love your cock. When are you going to put this beast to use?" she purrs, stroking my dick. I grab a fist full of her ratty assed hair.

"I don't plan on ever fucking you, whore," I spit at her as I nod down to my dick.

It isn't going to suck itself.

"That's cute," I hear a sweet voice behind me, and I turn my head to see none other than the object of my obsession standing there, arms crossed over her chest, pushing those mouthwateringly soft tits up.

48

Kentlee Johnson.

I kick Kitty off of me and stuff my semi-hard cock into my jeans before standing up to face the gorgeous little bitch, herself. Her nose is scrunched as she looks down on the half-naked Kitty in disgust.

"What the hell?" Kitty screeches.

"Go somewhere…. *else*," I bark at her. She quickly scrambles to her feet and runs off. "The fuck you want?" I turn my attention back to the smokin' hot blonde in front of me.

She's dressed in ripped up jeans and a baggy shirt. Kentlee isn't even wearing anything sexy, yet my dick goes from half-mast to hard as a rock with one sweep of my eyes over her curvy body. I know what's underneath all of that fabric, and my cock wants in there again.

"I need to talk to you," she says, grinding her teeth together.

I nod my chin in the direction of my office. She may want to talk to me, but I'm gonna end up fucking her. No way can I not get inside of that cunt with her locked in my office with me. I grin as I watch her go.

Kentlee takes the initiative and I follow after her fat ass as she sways it toward the door. I ignore the men's cat calls and odd glances. Kentlee is nothing like the women in this place, not even any of the Old Ladies can hold a candle to her.

A classy bitch, that's what she is—even in her tattered jeans and oversized shirt. She's too good for this place. If I get my way, and I always do, she'll be waiting for my cock to come to her daily. Never seeing the inside of this shithole again.

Kentlee

Fury is well… *infuriating.*

I shiver in disgust, imagining Katie Powell's lips on his cock.

God, he's a pig, and she's still the same slut she was in high school.

Once I step into his dingy, messy office, I turn around to face him. He is standing in front of the door, legs spread and arms crossed over his massive chest, his gray eyes focused on me *intently.*

"What do you want, Kentlee? Coming down here at night, after weeks of silence?" he barks harshly.

I jump slightly, not expecting his booming voice.

"Well… you know how…" I begin, not knowing how to say it without blurting it out.

"Speak," he growls, sounding like a damned lion. I narrow my eyes on him.

"*I'm pregnant, you asshole*," I cry out before I cover my mouth in surprise.

I hadn't planned on just yelling it like that. I wanted to ease him into it.

My eyes clash with his and the look on his face can only be described as — pure shock.

"*Knocked up*?"

I nod, unable to really say anything else. I am afraid to talk. If I speak the words again, they will indeed be true, and I am not one hundred percent convinced of them quite yet. I watch in awe as his eyes soften and he takes several long strides to stand right in front of me, only an inch separating our bodies.

"You gonna have my baby, babe?" he mutters as his hand wraps around the side of my neck, effectively making me weak in the knees like the idiot girl I obviously am.

"Yeah," I sigh before I push him off of me. That asshole had Kitty on her knees for him just five minutes ago.

"The fuck?" he asks, reminding of that night so many weeks ago.

"Katie Powell was just about to service your cock when I walked in. No way am I letting you anywhere near me."

"You think I give the first fuck about that whore?" he asks, stepping into my face and wrapping his hand around the back of my neck.

I shiver at the reminder of how his hand felt wrapped in the same place as he held me down and fucked my body into oblivion. I try to wrench myself from his hold, afraid to be so close to him, afraid that I'll crumble and accept him back into my body.

"I think she's a whore and you only care about getting off," I admit, turning my head away from his.

Fury's finger and thumb catch my chin and he guides my head back to look at me in the eyes. I gasp when he leans down and gently brushes his lips against my own before he rests his forehead against mine.

"Cut the shit, Kentlee. It's you I been thinkin' about for weeks. Now you're here and I ain't lettin' you out of my fuckin' sight," he growls before he presses his lips firmly against my own in a bruising kiss. "Gonna have to fuck my baby mama now," he growls.

I feel his big hand wrap around my ass and squeeze so hard I moan, throwing my head back as I press my breasts against his chest.

I throw up my hands to stop him, to ask him about his sudden change; but then his lips touch my neck, just below my ear, and I surrender to him — my willpower shattered.

"Fury," I moan when his tongue slashes out and licks my skin. It's warm, soft, and so fucking perfect, I actually purr.

"So sweet," he murmurs against my skin as his hands move around to unbutton, unzip, and push my jeans down my hips.

In a flash, his knees are on the ground and his palm wraps around my flat stomach. I watch in fascination as he takes me in, his eyes staring at the part of me that carries a piece of him deep inside. Slowly, his head lifts and his gray eyes focus on mine.

"Never wanted any fuckin' kids. Not 'til you walked in through that door and dropped the bomb that you're carryin' mine. Never thought someone sweet and good as you would carry my kid, either. Gonna try and do right by you, babe," he mutters, his eyes shining so brightly that I wonder if this is a dream or if he really means it.

"What about the other night? Everything you said? You don't even *know* me," I question. He stands up, pulling my shirt over my head as he does, leaving me in just my bra and panties.

"I was a fuckin' asshole. I know enough. I know you ain't a whore; you'd go to a club you didn't want to be at, wearing somethin' you didn't want to wear, just to make your sister happy. I know you have a sweet ride, and you work hard for it. I know you ain't cracked out, and you wanted me, so you took me the only way I offered it. When I was a fuckin' ass to you, you still came into this clubhouse – *which scared the shit outta you* — to tell me that I was gonna be a daddy. Know that your pussy's the sweetest I ever had. The rest I'll learn," he says, his breath hot and heavy.

My chest heaves with a confusing mixture of want, desire, fear, and *need*. I place my hands on his shoulders and jump into his arms, wrapping my legs around his waist. I kiss him, hard and on his lips, pushing my tongue deep into his mouth.

"*Fuck*," he hisses, breaking away from my kiss before his hands wrap in the sides of my panties. He rips them into shreds, throwing them on the floor.

My ass collides with his hard desk a second later, and I suck in a breath when he moves his hands to his belt and jeans, pushing them down his legs. I groan the second I feel his hard length plunge inside, stretching me. It's been a month since he was inside of me and it hurts — *so fucking good* — to have him back.

"Fury," I moan when he is seated fully inside of me.

"*Pierce*. You fuckin' call me Pierce when my cock's inside of you," he growls.

I shiver at his tone and then I shiver for a completely different reason as he slowly slides out of me before slamming back inside.

"*Pierce*," I cry out.

He grunts as his hand slowly slides up my back, unhooking my bra before he yanks it off of my body and flings it across the room. His hand then continues on its path, up and into the back of my hair, fisting it roughly. I cry out when he pulls my neck back. But not in pain. I like his roughness, the way he holds onto me like he needs me close to him.

"Sweetest pussy I ever had. *Fuck me*," he murmurs.

Fury's hand wraps around my thigh and his fingers dig into my flesh as his lips wrap around my nipple and his teeth

53

bite down.

I arch my back, pressing my chest closer, wanting more of his wicked torture.

Sweat beads on my skin as he continues to thrust deeply inside of me, continuously slamming his body, with mine. I can feel myself climbing toward my climax, and my nails dig into his tattooed biceps as I cry out in pleasure.

My body pulses around him, waiting for something to tip me over the edge. I *need* something, I *need* more.

"Come on my cock, sugar," he whispers against my sweat soaked breast as his thumb presses against my clit.

I do just that—I come around his cock. I cry out his name as I climax *hard*, my pussy pulsing, my body bowed and frozen in pure bliss. Pierce doesn't stop. He thrusts inside of me a few more times before he stills and roars — his release flooding my body.

I start to go completely limp, but he catches me, gathering me in his arms, his semi-hard cock still inside of me. He carries me to the beat up couch, sinking down as I collapse on his chest, burying my face in his neck. Pierce's hand gently strokes my back and I find the move odd, *comforting*, and perfect all at the same time.

"You okay, baby girl?" he murmurs against my forehead before pressing his lips to my skin.

"I didn't plan on sleeping with you," I sigh, kissing his sweat soaked neck.

I feel his body move and shake before his laugh reaches my ears.

"Never planned on fucking you again, no matter how badly I wanted that sweet cunt. Thought I fucked up," he grumbles. I sit up and narrow my eyes on him.

"You did fuck up," I confirm. He smiles widely, the look so beautiful on his bearded face that my breath stops at the sight.

"Did something right. Put my baby inside you, made you come back to me. Pride saved, and I got the girl."

I open my mouth to say something but I can't. He's right, the *bastard*. Just when I am about to say something else, his office door slams wide open. I scream and plaster my chest to his, in a lame attempt to hide my naked body, well aware my ass is in clear view of whoever opened the door.

"Fuck me," I hear a familiar voice, *Johnny Williams*, say from the doorway.

"What the fuck man?" Fury yells his hands wrapping around my ass.

"Fuck, Prez. Sorry as shit man, but we got trouble," Johnny says. I can hear the smile in his fucking voice, before he leaves, closing the door behind him.

"Give me a minute, yeah, sugar? Stay in here I'll be right back. Lock the door and don't open it for anybody but me," he murmurs, his eyes focused on mine and his face serious—*too* serious.

I nod and cringe when he turns me around, placing me on the couch before reaching down to snag my shirt; he then slides it over my chest.

"Get dressed soon as I leave, baby," he murmurs.

I have no clue what's going on, but it's critical, I can tell that much just by the change in demeanor. He has shifted from Pierce to Fury in just the span of seconds, and it's painfully obvious that *Fury. Is. Pissed.*

As soon as he walks out of the door, I rush over and flip the deadbolt. Then, I run and quickly dress in my jeans and t-shirt. My leg bounces as I sit on the sofa... *waiting*... for what, I have no damn clue, and it's killing me.

Chapter Six

Fury

Fuck. Fuckin'. Fuck.

Fuck.

The second Dirty Johnny walked into my office— after initially wanting to beat his ass— I knew something bad was up. His nervous pacing in front of the door solidifies my suspicions.

"Who's here?" I bark, making him jump.

"Sorry, Prez, *Bastards* sent a message. Thought you'd want to see it," he mumbles, lighting a cigarette.

The smell wafts over to me, making me want the stupid stick. I've been trying to put that habit behind me. As I follow him outside behind the clubhouse, I groan when I see exactly what the Bastards' message entails.

Red, an Old Lady, beaten and naked, left dead on the back of our property. Buck is gonna lose his shit—not that he really cared much about the bitch. She was a crackhead, turned tricks on the corner; but at one time, she had been in the fold.

Buck kept her, clothed her, and gave her a roof over her head because she gave him two kids, but they weren't together—not really. The Bastards had no way of knowing what their relationship status was; they are going after women for the sake of going after *our* women. Trying to run us out because they want the full reign on the entire town. *Fuck them.*

"Get her the fuck outta here before Buck sees her. I'll talk to him. Get the bulk of the whores and hang-arounds outta here. Party's over. Get all the kids and old ladies here—fuckin' lockdown starts immediately."

I nod to Dirty Johnny, lifting my chin so he'll get started ASAP on the orders I gave. I watch as a few prospects are given the duty of getting rid of Red's body, and then I slowly make my way inside to talk to Buck.

I walk to the bar where Buck is perched with Kitty on his arm. He's licking her neck and I can't help but be glad I didn't touch any part of her whore ass. I nod to her and she gives me narrowed, pissed off eyes before she scoots her ass away. Buck turns around and his eyes narrow for a second before his face pales, knowing something ain't right.

"Its Red, brother."

His eyes go wide and then he nods. "Knew her drugs and whoring would catch up with her. Give it to me," he urges. I shake my head.

"It wasn't either, brother. It was the *Bastards*."

"*Fuckin' shit*," he roars. I can't help but feel the same way.

"A message. We're on lockdown for the time being. We're gonna find these fuckers, don't you worry about that. *Retribution*," I offer, slapping my hand on his shoulder.

Buck's shoulders drop and he rubs the back of his neck before speaking.

"She was a sweet kid when we met. I fucked with her, fucked her over a million times, then she got hooked on the shit and never could get off. Loved that bitch, deep down; loved the way she was when we met," he mumbles. I watch as wet shines in his eyes.

"Vengeance. Don't doubt it," I murmur. He nods before taking a shot of whiskey.

I sit down next to my brother, a man who just lost his Old Lady. She has been gone for years, but she's *gone* now – *forever*.

I flick my fingers to the prospect behind the bar and wait until he brings me a bottle of jack and a shot glass. Tonight, I help my brother mourn. Tomorrow, I put some Bastards into the ground.

Kentlee

I look down at my phone. One in the morning. *Unfucking-believable*. He's left me locked in his office for almost three hours. *Fuck this. I'm outta here.* I reach for the handle of the door, but then remember the panic on his face—the worry, the seriousness.

I release the handle and step back over to the gross sofa, falling down on the cushions. I open up my Facebook app and contemplate announcing my pregnancy. *Nothing would embarrass my mother more,* I think to myself with a chuckle before I close the app.

I'm exhausted, and hungry, and pissed off.

I stand up from the sofa and walk over to the door, my hand lingering over the handle. I should just leave. My car is here. I can sneak out undetected. I close my eyes for a moment and remember Fury's face before he left. Maybe I don't want to know what lies outside of this little office. I take my ass back to the dirty sofa, yet again, and I lie down.

I need sleep.

"*Shit,*" a voice hisses. I open my eyes to the pitch black room, a large shadow hovering over me.

"Pierce?" I ask drowsily.

"Baby girl. I forgot you were still in here. *Fuck,*" he murmurs before I feel his large arms slide under my body.

I don't even want to think about the fact that he forgot about me and how that makes me feel, so I ignore it.

"Is it late?" I mumble, the words sounding slurred even in my own head. I am so tired. I just want to sleep longer.

"No, baby, it's early. Let's get you to a bed," he grinds out as his big body moves with me wrapped in his arms.

Safe.

I feel safe.

Warm.

Content.

I close my eyes, leaning against his chest, letting him take care of me as he carries me wherever he wants. I don't trust him; I don't know that I ever will, but I'm willing to try. I'm willing to give my body over to him, surrendering to my desire to have him. I want him that bad. I want whatever piece of himself he's willing to give me right now. I feel so fucking pathetic about that, too.

"Let's get you undressed," he grumbles as he lies me down on a bed.

It isn't as comfy as mine at home, but it's a step up from the gross couch I was sleeping on. I moan when I feel my pants being pulled down my legs. I reach under my shirt and unhook my bra, taking it off through one of the oversized sleeves before flinging it across the room.

"Damn, don't know why that shit was as hot as it was. But fuck," Pierce mutters as I slide beneath the sheets.

"You're a pig," I grumble unable to open my eyes, I'm *that* exhausted.

"Well, yeah," he admits as I hear him move around the room. He's making so much noise I can't fall back asleep.

"Come to bed, Pierce," I order hazily.

"Yeah, sugar. No place else I'd rather be right now," I hear him say, his voice fading as sleep takes over again.

Before I completely pass out, I feel his large, warm body behind mine. His hand slides up my thigh, over my hip, and then around my breast.

Heaven.

There is something warm sliding over my breast, down my stomach and then back up. The slight tug on my nipple has my eyes popping open, and I stiffen when I look around and realize that I am not in my room. It takes me a moment to register exactly where I am and exactly what happened last night.

Fury. Sex. The baby.

It comes back to me in pieces, but it all comes back, and then I take in my surroundings. The room is bare with only the bed, a dresser, and a crate for a nightstand. It's neat, tidy, and a total contradiction to the man behind me. The rough and rowdy man who goes by the name of Fury.

"Mornin'," he whispers against the side of my neck as his fingers dip between my thighs.

I whimper when they swirl around my clit. Fuck, the man knows *just* how to turn me on.

"Fury," I warn. He slides his finger inside of me and I throw my head back with a moan instead of telling him to stop.

"Love the sounds you make. So fuckin' sweet," he murmurs before his thumb presses against my clit, his finger working in and out of me.

"We should talk about everything," I grumble. He just chuckles behind me.

"I fuck you nice and sweet, then I'll tell you how we're going to play this," he cajoles.

"*Fury*," I warn.

"Any part of me is inside of you, babe, you call me Pierce," he orders.

I whimper again—not in pain or fear, but in lust.

God – just his voice could send me over the edge. Hard and unrelenting, just like he is.

"Yes, Pierce," I whisper.

I hear him groan before his hand leaves my pussy and slides to my knee, lifting and spreading me wide. I cry out in pleasure when he glides his cock inside of me. I'm sore, but he feels too good to stop.

"So good. Feels like I've come home," he moans as he gently fucks me; his cock hard, but his movements precise, slow, and gentle.

"You feel so good, baby," I moan when his leg hitches, holding me open and his fingers return to my clit.

So fucking good.

Pierce doesn't say anything else as he continues to fuck me slowly. I whimper, moan, and beg for more. I want it hard. I *like* it when he's rough, but he refuses to *be* rough.

It doesn't matter what I want; he's going to give it to me the way he wants me to have it. Even *that* is a turn on.

"Pinch your nipples, sugar, I wanna watch," he grunts.

I'm so close, I can feel my body building toward my climax, so I do as he asks.

I throw my head back against his shoulder and wrap my fingers around my nipples and pinch. *Fuck.* I cry out as my release washes over me. My thighs shake, along with the rest of my body. Pierce rolls me to my stomach, wrenching my hips back with his hands and he takes me – *hard*.

Exactly the way I need it.

I slide my hand beneath my body and start to play with my clit. I don't want to lose my orgasm, I want to extend it, or bring myself to another. When he's inside of me, rough and so fucking unbelievable, I want to come over and over.

I need him to feel how he affects me, even if it is only physically.

"Fuck yeah, baby girl. Play with that pussy while you take my cock," he growls.

I can't help the scream that comes from my mouth. I'm being as rough with my clit as he's being with my pussy, and I know that my hips will be bruised by his fingers, but fuck me — I love it.

"Come on my cock again, Kentlee," he orders, and I do.

It's like he can just order me to come and my body throws up the white flag, coming on command.

"*Pierce*," I cry out.

"Yes, fuck yes, take my come, baby girl," he roars as he releases inside of me.

I am a boneless pile of flesh as I collapse onto the bed. He soon follows, his weight heavy against my back with his cock still inside of me.

"Sweetest cunt I ever been inside, sugar," he murmurs against my shoulder before he places a gentle kiss there.

"We should talk," I say breathlessly.

Pierce grunts before he slides out of me and rolls to the side, his back propped against the headboard.

"C'mere," he murmurs, holding out his arms.

I do as he asks. I cuddle into his warm, hard body, lying my head on his chest while I wrap my arm around his middle.

"So, I'm going to sell my car and get something more affordable. I make okay money, but not a ton. I can work as much overtime as possible until the baby gets here, but I'm sure I won't be able to afford daycare afterward for overtime, so I'll have to cut that out. Hopefully, I'll be able to save enough from now until the time I'm due that I'll be okay," I babble as I begin with my plan. Pierce squeezes and shakes me a bit rough.

"Can it, babe," he barks harshly. I wrench my head back to look at him in the eyes.

"Excuse me?" I ask bitchily.

"You ain't sellin' that sweet ride and you ain't workin' your pregnant ass to the bone. You got a man now, and I take care of what's mine. Namely, you and my baby," he declares.

"Pierce, if I had a cheaper car, I could save even more money; and the overtime would just be until the baby is born," I try to defend. He shuts me up with a hard kiss.

"Gonna help out in every way I can, including financially. First, we're gonna get you outta that small as fuck pad you're livin' in. Baby needs a room. Then whatever you need, I'll buy it for you. Your income will be just that, yours. You pay for nothin' except whatever it is girls wanna spend their dough on," he announces. I blink before my mouth falls open.

"*What?*" I breathe, unbelieving.

"New place and a man who pays your bills, babe," he consolidates. I continue to gape up at him.

"Seriously?" I ask in awe.

"Babe, the fuck you thought I meant when I said I was gonna do right by you?" he asks.

It suddenly hits me that all this is because of the baby. Though, that thought should have been the first to cross my mind, but I was still basking in my orgasm induced haze.

"Because of the baby?" I ask, feeling insecure and stupid all at the same time.

Of course he's taking care of me solely for the baby. We've only seen each other a handful of times.

I need to get it together.

"Partly because of the baby, and partly because I like you. I wanna see where this goes. Thought I fucked up for good and wouldn't be seeing you again. Hated that feeling; wanted more of you, more of that sassy assed mouth of yours, and more of that goddamned perfect cunt," he volunteers as his hand slides behind my neck, gently holding me, like he did the afternoon we met.

"You're an asshole and sweet all at the same time," I mutter as a tear falls from my eye, landing on his chest.

"Baby girl," he mumbles. His head dips down and he places a gentle kiss on my lips.

"I'm just hormonal," I offer as an excuse for my tear.

"Yeah, I got that, sugar. Let's get some food in you and get you home. You shouldn't be hangin' around this shithole," he says. I bite my tongue.

I want to ask him about Katie Powell and her mouth being near his cock. I want to ask him about the other women I saw, but I don't. We aren't really much of anything yet. Sure, he feels the need to care for me and he wants to get to know me better, but I'm under no illusion that this is some insta-love, committed relationship we have happening between us.

Pierce and I take a quick shower in his attached bathroom and, once again, I am impressed by his cleanliness. I want to ask him why he's so clean; he's nothing that I have been imagining on that front. I don't, though; I'm too busy following him downstairs and through what I now know is a common room— a bar and a party place. Bodies are passed out everywhere. Most are naked or in various stages of undress, and my eyes widen as I take it all in.

"Don't get used to seeing this shit, Kent," he mumbles as we step outside of the building.

"Why?" I ask, digging my keys out of my purse.

Once I have them in my hand, Pierce wraps his hand around my waist and pulls me into his body. I look up and am captured by his gray eyes as his other hand wraps around the side of my neck. His head dips so that his lips are a hairsbreadth away from mine.

"My woman, my baby mama, ain't gonna be anywhere near these dirty bastards. You're mine. I don't share well, and

I don't want nobody lookin', either. I had my way, I'd lock your pretty ass up and nobody would be able to see all that is you."

My breath hitches at his disturbingly beautiful words and I feel tears well up in my eyes, *again*. No man has ever felt that way about me – *ever*.

It's creepy, but it's equally lovely.

"Pierce," I sigh before I lean in and take his lips with mine. They're soft and warm, and when his tongue slides out, I open to let him into my mouth as I melt. I melt into him, and for him, all at the same time.

"Now, let's get the fuck outta here so I can feed my babies," he grunts.

I can't help the smile that forms on my lips. Pierce tells me which restaurant to go to and informs me that he'll follow me there on his bike. I don't ask questions, I just drive, in a complete lover's daze.

I want him.

I want everything he's promising me.

I want this dream to be a reality.

I just hope and pray that it will be.

chapter seven

Kentlee

The diner is busy for a Saturday morning, and I am feeling a bit disheveled and uncomfortable in yesterday's clothes, looking exactly like the classic walk-of-shamer that I am. I look around, praying I don't see anybody that I know.

I'm relieved when I find that I don't know a single soul in the room. Pierce wraps his hand around my waist from behind and places a kiss on my cheek before he murmurs to the hostess that we need a table for two — *in the back*.

"Why in the back?" I ask as the hostess gathers plastic menus and two napkin rolled sets of silverware.

"I don't like people behind me, ever," he grunts before taking my hand and leading me toward our table.

"Specials today are eggs, potatoes, bacon, and pancakes

with a side of me if you're interested, *again*," the hostess suggests with a wink once we have sat down.

Pierce is sitting across from me, his hand wrapped around mine lying across the table. I cannot believe. *This. Bitch.*

I feel my face heat with anger and I tighten my hand in his. I open my mouth to say something but the little bitch walks away. Naturally, I turn my anger toward him, the man who seriously brought me to a diner where he fucked the whore of a hostess.

"Don't," he warns.

It doesn't matter. I narrow my eyes on his and take a deep breath just as the infuriating man speaks first.

"One thing you gotta know. I've fucked a lot of bitches, Kentlee. Nothin' can be done about it. It's life. You can't go gettin' pissed off every time one of them says something. This is one of the reasons you won't *ever* be at the clubhouse," he informs me. My eyes widen.

"What are *all* the reasons I won't be there, Pierce?" I ask, taking my hand from his and crossing it over my chest. I'm ready to throw a bitch fit. I'm ready for a fight.

"I already told you the first reason, I don't want my brothers getting any ideas about you—at all. Secondly, the shit that goes down there, the whores, the drugs, and the booze. You don't need to be around any of it while you're knocked up," he states casually.

I look down at my lap and try to hold my emotions together. *I can't.* My first tear spills over at the thoughts of *him* being around all those things, especially what he refers to as *the whores.*

"So, you want me to stay home and be oblivious to what you're doing while you're down there. Then you want me to

69

just accept you into my bed after you sober up?" I ask as I look up at him, my tears falling from my eyes uncontrollably.

I'm so angry that I'm crying, but I can't help myself. The thought of him fucking women he so loosely refers to as whores and then coming home to me, it makes me miserably sad and uncontrollably angry.

"I say I'd be fuckin' anyone else?" he asks harshly. I shake my head. "You're *mine,* Kentlee. You keep giving me what I want and I won't go lookin' for cheap, easy pussy. I'll come home to you, to my sweet cunt."

Disgusting.

I scrunch my nose and wonder why I'm flattered by his grotesque words. He's rough and his no bullshit attitude is real. He's giving it to me straight. I may not know much about Pierce Duhart, but I do know that he can be sweet, if you can read through the gruff, the rough with the coarseness of his words. I have a feeling I'm one of the only people in the world to get his brand of sweet, too.

He wants me. In his own crass way, this is him being sweet, offering me what he can give me. It's up to me to decide if it's enough. Is what he's offering enough for me? Can I live with him being down there in that environment and then coming home to me?

"You're a pig," I grumble as the waitress walks up to take our order.

Pierce throws his head back in laugher. I try not to look at the infuriating man, but I can't help myself. His smile, his laugh — he's intoxicating.

Once we have ordered, a silence falls between us. I want to know everything about him, but I fear he's closed off. We hardly know each other, and yet we're making plans for a future together. It feels oddly comfortable to be with him, our physical connection is spectacular, but conversing with him—it's frightening to me.

"You only got the one teenie-bopper, Barbie sister?" he asks, finally breaking our silence.

"No, I have an older brother, too. Connellee. He's in medical school," I offer as I cut a piece of pancake and shove it into my mouth — *fuck, carbs... so damn good.*

"Medical school?" he chokes.

"Yeah. My dad's a doctor; Connellee's been on that path since he was born. My sister, Brentlee, and I weren't ever really encouraged in school. We were told to marry someone who would take care of us. Brentlee's followed through, she's marrying a lawyer, but I wanted to do my own thing. Take care of myself. I guess that's all over with now, *right*?" I ask, looking up at him, unable to stop babbling.

"Class, one hundred percent," he mumbles.

I don't understand.

"I don't know about all that," I grumble.

Pierce takes my hand with his own and squeezes it.

"You're classy, babe, no way around it. Born and bred to be with someone a fuck've a lot better than me," he says before taking a drink of his coffee.

I look down at my empty plate and sigh. *His own brand of sweet.* I open my mouth to respond to him but the waitress appears and gives him the check, along with her number.

"Seriously?" I ask, loud enough for the bitch to hear me. She turns and just grins at me before she shakes her ass as she continues to walk away.

"Gotta let that shit slide, sugar," he mutters as I wiggle out of the booth.

"Thirsty, dirty bitches," I mumble.

I am awarded with a laugh from Pierce as he slides his arm around me, pressing his hand around my lower back.

"You get enough to eat, baby girl?" he asks as his other hand rests on my stomach for a beat. The gesture is so touching I have to hold the tears back, *again*.

"Yeah," I breathe as we step up to my car.

"I'll follow you home so you can rest today. You're the real estate girl; there anything worth lookin' at for us to rent that's a bit bigger?" he asks. I suck in my lips. He's serious. Last night, he was totally serious. I blink once and then I smile.

"Yeah, we can go over budget and stuff when we get to my place. Thank you, Pierce. Thank you for really wanting to do this," I praise as I shove my face into his neck and my arms around his waist, hugging him close.

"Baby girl, never gonna lie to you, sugar. What I say, I'll deliver," he promises as one hand wraps around my waist and the other sifts through my hair.

A few minutes later, I am in in my car and driving toward my little house with Pierce behind me.

Once we pull into my driveway, I get out and go straight to the door. I'm tired—exhausted, really. I need to change my clothes and actually put on panties, since he ruined mine the night before. I am a mixture of excited and nervous about everything that is happening so quickly. Last month, I would have laughed in anyone's face if they said this is the turn my life was going to take.

Pierce walks in, locking the door behind him before he begins to stalk toward me. I hold up my hands to stop him, to slow him down, but it doesn't work. His hands wrap around my ass as he picks me up – *mid-stride*. He carries me into my bedroom and without a word, I am dropped onto my bed as his body slowly lowers over me, his lips pressing to mine.

"Don't want any other bitches, Kentlee," he groans. One of his hands slides up the inside of my shirt and wrenches down the cup of my bra. I moan when his thumb glides across my nipple before he pinches and tugs it gently.

"*Pierce*, please," I beg.

I need more. I need him inside of me. It feels like he hasn't been there in weeks, the need is so strong. I've turned into this hormonal, horny, sluttastic girl and I don't even care. Suddenly, I'm not longer exhausted; instead, I'm horny as all hell.

"Need you to understand, Kentlee. No other bitches. No matter where I go, or what's happening. You don't need to worry about that from me," he grunts as I unbuckle his pants and wrap my hand around his hard cock. He went commando, and I can't even begin to think about how fucking hot that is right now.

"Okay. Only me, Pierce. I understand," I whisper breathlessly. I have never been as wound up as I have been around this man.

"I'm going to take you every way I can, Kentlee. You're mine," he grinds out before he wrenches my jeans down my legs. "This," he cups my center before he plunges two fingers inside of me, "is mine. My woman, my cunt, my baby, all fucking mine." His head slants as he kisses me, removing his fingers to plunge his cock inside of me to the root.

I whimper, unable to form words as he fucks me, hard—his eyes focused on mine, so clear, it is as if I can see inside of him. He wants this. He wants me and he wants us.

I dive my fingers into his shaggy hair and hold on to him,

my eyes never breaking from his. His grunts and my whimpers fill the silence of the room. When I come, it is looking into his eyes. He follows shortly, doing the same. His lazily slides in and out of me after his climax, and then he places a soft kiss on my lips.

"*Mine*," he murmurs quietly before he slides out of me and wraps me in his arms.

I should go clean up. I should do about a million different things, but with this man's strong arms wrapped around me from behind, his warm body nestled next to mine, I can't do anything but let the exhaustion swallow me up.

I am safe.

In his arms, with him in my bed, nothing can hurt me.

He's more than I ever thought possible and I don't even know him yet.

Fury

She sleeps.

Pure fuckin' beauty, and she's mine.

There is no way I can let the bad part of my life touch her.

Kentlee is good, so good, and I can't corrupt her – not like that.

She'll never know about the way this life is.

Kentlee isn't Old Lady material; not that'd I'd ever have one. She's not strong enough. I can see it in her eyes. She needs someone to take care of her, and I'll do that. I'll be hers and she'll be mine, but I can't declare her as anyone to the club.

No way in fuck could she deal with the shit Old Lady's deal with. My mama was strong and she was tough; she dealt, but I don't see those traits in Kentlee. She's soft, sweet, and pure. I'm going to keep her *for* myself, and *to* myself.

My phone starts ringing in my jeans, and I break away from her sleeping form to answer it.

Torch.

"What's up?" I ask, knowing that it must be something big if he's calling me right now.

"Got a problem with the shipment to Canada, brother. The club says they're having issues with the Mexican Cartel there. They need muscle—they need backup. The shipments are getting intercepted by the Cartel and the club hasn't been able to make their deliveries. The Aryan's are *pissed*," Torch explains on a hiss.

"I fuckin' hate the Aryan's. I don't know why that deal was ever made in the first place," I grumble, walking into Kentlee's living room.

"Money talks, brother," Torch sighs. I know he feels the same way about those racist fucks.

"So they want us to come up to Canada, guns hot, full force, to protect their shipments? Do they not understand the word incognito?" I ask, not expecting an answer.

"You know them. They don't give a fuck. They just want their shit. Douchebags," Torch answers. I stretch my neck from side-to-side, trying to relieve the tension I feel building.

"We try one more shipment, the one going out next month, on a different route. If it's intercepted, then we come in and make ourselves fucking known," I explain.

No way in fuck do I want to help those assholes, but they pay us well, and Torch is right. *Money talks.*

"I'll spread the word," he offers. I thank him.

I'm not contacting them unless I absolutely have to.

I never agreed to doing business with them. I've never wanted it, and I've never liked it. The original charter set all that shit up. While I was a voting member there, I was too busy fucking and drinking to give much of a shit about the business side of it. I took my orders like a good solider and did what I was supposed to do, but that was about it. Now that I'm in charge and have a fairly decent clear head, I don't like it at all.

I walk back into Kentlee's bedroom, which is about two steps away—seeing as her house is the size of a fuckin' postage stamp—and crawl back into her comfortable as shit bed. When I wrap my arms around her again, I hear her let out a sigh and I smile.

Fuck, this little girl and what she does to me. *Unbelievable*. I close my eyes and sigh out my own breath.

I'm happy.

Never been happy like this before.

My woman.

My baby.

Fuckin' bliss.

chapter eight

Kentlee

The heavy arm that is pressing me into the mattress should feel uncomfortable. *It doesn't.* In fact, I like it – a lot.

I roll over to face Pierce and see that he is still asleep. He looks younger when he's asleep, his jaw slack instead of clenched.

I trace his eyebrow with my fingertips and then drag them along the edge of his face, down along the underside of his jaw, feeling the scruff of his beard.

"Feels good, baby," he mumbles in a hazy sleep-filled voice. I slip my fingers through his shaggy hair and gently rake my nails along his scalp.

"Good afternoon," I remark as his eyes slowly open.

"Yeah. *Fuck.* Passed out," he says as he stretches next to

me.

"You want me to make something to eat while we discuss budgets and stuff?" I ask, hoping that he's still on board—that sleeping and time haven't changed his mind.

"Yeah, sugar, that'd be good," he says, smiling as his stomach growls.

I laugh slightly as I crawl out of bed in search of something to wear.

I slide a clean pair of panties on over my hips and turn around to see him watching me from the bed. His eyes are a bit darker than their normal gray, but they are completely focused on me. Biting my lip, I put on a bra and grab an oversized shirt before slipping a pair of leggings on. I don't plan on going anywhere else today.

"Gorgeous," he breathes as he climbs out of bed and heads my direction. I jump when his hands grasp my hips and he angles his head to plant a hard kiss on my lips.

"Peirce," I moan after he lets me go. He doesn't say another word.

He pats my ass and then turns and walks to my bathroom. I watch him as he goes, enjoying the view of his bare ass and the muscles that move with each step he takes. As soon as the bathroom door closes, I sigh and make my way toward the kitchen.

I don't have much in my refrigerator, because I really don't like cooking for just one person. It's sad and makes me feel lonely, so I don't do it often. Luckily, I have all the ingredients to make meat sauce spaghetti and I have a new loaf of bread that I can turn into cheesy garlic bread. My mouth waters at the very idea of more carbs, so I quickly get to work making food for my man and myself.

My man.

I still can't believe that Fury is mine.

Pierce "Fury" Duhart is *mine*.

I am Pierce "Fury" Duhart's *woman*.

I shiver slightly at the thought.

I am taken out of my daydream when two strong arms wrap around my middle and a pair of soft lips touch behind my ear. I inhale his scent; sweat, spice, and Pierce fills my lungs.

"Smells good, baby girl," he rumbles behind me, his chest vibrating against my back.

"It's ground beef, Pierce," I chuckle. His arms squeeze me slightly before one of his hands drifts up the inside of my shirt to wrap around my breast. I moan when he pinches my nipple through my bra.

"Haven't had a woman cook for me since my mama did before she died. Smells good, baby girl," he says, repeating the phrase, rocking me to my core.

I realize that I truly know nothing about the man. He lets me go and grabs a coke out of the fridge before settling down at the bar to watch me.

"You're mom passed? I'm so sorry," I say quietly as I turn to face him.

"I was fifteen; twenty years ago, sugar. I miss her, but I've dealt with all that sorrow," he confesses. I blink, realizing that he's well over ten years older than I am.

"Does it bother you that I'm twenty-three and you're thirty-five?" I ask. He smiles slightly before he speaks, his eyes roaming my body.

"Not even a little. Now, if you acted like a young idiot chick, it would probably bug the fuck outta me, but you don't.

You're a woman, you're responsible, and you're fuckin' heaven around my cock. Plus, you cook. How could I fuckin' complain?" he asks as he chuckles.

I want to throw my spatula at him, but I can't. He is being his own brand of sweet again, and I'm falling all over it.

"*Pierce*," I hiss before I turn around and smile into my pan of browning ground beef.

"You love it, baby girl," he grunts.

I shake my head. *I do. I absolutely love it.*

Pierce and I exchange small talk, very small talk, while I make dinner. I find out that he's not from Idaho but California, and that his club's original chapter is there. Not that I even understand that. I tell him that I've never left Idaho. My brother goes to college at Notre Dame, but I've never left state lines. I ask him about his father, where he is and if he misses him. He tells me that his father is the President for the club he was raised in, back in California.

"So, what do all the patches mean on your vest thingie?" I ask as I continue to cook.

"It's called a *cut,* baby girl, and they stand for different things. My position, my charter, and some of them are for shit I've done," he explains in a roundabout way.

"Oh, okay."

I don't push the issue or try to get him to tell me all about the things he done that earn those patches. In all honestly, I don't think I want to know.

"I'd like to meet him soon—your dad," I say as I plate the food, trying to avoid conversation about the *cut* he wears, or anything to do with it.

"Yeah. I got some shit coming up here at the club, but once that settle's down, we can go out there. I want him to meet you before the baby comes, anyway," he offers. It makes me smile that he really does care.

"I need to tell my family about this—about you and the baby," I say. He grins.

"You want me there for that?"

"No, I should probably go it alone. My mother and I don't always get along. Odds are, it will turn into a scream fest. Brentlee will probably kick me out of her wedding, too, which is fine with me."

"Why would she do that?" he asks, taking a bite of bread.

"Her maid-of-honor gave all of us a diet plan, along with a workout regime to follow. No way would she be okay with me being pregnant for her perfect day. I'll be, like, seven months along and as big as a house," I explain, taking a bite of food. "Especially if I keep eating carbs like this."

"First of all, that girl sounds like a cunt. Secondly, you look fuckin' *smokin'* hot. I'm gonna keep feeding you carbs. Love that big ass of yours," he murmurs, then grins.

"I'm not sure how I feel about you calling my ass big," I mutter. He laughs as he leans in and places a kiss on my neck.

"Well, I know how I feel about that big ass of yours, and I like it just as it is. Don't listen to that anorexic, little girl. You look like a woman and I like all that is you, Kentlee," he mutters before taking another bite of food, essential shocking me — *once again*.

"Pierce," I admonish.

I decide to leave the talk about my ass alone and start the conversation about budgets instead. I ask him how much he would like to spend on a house to rent and he shakes his head before answering.

"Whatever you want, baby girl. Just find what you want

and I'll lay down the cash for it."

"That's insane, Pierce. We need a budget. You said you wanted to pay for all of it, but I can't accept that. And adding no budget on top of that? It's *insane*," I say as I finish up my last bite of pasta.

"I'm a man, Kentlee. I don't pay anything right now for rent, and I have plenty of money. I can take care of you, and I will," he announces. I blink at him.

"Okay, well, how about I put together a few rental listings and then we can look at them together?" I offer. He shakes his head.

"Baby girl, pick what you want. You'll be decorating and cooking and shit there. I'll be happy if it has a garage for my bike and your ride." He emphasizes his need for a garage and it makes me smile.

I like that even though he wants one, specifically for his bike, he wants my car in there too – *safety*.

"Okay. You want to look at a few online with me?" I ask, willing him to say yes.

"Sorry, babe, I gotta get back to the clubhouse. Been gone all day. Still got some shit going down that I need to reign in," he says, standing up and stepping closer to me. I widen my legs so that he can get close.

"Get some good sleep. Let me know what your parents say. I'll touch base with you tomorrow, yeah?" he asks, his eyes searching mine, looking for something. I'm not sure what, exactly.

"Yeah, okay. I'm going over for wedding planning and dinner tomorrow night, so I'm going to tell them then," I explain. He nods once before he leans down and places a gentle kiss on the corner of my mouth.

"Saw your phone on your nightstand so I added my number and got yours. I'll text you tomorrow night. You can tell me how it all went down," he says. I nod, wrapping my arms around his waist.

"You aren't coming home tomorrow night, then?" I ask, sounding needy and pathetic.

Home.

This isn't his home and I damn well know it, but last night and this afternoon, wrapped in his arms – I don't want to face another night without his strong body next to mine.

"Can't, baby girl. I won't be home with you every single night. Like I said, I need to keep you and the club separate. I'm the president there, I have to be there more times then not," he explains.

In the back of my mind, it sounds like complete bullshit; but I'm so fucking needy for him, I accept everything he's saying.

"All right. Well, okay, I'll just talk to you tomorrow then?" I ask.

"Yeah, sugar, you will," he says before leaning down and brushing my lips with his.

I spend the rest of my day searching my company's online database for rentals in the area and I find four that I want to look at. Three of them have huge yards that I envision Pierce and our little baby playing in. I wonder if he is going to be the hands-on dad that I dream of, or will he be like mine? Home for some evenings and only making it to half of our events as children. I hope that he's hands-on. I hope that he's really *in* this like he claims to be – *I hope that we fall madly in love.* It wouldn't be hard to fall for him. Our connection is there; we just need our hearts to fall into line.

Fury

Leaving her is harder than I imagined.

I need to go, though.

Being dependent on her will make me weak.

In this life, I cannot afford to look weak.

Kentlee is carrying my baby, which in and of itself is a weakness. But the way I feel about her already — *fucking ridiculous.*

I ride back to the clubhouse, trying to push thoughts of her aside. The way she feels around my cock, the way she looks in her oversized shirt making me spaghetti. *Fuck,* the bitch can cook, too. If she were Old Lady material and I was down to have one, she'd be it – *one hundred percent.*

I park my bike outside of the clubhouse doors and walk inside to see that Saturday night's party is gearing up, at least for the brothers. We're still on lockdown, but that just means that they'll corral all the kids to one room while the adults party. They're already drinking and smoking green. Harder drugs aren't encouraged, but some guy's party with coke on the weekends. I prefer the mellowness of green. I'm usually jacked up and need something to calm me; booze, and weed always does the trick, along with a good fuck.

"Hey, Fury. Missed you last night," Kitty whines, sliding right up next to me, her big, fake tits out and bare.

"I was busy," I say, signaling for the prospect to hand me a beer. He does. Once I take a pull, I turn to look down at the little slut hanging off of me, obviously wanting my attention.

"We didn't get to finish what we started," she says, pouting her lips and giving me innocent eyes.

"Don't want you, Kitty," I mutter as her hand goes down

her little shorts, obviously to her pussy.

Fuck me, she's a train wreck. I don't want her, but nothing is hotter than a woman playing with herself.

"Let me show you what you're missing, Fury. I could be so good to you—best you could ever dream of—if you'd just give me a chance." She moans before she bites her lip, her hand working her pussy. It's making me hard even though I can't see a fucking thing.

"I ain't gonna fuck your pussy, Kitty. I'm not available anymore," I grunt.

"No Old Lady, though?" she asks.

"Nope."

"That Kentlee bitch, then? She's got your balls in a vice?" Kitty bites harshly. My back goes straight and I look down at her.

"You know her?" I bark, which startles Kitty. She removes her hand out of her pants and takes a step back.

"Went to high school with the bitch," she spits angrily.

"You don't know her. You don't talk about her. You pretend she doesn't fucking exist, do you get me?" I ask, grinding my jaw and glaring at the whore.

"Yeah, I get you, Fury," she says, her voice quivering.

"Good. Now take off your shorts and get on this bar. I want to watch you make yourself come. Finish the goddamned show, Kitty," I say with a grunt.

I watch her strip her little shorts off and then make a show of climbing onto the bar and spreading her legs right in front of my face. Her feet are flat on the bar top, and I watch her fingers trail down her stomach to her pussy.

I watch, but it doesn't affect me like it should— like it used to. I love watching a woman get off, it's hot as fuck; but right now, with Kitty, I can only think of Kentlee and how fucking sexy it would be to watch her play with her perfect pink pussy.

Kitty shoves two fingers inside of her cunt and throws back her head with a cry. I feel my brothers at my back and side, watching the show from all around me. I should be into it. Kitty has a great body, even if her hair is a mess, and her face ain't much better.

I can't, though.

Kentlee Johnson is on my mind. Her soft tits and her greedy cunt. The way she whimpers and the way she takes me inside of her. Everything about her is fuckin' perfect.

I take my beer and stand up.

I need to breathe.

"Where ya goin', man?" Dirty Johnny asks me.

I just lift my chin toward the back door and head out. He doesn't follow me. He's too into the Kitty finger-bang show.

Once I am outside, I see Sniper leaning against one of the picnic benches we use during cookouts. I make my way over to him and pop a squat right next to him. He's quiet. I don't know his story, other than he is ex-military, as are a few of our other guys. He showed up fresh out of the Marines, back in his hometown, but not the same guy as he once was. Now, he's a brother.

"Hey, Snipe," I say, taking a joint out of my cut pocket.

"Prez," he offers with a head nod.

"You ever been in deep with a woman before?" I ask as I light my smoke.

"Once," he offers but doesn't go any further.

"You ever think about settling down then?" I ask, knowing damn well that he and his girl never did.

Snipe is single.

He fucks whoever he wants and lives at the clubhouse, much like me – *or the me I used to be.*

"If I had the chance to go back and make that little girl mine? I'd do it in a heartbeat. I'da made her fuckin' miserable, I'm sure, but she'd be mine and I could spend a lifetime tryin' to make her little ass happy. Don't worry about what other people think, brother, it's a waste of fuckin' time. Only thing that matters in the end is your happiness. If some bitch makes you happy, claim her ass," he advises. I stare at him in shock.

"In this life, it ain't that easy, man," I say, taking another hit and staring at the setting sun.

"Who the fuck says? You're the president. You want some hardcore cunt, or some soft sweet piece in your bed? Ain't nobody gonna say shit to you, man," he points out. He's right, to an extent.

"A soft bitch makes me weak," I explain. He shakes his head before standing up.

"A man is any kind of man, he's weak for the woman he loves. Don't matter if she's soft, sweet, or a total fucking hardcore cunt. He loves her, and she's his weakness. In our life, we have to protect that with a vengeance. You wanna hide that from the world? Maybe that's your way of protecting her. I don't know; but don't crawl to her with broken promises and expect her to be all for it, brother. Kentlee's not gonna accept that shit," he says. My eyes narrow on him.

"How'd you know it was Kentlee?" I ask suspiciously.

"Saw her last night with you; watched you take her outta your office after all that bullshit went down; and now, today, you're asking me this shit. Doesn't take a genius," he says before taking a step away.

87

"You know her then?" I ask.

"Know her sister. Know that she comes from good people. Know that she'll take the absence of you, but she won't accept that shit you just pulled with Kitty. I won't tell her dick, 'cause I'm your brother, but Kitty's a bitch and Kitty has hated her since they were kids. She'll blow it up and she'll flap her gums all over town to get to Kentlee. It were me, I'd treat Kentlee like the good girl she is. Show her respect while I had her, and definitely not fuck around, especially in this small as shit town," he clarifies, then walks away to leave me alone.

I made a promise to Kentlee.

I said I wouldn't fuck these whores and then go home to her.

I need to keep my promises.

Kentlee isn't just some sweet piece. She's the mother of my child and deserves my respect.

I pull out my phone and call my dad.

chapter nine

Kentlee

Saturday evening is lonely without Pierce, or Fury, or whatever the fuck he wants to be called. *How did I get so attached so quickly?*

I try not to get upset, and just keep reminding myself that it's all hormones. I'm an emotional wreck because of the baby, and that's why I am the way I am. It doesn't have anything to do with Pierce, not really. It's just damn hormones. That's why I'm lying in bed, crying my eyes out, because I'm alone and he hasn't called or texted me. *Hormones.* Eventually, my eyelids become heavy and I fall asleep.

Something solid presses against me and I open my eyes as my heart slams against my chest. I try to roll over, but I'm trapped. I open my mouth and start to scream, but a hand presses against my mouth. Tears immediately prick my eyes and I begin to struggle until I hear his voice.

"Ssshhh, sugar," Pierce murmurs, his body now halfway on top of me and pressing against mine.

"What are you doing here?" I ask, after he releases my mouth as I wipe the tears from my eyes.

"Missed my baby girl," he murmurs before dipping his head to gently kiss my lips.

"Scared the fucking hell out of me," I grumble, which makes his body shake with a low rumble of a chuckle.

"I'm sorry, sugar, but I made a shit ton of noise and you were sleepin' like the dead," he explains.

"Well, you need to be even louder next time," I snap. "Why didn't you call?" I almost pout, still upset about his not calling me.

"Got busy, baby girl, couldn't get away," he admits.

He scoots off of me but wraps me into his arms, pulling me against his chest. I slowly melt as he begins to stroke my arm with his fingertips, languid and sensual.

"Don't like that you sleep like the dead. Means anyone could have come in here and hurt you," he murmurs against my shoulder before placing a quick kiss there.

"I've always been a hard sleeper. That's why I make sure my doors are locked," I confess. He squeezes me a bit tighter to his body.

"Not gonna be able to let you sleep alone from now on, am I?"

"You can do whatever you want, *Fury*. If sleeping at the club is what you want to do, then go do it. I've been on my own a while now, I'll be just fine," I argue, feeling angry and irrational.

"Baby girl," he moans before he rolls me over onto my back, quickly rolling himself on top of me. His arms cage my head so that he doesn't put too much pressure on my body.

"Fury," I snap. He smiles.

It's infuriating and gorgeous all at the same time.

"Don't get all bitchy on me, sweet girl," he murmurs, pressing his lips to the underside of my jaw. I can feel myself melt with each touch of his lips.

I'm irritated with him, but I shouldn't be. We don't technically live together, *yet*. He can come and go as he pleases without telling me. But I *want* him to *want* me and to *want* to be with me.

I *need* him to want to be with me, to stay by my side.

I want him — all of him, all of the time.

"I thought you wanted to keep me and the club separate?" I ask as his lips travel the column of my neck.

"I plan on it, but I also plan on being next to you, and inside of you, as much as possible. I'll have to tell the club I'm living with someone, but I won't give them anything else – including the address," he mutters, kissing down my chest to my panties.

"You didn't wear nothin' to sleep in, Kentlee," he grinds out through a clenched jaw.

I don't know if he's angry or turned on, and it is slightly terrifying.

"I'm wearing panties. I always wear a tank and panties. I get hot," I say with a shrug. Then I gasp when my panties are yanked down my legs and his cock presses against my already wet entrance.

"You're wet, too. You like having me here, baby girl?" he

grunts as he teases my entrance with the head of his cock.

I moan but refuse to answer him with words. *The bastard will probably gloat.*

"Answer me," he says with a smile as his hand loosely wraps around my neck.

"Yes," I hiss, crying out as he slides inside of me, stretching me, filling me, and owning me — all at the same time.

"I like being here with my girl, too," he announces as he begins to slowly pull out of me. He then glides back inside with purpose – *to drive me crazy.*

"Pierce," I cry out as I wrap my hands around his forearms.

"Take me, Kentlee. Watch me fill you," he orders. My eyes trail down between us.

We're both focused on the way he moves his body in and out of mine. *It's beautiful.* It feels spectacular, but watching it fills me with emotion. He's giving me a piece of himself, just as I am giving him a piece of myself.

This isn't the act of a hook-up, this is slow, deliberate, and *loving.* He stretches me, but I accommodate him, all of him. He fits inside of me like I was made for him, for his big cock, for his body.

Nobody else could take his place inside of me – nobody else would fit.

"This cunt is mine—all mine," he mumbles to himself. It makes me smile. Yes, it is his—all his.

"I need to come," I moan, digging my nails into his forearms.

I feel like I am going to explode, but I can't. Fuck, I can't get there with this slow as hell pace he's set.

"Get yourself there, Kentlee. I want to watch your play

with that pretty clit," he says with a grin. I shiver.

"Pierce," I warn.

"Do it, Kentlee. I *need* to watch," he says, his eyes flicking over mine for just a brief moment.

I take a deep breath and slide my hand down my stomach to my clit. If he needs this, *needs it*, then he'll have it.

"Fuck, yes," he grunts as I begin to play with my clit while he continues to fuck me slowly.

One of his hands slides under my knee and he spreads my legs even farther for him. I continue rubbing my clit as I feel the release wash over me, and I cry out, whimpering and clutching his cock with my pussy. My back bows as my body tightens.

"Fuck yes, strangle me," he grunts as he begins to fuck me wildly.

I cry out again when I feel his cock grow and then twitch inside of me, filling me with his release. Pierce buries his face in my neck as he slumps against my body, his hips still moving his cock in and out of my pussy – feeling so fantastic.

"Pierce?" I ask a few moments later. He hasn't moved. His breathing has finally calmed, but he's still wrapped around me and inside of me.

"I'll be in this bed every single night, sugar," he says once he finally breaks away from me.

"You will?" I ask as I begin to get out of bed to clean up.

"Your ass is here, that's exactly where I'll be," he says. His feet hang off the side of the bed as he grabs me by my waist and pulls me into his lap.

"Pierce, I need to clean up," I squeal as I wiggle on his bare thighs.

"This," he silences and stills me by pushing two fingers

inside of me, "is gorgeous. It's me inside of you. Fucking per-fect," he grins. All I can do is gasp.

"Pierce," I whisper as he continues to thrust his fingers in and out of me.

"Nothing sweeter than you taking my come, Kentlee, no matter how I give it to you," he murmurs, placing a kiss over the flesh of my breast before his tongue snakes out. He swirls it around my nipple.

"I'll always take it, Pierce. *Always*," I vow. He shakes his head as he lets my breast go with a pop of his lips.

"Might not always feel that way, baby girl, but I hope you do. I'll never get enough of this sweet cunt," he expresses as his thumb grinds against my clit. His touch causes me to clutch his shoulders and throw my head back with a moan.

"Climb on my cock. I want to watch your tits bounce while you ride me," he grins.

I do it. I climb on him and I slide down on his cock, moaning when he fills me full.

I ride him. I ride him as if my life depends on it, because with him, you cannot do anything half assed – he wouldn't allow it. He orders me to touch myself for him again, to make myself come undone around him. He's focused on our con-nection, his eyes taking my body in—the way I touch myself, the way he fills me, and the way my tits bounce just for him. It turns me on; it makes me want to be sexier for him, to give him a show to enjoy.

I grab onto his thigh behind me as I touch myself with my other hand and ride his beautiful cock, my back arched and my head thrown back.

His heated gaze is everywhere at once, and I feel every piece of me that it touches.

I'll never get enough of him, just as he'll never get enough of me.

Fury

Kentlee fucks like no woman I have ever had before. That's saying a lot, considering I've fucked a shit ton of pussy in my thirty-five years. Something about her, though, makes me want to live inside of her.

I need to watch her come; I need to see her smile that lazy smile when she's satisfied by my cock. I want her to smile and I want to be the one she's smiling for.

I wrap my body around hers after our hours of fucking. I'm exhausted, but I can't sleep.

I can't believe how hard she sleeps. I wasn't lying when I said I made noise breaking into her place. I didn't want to scare her and I even called out to her. She never woke. It fucking terrified me. All I could think about was the *Bastards* getting to her—like if somehow they already knew that she was mine and decided to hurt her.

I have never wanted a woman like I want Kentlee. It's too much. I feel too much for her way too soon. I want to protect her and our baby. It's irrational, yet feels completely right. I try to sleep, but it doesn't come. All I can think about is every single scenario I can come up with of this going wrong between us.

Kentlee's parents will hate me, of that I'm sure. Her father's a doctor, so there is no way he'll be down for an outlaw knocking up and living with his daughter, even if I can financially take care of her. That's the first strike we have. My dad'll like her, but he'll see her as soft, weak, and not made for MC life.

Then there are outside forces, like the Bastards, the Aryan's, the Cartel, along with numerous other groups and clubs who will try and use our women as bait, as leverage. They'll hurt her, if they can, to get to *me*. I don't even want to think about what law enforcement will try to scare her with, either.

There's nothing going for us, not really—except fucking and the way she makes my heart beat. The way she makes me smile just thinking about her. We've only been together for hours, and we've spent most of that time fucking each other, but she's it. *I can feel it down to my fuckin' bones. I know it.*

Man like me knows what he wants and what he doesn't want. I know I want a soft woman like Kentlee; I know how Kentlee makes me feel. She's more than just a hole to get off inside of. She's been more than that since I saw her sweet ass walk up to her cool-as-shit ride.

Something inside of her calls to me in such a way that I know nobody can replace her in my life. I close my eyes and finally fall asleep, my woman at my side.

I hear a banging on the door and sit straight up in Kentlee's bed. I reach for her but she isn't there and panic sets in. I grab my pants and pull them over my hips as I run out to her living room. I see her opening the door and then gasp at who is on the other side.

"Where's Fury, LeeLee?" the voice asks. I furrow my brows at the familiarity they share.

"Bates?" she asks.

I blink once before I get my shit together and walk up behind her, taking the door in one hand and wrapping my arm around her waist with the other.

"Snipe?" I ask, my voice raspy and hard.

"Got a problem. Dirty Johnny and Torch tried callin'. I didn't tell anyone where I was goin'," he says, answering my questions and relieving them all at once.

I move the door to the side, along with Kentlee, and lift my chin for him to come inside.

"How do you know Bates?" Kentlee asks, looking up at me.

"I should ask you the same question. He's one of my brothers," I tell her. She looks back at Sniper with confusion.

"No, he's a Marine," she says to me before she turns to him, "you're a Marine," she informs.

"Was, LeeLee. I *was* a Marine," he clarifies. She nods once before shocking the fuck outta me.

"You tell Brent you were back?" she asks.

He looks down at his boots before bringing his face back up to her, his eyes full of fucking anguish. That's when I know—Brentlee was his.

"She obviously don't want me now, LeeLee. Would do no good to tell her I'm in town."

"No, Bates, it would change everything," she pleads. Sniper just shakes his head and looks away, subject closed.

"Go take a shower, get ready for house hunting today, sugar. I need to talk to Sniper," I murmur, brushing my lips across her cheek.

Surprisingly, she doesn't argue. Instead, she takes one long look at Sniper before she turns and heads to her bedroom.

"Brentlee the one?" I ask. He looks up at me, his eyes shuttered and completely shut down.

"Don't matter. Got bigger shit to discuss then who's suckin' my cock at the moment," he explains.

I can't help but chuckle at his words, then I take him into the kitchen and start up Kentlee's coffee. I'm gonna need this shit to get through today. I'm tired as fuck from tossing and turning with worry all night.

"What's up?"

"Bastards struck again, but this time at the club. Last night. Fuckin' vandalized our bikes, man. Like school aged punks. Spray panted their shit all over our bikes. It's fucked up, but they're a thorn in our side that needs to be taken care of. Red's dead, and whose bitch is next?" Snipe asks.

Involuntarily, my eyes go back to the closed door where Kentlee is showering. She could be next, and that would fucking gut me. Nobody knows that she's carrying my baby yet, either. Just me being right where I am is dangerous enough, add the fact that she's got my baby inside of her and I'm spending my nights here—that makes her a target. Plain and simple fact. It wouldn't take much for someone to watch and figure it out. Figure out that she means somethin' to me.

"Yeah, it's time for war," I grind out.

"What are you gonna do with her?" he asks, lifting his chin, knowing damn well what we do with Old Ladies is put them on lockdown. But Kentlee isn't my Old Lady, and she's not going to be, either.

"We're movin'. I'll stick with her secretly. I'll come through the back and leave the same way. The new place will have a garage, so hopefully nobody will notice me coming and going," I say with a shrug.

Sniper looks at me with disappointment and nods once before he stands and claps my shoulder with his hand.

"Call Torch and Dirty Johnny," he grunts.

"Church in an hour. Start making calls," I order. He nods before he leaves.

I sit back on the sofa and wonder if I'm making the right call by not claiming Kentlee.

Am I keeping her safe or putting her in harm's way by not locking her ass down with the rest of the Old Ladies?

I don't need the questions about her to surface, so I decide to stick with my plan. She's mine, but she's a secret. Makes me feel like shit, but I need her safe. I don't need the club to touch her and muddy her up. I need her clean, sweet, and waiting for me.

chapter ten

Kentlee

I used to think that lazy Sunday mornings were heaven. *I was wrong.* Lazy Sunday mornings being wrapped in Pierce's arms are heaven, with a cherry on top. I couldn't lie with him another minute longer, though.

I was nauseous and I had found that having a piece of bread with peanut butter slathered on top tamped that nausea right down. So I slid out of bed and made myself one. Once I was finished stuffing my face and drinking a whole glass of milk, another thing I noticed I absolutely adored now that I am pregnant, there was a knock on the door. Bates Lukin graced me with his presence.

I didn't talk to him for long. Pierce ordered me to the bedroom, and the look on his face had me more worried than curious, so I didn't question him.

I think about Bates as I wash my hair. It's been years since I've seen him. So many, in fact, that I hadn't known he was even back from his duty in the Marines.

Bates Lukin – talk about a blast from the past.

He dated my sister when she was fourteen and he was seventeen. She loved him, *really loved him*. I watched her fall apart the day he left for boot camp, and she was never the same. Something happened between them, something I couldn't understand, and she's been changed since.

"Sugar," Pierce calls into the bathroom as I turn the water off and grab my towel.

"Yeah?" I ask, drying off before stepping out of the shower.

"Gotta go. Got shit to do. You gonna be okay the rest of the day?" he asks, pressing his hand against my lower back, bringing my body closer to his.

"Yeah, I have some houses I'm going to go and look at in a little while, then dinner with my parents," I shrug as I trace my finger along the black swirl tattoo on his shoulder.

"You got someone you can take with you to those houses?" he murmurs as he tips his head down to watch my finger on his shoulder.

"I can go it alone. The keys are at the office," I say, tipping my lips in a half smile.

"I don't want you goin' alone to a bunch of empty houses, baby girl. Be better if you took one of your bitches with you, at least," he says.

I take his words into consideration. He's being protective and I like it. *I love it, actually.*

"Yeah, I'll find someone. Maybe Brentlee will want to

come."

I smile and he leans down to place a sweet kiss on my lips. He doesn't need to know that I don't really have any friends. That's what happens when you're kind of nerdy in school. Brentlee has a slew of fake friends, but I couldn't handle that. Not at all.

"Good girl. Now, I gotta go. Call me when you're done with the family and I'll come over." He squeezes my hip before he turns to walk away from me. I stand in the middle of my little bathroom, wrapped in a towel, watching his perfect jean encased ass go. Then I shiver.

Fuck, he's hot.

Once Pierce is gone, I call my sister, and it only takes two words—*house hunting*—to get her raring to go. Brentlee likes to shop, she doesn't care what she's shopping for. As long as it's shopping, she's in her element.

Pierce never did give me a budget, so I found four homes to look at—all rentals, all with a garage, and all with a moderate price. It's more than I could ever afford on my own, but with him pitching in, I'm fairly certain we can make it work.

"I didn't know you wanted to move?" Brentlee asks as I give her directions to the first house. I don't feel the best and talked her into driving.

"I wasn't, but things change," I say, trying not to give it away. I won't be able to last. I never could keep secrets from Brent. She can keep them from me, but I'm an open book.

"Spill it, woman," she says, grinning as we pull up to the first place.

I take a look at the house and sigh. It's in a decent neighborhood, not the best, but not the worst. They are fifties style houses, all lined up. If they weren't different colors, you wouldn't be able to tell them apart. The yard is neatly kept by our company's lawn service, and I wonder if Pierce will be outside pushing a mower when we move.

I bet he'd look spectacular all sweaty and hot doing yard-work.

"Well…" Brentlee says as we walk up the front porch.

I ignore her while I open the house. Once we've walked inside, I lock the door and turn to face her.

"I'm pregnant," I confess. Her mouth drops open as her eyes bug out.

"*Shut.Up,*" she screeches.

"I am," I say, tearing up.

Then, to my surprise, she wraps her arms around me and pulls me into her body in the first sisterly bit of affection we've had in years.

"Kentlee," she murmurs into my hair, "who is this bastard? Where is he? I'll kill him," she cries out.

I take a step back from her and am surprised by her fierce protectiveness. Seems like this pregnancy is bringing out people's need to take care of me. I've been taking care of myself for so long that I'm not used to other people caring about what I'm doing, or what's happening to me. It feels good, though — It feels nice that Pierce and Brent are both willing to take care of me, in their own way.

"He wants to be with me—wants this and wants us. This house is for us to start a family," I explain. Brentlee's eyes widen once more.

"That hot dude that dragged you out of the club?" she asks.

"Fury, yeah," I admit.

"Kent, that guy is a *Notorious Devil.* You can't have a relationship with one of them. You can fuck them for a good time, but you can't actually *be* with them. They're dangerous," she says.

I know she's saying it out of concern and not anything else, but her words still sting. Pierce doesn't feel dangerous to me. But from the outside looking in, I can see why she would think that.

"We're going to try, Brent. Maybe he'll be bad for me, but he cares for me and he wants this," I say as my voice wavers and tears fill my eyes.

"I just… *he was old*… I don't understand it at all," she says, pressing her lips together as she shakes her head.

"He's thirty-five. Yeah, he's older than me, but we have something, Brent. I honestly don't understand what you and Scotty have, but I don't meddle in your choice when it comes to him," I confess.

I watch her eyes dull slightly before she shakes her head and the look vanishes.

"He's safe," she tells me as we walk into the tiny little kitchen.

It isn't the best kitchen I've ever seen, but it would be do-able.

"Because Bates wasn't?" I ask.

I watch her from the corner of my eye as she bites her bottom lip, something she does when she feels emotion.

"Bates was… *Bates*. No man will replace him. But yeah, he wasn't safe," she says, nodding.

I drop it. I want to tell her that I just saw Bates, that he's back in town, but I don't. He thinks she's happy. *She* thinks she's happy. There is nothing I can say that would change anything at this point.

We stay silent as we finish looking at the first house. It's not the best, so I hope the rest are better.

Maybe I should have upped the budget I set for myself. This first house is kind of dumpy.

Brentlee and I get in her car to go to the second home. We don't talk about anything as I give her directions to the home. It's an uncomfortable silence and I look over to her, knowing she's thinking about something, practically watching the wheel's spin in her brain.

It isn't until we step inside of the second house that she finally speaks.

"Is he your Bates? Is he the one, then?" she asks.

"I think he could be," I say as I step into the kitchen.

It's beautiful for a rental. I can't help but imagine myself behind the stove, with Pierce standing at my back, his hands on my hips and his lips on my neck.

Perfect.

"I hope he is. *God*, I hope one of us gets to keep the love of our lives," she says, grinning.

I wrap my arm around her.

"Scotty *is* the love of your life," I tell her. She scrunches her nose at me.

"Scotty is comfortable; he's safe, he's predictable, and we'll be happy together. I love him, don't get me wrong, but he's not the one who makes my stomach clench and my pussy ache. That was always Bates, and always will be. He's the only man who has ever made me feel that way," she admits.

Brentlee's words are telling, *so telling* and so damn *sad*. I want her to have him. I want him to have her. They deserve epic happiness and I wish they could have that, but it doesn't look as if it is in the cards.

That makes me depressed for them.

"I want you to have it all, Brent," I say as I step into the backyard of the home.

It's small and manageable, but big enough that maybe we can put a small play-set in the corner.

"I'll have it all, Kent. I'm going to be a fancy lawyer's wife. I'll be able to stay home with our kids and be the perfect wife and mom. I'm going to have a husband who dotes on and adores me. I'm going to be the *envy* of all my friends. What more could I want?" She sounds so spoiled, so vain—that's not her.

This is the Brentlee she shows her girlfriends, the phony party girl.

I don't care for her.

I like the real Brentlee, but she's hiding from herself, and hiding herself from the world.

"Okay, baby sister, you'll have it all. I want you to have everything you want," I say, wrapping my arm around her tiny waist.

"Mom's going to flip her shit," she says on a sigh.

"No joke."

"This is your place, you know?" she states.

"Yeah. This is it, isn't it?"

"You'll be happy here, with your man and your baby."

We don't say anything else. There isn't anything else *to* say. Brentlee is making the life she thinks she wants. She's nineteen and thinks that she *knows it all*. There's nothing I can say or do to advise her at this point. I don't think Scotty is the man for her, but she's determined to make her relationship and future marriage with him work out. I can only hope that it does, for her sake.

I look out the window and sigh as we drive toward my parents' house in silence. I'm starting a path I never thought I would be on. I'm going to move in with an outlaw biker—the president of his club, at that.

Nothing is as I had planned.

Plans have a way of never working out, and I am okay with that—so far.

I have a man who wants me, who wants to take care of me, and who wants our baby.

How can I complain about life being not as I planned when life is giving me so damn much right now?

My parents' house comes into view and I suddenly feel sick to my stomach with nervousness. I am dreading this conversation, but it needs to happen. They need to know what is going on in my life, even if they won't approve of it.

I just hope that they can be open-minded enough to accept my decisions on the matter. I shouldn't hold my breath, though. They barely tolerate the fact that I'm unmarried and not relying on a man.

Little do they know that they're about to get their wish, it just isn't what they had envisioned.

"Girls," my mother cries as soon as we open the door.

I want to roll my eyes.

Brentlee lives here at home still, and I just saw my mother last week. Yet, she acts like we haven't seen her in months. *Drama-Queen.*

"Mom," I mumble as I hang my purse up on the hook by the front door.

"You're just in time to set the table, Kentlee," she directs. I do as she says, knowing that if I don't, she'll raise hell until I do.

107

I need to stay inside of my own head until it's time to spill my secret. Brentlee, *surprisingly*, helps me set the table, and it feels like we're little again—like it's us against the world.

I know that this feeling won't last. Once my secret is revealed, Brent will fade away while I'm roasted on a spit; but it feels good to have her at my back for the moment.

Once the table is set, I go in search of my dad. I find him in his office on his computer. *He must be on call.* He is studying the computer monitor so intently that he doesn't hear me walk inside or shut the door. I clear my throat to alert him to my presence. Only then does he tear his eyes away and finally focus on me.

"Kentlee," he murmurs.

"You on call?" I ask, lifting my chin toward his computer.

"Yeah. I'm monitoring three patients right now," he says before he stretches his body.

My dad still looks good for his age. He's tall, with an olive complexion and thick dark hair, only a touch of gray at his temples. He's still fit, too, spending too many hours living off of coffee alone, then visiting the gym at least four times a week to play tennis or basketball with his friends.

"I have to talk to you and mom tonight. You'll be eating with us, right?" I ask, knowing that sometimes he'll take his dinner in his office when he's on call.

"Wasn't planning on it, but if you need me to, I will," he offers with a smile.

"Yeah, probably should. It's important," I say, looking at my feet.

I can't look him in the eye. We aren't very close, my father and I, but he's still my dad and I still seek his approval in everything that I do.

"I'll be there in five minutes. Just let me open up my iPad and get it set up," he says with a serious nod.

I leave my father's office and head toward the kitchen to help my mom finish setting the table. My thoughts travel to Connellee. I wish my big brother were here. He's always the one on my side. We aren't best friends, but when my mom gets on my case, Conn is always there to tell her to back off. He would support me; he would offer help in any way he could give it – or any way I would accept it.

I miss my big brother, but he's off living the college life, studying and becoming a doctor. *He amazes me.* He succeeds in everything he attempts. I wish I could be more like him.

"Well, what's this you wanted to talk to us about then, Kentlee?" my father asks as we sit down at the table.

My mother's head pops up and her eyes widen in surprise. I didn't want to tell her ahead of time that I wanted a chat. She would have been relentless trying to find out first.

"I – uh – I met someone," I begin.

My mother's eyes round as her face lights up.

"What's his name? What does he do?" she immediately asks.

I pinch my eyes closed for a moment, taking a deep breath before I continue. I'm just going to spit it out quickly, like ripping off a band-aid.

"His name is Pierce and I'm not exactly sure what he does, but we're moving in together, and I'm pregnant with his baby," I blurt out.

I then watch my mother's face go from excited to absolutely shocked. Then I chance a look over to my father, who is emotionless. However, I don't miss how his fists and his jaw are clenched.

He's pissed.

"*You're pregnant?!*" my mom screams.

"I am," I answer.

"Who is this man, Kentlee? Don't lie to me," my father grinds out.

"He's the president of the *Notorious Devils*," I confess. My father's face turns bright red in anger.

"Are you fucking serious?" my mother screeches. I stare at her in complete surprise. I have never heard my mother curse before—not in my whole life.

"Mom…" Brentlee begins. My mother shuts her up with a side-long glance.

"You've just ruined your life and this entire family," my mom says.

"That's not fair," I begin.

My dad holds his hand up, which shuts *me* up.

"I cannot have trash like that in this family, Kentlee. We have to uphold a certain image in this society, and a man like that? He doesn't belong. Men like Scotty belong here. I could overlook it if you fell for a man with a blue collar job. I wouldn't be happy about it; but if you dated a police officer or a firefighter, at least it would make us still look decent. This guy? No, Kentlee. I won't stand for it," he announces.

"So if I move in with him, then what? I'm out of this family?" I ask, my lips trembling with each word.

"I'm sorry, but yes. You either take care of that baby and break it off with him, or you're out," he says.

I blink in shock.

Of all the ways I saw this going, never in a million years would I think my own father would suggest an abortion.

"Dad, I could never abort my baby," I say, my voice shaking and tears forming as I place my hands on my belly.

"That's your answer?" my mother interjects.

I stand and my eyes flick back and forth between them, unbelieving that my parents would do this to me – would make me choose between my baby and my family. Even if things don't work out with Pierce, I will never regret keeping this baby. *I couldn't.*

"I will never destroy a life to appease you. This wasn't planned, *at all*, but it happened. I'm not ashamed that it happened, and I'm not ashamed that it happened with Pierce. He's been good to me and he's willing to do what it takes to make this work – or at least give it a try. I'm sorry that you feel a baby would give you so much shame," I say before turning to Brentlee. "I love you, Brent. You're always welcome in my home and in my life."

I turn and I leave.

There is nothing left here for me.

Grabbing my purse off of the hook by the door, my fingers linger on the knob—waiting—*hoping* that my parents will realize their mistake and stop me. They don't.

I walk out of their house, leaving them to their small-minded world.

I have a life to live, a beautiful life with a new family of my own. I begin to walk, irritated that I allowed Brentlee to drive me, because now I'm without a ride. I dig my phone out of my purse and place a call to Pierce.

It goes straight to voicemail.

"Pierce, things didn't go well with my parents. My sister brought me over to their house, and I have to walk home. If you get this, maybe you could call me and give me a ride?" I ask before ending the call.

It's dark and lonely on my walk home, so I decide to call Connellee before my parents get to him first.

"'Ello," he answers with a yawn.

"Hey, big brother," I say, smiling. Even his sleepy hello makes me smile.

"Kent? What's up?" he asks with concern laced in his voice. I never call him, like ever. He's my brother and I love him, but he's been gone for years and hardly comes home from school.

"A lot," I admit before I take in a deep breath.

"Well, are you going to tell me or keep me guessing?"

"I met someone," I confess, afraid to tell him the rest of the story immediately.

"And…"

"And, we're moving in together, I'm pregnant, and mom and dad don't approve of him. They just disowned me," I rattle off quickly. Connellee grunts.

"Black sheep syndrome, Kent. Total black sheep," he chuckles.

"This isn't funny, Conn. They are so pissed. They told me to get an abortion if I wanted to stay in the family."

"Are you fucking kidding me?" he shouts.

I can tell he's just as angry as I am about it.

"Wish I were," I murmur.

"Assholes. Don't worry about them, Kent. You're a big girl, you make your own decisions. They're being their normal close-minded selves. They'll either get over it or they won't, but don't you change the course of your life for those petty assholes," he lectures. I smile to myself —*I love my brother.*

"No worries. I basically told them to fuck themselves," I admit.

"Good. Now who's this guy, and is he going to take care of you?" he asks.

I spend the rest of my walk home with a smile on my face as I talk to my big brother. It's the first time we have ever talked like this before in our adult lives, and it's nice. I didn't realize how much I had missed having him around until this moment. It feels good to have his support, even at a distance.

Once I reach my house, I promise to call him more often with baby updates, and to send him pictures of my growing belly—something he thinks is going to be freaky, but awesome—and then we hang up.

When I am inside of the house, I lock the door behind me and strip off my clothes and shoes. *My feet ache.* I look down at my phone and frown, only just realizing that I walked for over an hour and Pierce never called me back.

I decide to text him before I shower and crawl into bed.

Me: I made it home safely, walking home from my parents. I'm going to bed now. See you…. Whenever.

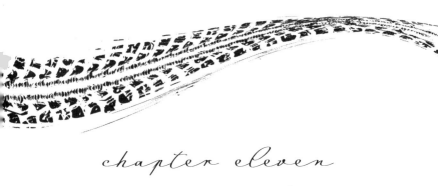

chapter eleven

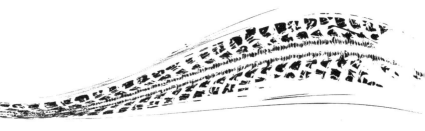

Fury

W*ar.*
      The word lingers, tasting vile on my tongue, but it
is a necessity in this life.

I close my eyes and take a hit from the joint in my hand. *I need the green to calm down.* Brothers are gathering their Old Lady's and children, packing clothes for a few weeks and shopping for food that will hopefully last a month.

We'll probably need to take a few runs for fresh shit as the weeks go on.

The temporary lockdown I insisted on a few days ago has just been blasted to semi-permanent. No end in sight, at this point.

"Notice you ain't goin' to pick anybody up," Sniper remarks, lifting his bearded chin at me.

"*Nope.* Gonna enjoy this smoke right here and bake a while," I reply, knowing exactly what he's referring to—the fact that I didn't rush out of here like the other guys and grab Kentlee to keep her safe from the *Bastards.*

"You need me to keep an eye on her, I'll be more than happy to stick around her for protection," he says, his eyes searching mine.

"Don't want you anywhere near her," I growl.

He nods once with a tip of his lips.

"Didn't say I'd fuck her, man. She's like a sister to me, anyway. A hot as fuck sister, but a sister, nonetheless."

I want to stab him in the throat and gut him for calling her hot—*she's mine.*

But is she?

If I don't claim her in front of my brothers, is she really mine at all?

"She'll be fine," I reply, ignoring his bullshit taunting about her being hot as fuck.

"You're the boss, *prez*," he hisses in obvious disagreement of how I'm handling this situation.

I couldn't give a fuck.

My phone dances around on the table, ringing, and I look down to see her name flashing. I don't answer it. Not in front of him. I answer it, and he'll know she's got my nuts in a vice. She does, too. That woman could say jump and I'd ask how high.

Fucking pathetic.

I take the phone and shove it into my pocket as I walk to the bar. I need a beer and to finish this joint. I need to relax before this whole war breaks out. I look around, noticing many of my brothers are thinking along the same lines as I am. Kitty's busy at work, sucking on one cock while another brother fucks her from behind. I shake my head with a laugh.

Dirty assholes.

I sidle up next to Torch at the bar. He's pouring himself a shot and grabs another glass, doing the same for me. It burns as it goes down, but it feels good, *calming*, and normal. I haven't had my brand of normal these past few days, not since hooking up with Kentlee. *I need some normal.*

"You been missin' around here the past few days," Torch comments. I nod.

"Yup," I say, not elaborating.

"Get a piece of town pussy?" he asks, looking straight forward.

"Something like that," I admit.

"Keep that close to the vest then, brother," he grumbles.

I look over at him in surprise, but don't say anything else. He takes one more shot before he leaves me alone to drink.

I don't know how long I sit at the bar, but the music is blaring and the place is filled with Old Ladies, club sluts, and brothers.

The party before the hell; the calm before the storm.

I stumble away from the bar and into my room. I blink in surprise to see Kitty sitting spread eagle on my bed. I grin lazily when she slides her fingers into her pussy and starts to pump in and out.

"Fury," she moans.

It sounds screechy and horrible; it grates in my eardrums, and I don't like it.

I move my eyes back up to her face and cringe. She's nothing but three holes. I feel absolutely *nothing* for her. I wouldn't care if I never saw her again.

My cock doesn't even twitch at the sight of her. I shake my head and take a step toward her. She giggles thinking that this is going somewhere. *It's absolutely not.* I wrap my hand around her bicep and drag her out of the room. I feel her struggling, kicking and screaming, but it doesn't bother me.

"Keep your nasty as fuck snatch out of my room, bitch," I bark slamming the door and locking it behind her.

I grab the top sheet that she had her naked ass on top of and peel it from my bed, tossing it to the floor before I strip myself down to nothing and fall face down on the mattress.

What seems like minutes later, I'm woken by the sound of pounding on my door. I stand on wobbly legs, still drunk from the night before, and rub the sleep out of my eyes, as I wrench the door open. Dirty Johnny is standing there with a shit eating grin on his face.

"What the actual fuck, man?" I growl.

He doesn't say a word, just starts shaking with laughter.

"Got a visitor, brother," he chuckles.

I slam the door in his face before I grab my jeans and slide them on, along with last night's shirt and my cut. I pull my boots on quickly before I walk out of my room and toward the common area.

I groan when I see my visitor.

Kentlee.

She's standing with a hip popped out and her arms folded under her delicious tits, wearing one of her hot as fuck secretary getups. My cock presses against my zipper with need, the need to be buried inside of her *sweet, wet cunt.*

"C'mon," I motion to her and watch her eyes narrow.

I don't give her a chance to say another word before I'm walking away from her and into my office. Once we're inside, I close the door behind her and lock it.

"Pierce," she huffs.

I hold my hand up as I collapse on the chair in the corner.

"First, you can't come in here and bitch me out in front of my brothers. You wouldn't like how I would have to put you in your place if you did that. You get pissed at me, you run your mouth in private where nobody can hear you. Secondly, I wasn't fucking around when I said you weren't allowed here," I inform her. I watch as her spine goes straight and her eyes narrow into slits.

"Do you give the slightest fuck about me, Pierce?" she asks, going in a completely different direction than I thought this was headed.

"What is this about?" I ask, not willing to play any games. *I'm too fuckin' hung over for that shit.*

"I called you last night when I needed you. Not only did you not answer, but you never returned my call after I left you a voicemail. Then I texted you when I got home, and you never responded to *that*. You said you'd be over last night, and you never showed. I mean, is this what I have to look forward to?" she rattles.

My head fucking spins.

"I didn't listen to your voicemail, and I was too fucked up to go anywhere last night. I didn't even get your text. I passed out drunk and alone," I clarify, so she doesn't think I was here getting my rocks off while she was in her bed alone.

"Well, if you had listened to your voicemail, you would have known that things didn't go well with my parents. They disowned me, Pierce. My sister gave me a ride to look at houses and then over to my parents, so I had to walk home alone, *in the dark*. I needed a ride last night. More than that, I needed *you*. My own father told me I had to choose, either abort this baby or be part of his family," she says.

She holds her shit together for about a second before tears start falling down her face.

I don't think.

I do.

I grab her and pull her down into my lap. She shoves her face in my neck and cries.

I'm the worst kind of man.

I was busy voting in a war, drinking, and smoking. I wasn't there when she needed me. One of the *Bastards* could have snatched her up and I wouldn't even have known about it.

"I fucked up, baby girl," I murmur into the top of her hair. "I had some shit go down here and I got drunk."

"You're an asshole," she mutters as she lifts her face from my neck.

"Yeah, I already know that shit," I admit with a grin.

"I have to go to work now," she sniffles. I wipe the tears from her eyes with my thumbs.

Fuck, she's pretty—even when she's crying. Those blue eyes pop, and her lips puff out even more from being swollen.

Christ.

"Not until I fuck you," I growl.

"You smell like a brewery and pot. Were you smoking pot last night?" she asks wide eyed.

"Uh, yeah, sugar," I nod as I unbuckle my pants and pull my already hard cock out.

HAYLEY FAIMAN

"You're a grown ass man, Pierce. You shouldn't be doin' that shit anymore," she admonishes.

I throw my head back with laughter.

"Baby girl, I'm grown, so that means I can do whatever the fuck I want. Right now, I want to fuck you, so bend over my desk like a good girl and lift your skirt," I order.

I watch her whole body shiver before she narrows her eyes on me as she stands up.

"I should tell you to fuck off. I mean, I'm so pissed at you right now, Pierce. *Seriously, I needed you*," she rambles.

I don't hear her because she's lifting her skirt as she shoves her pretty pink lace panties down her thighs.

I wrap my arms around her waist and press my cock against her ass.

Fuck, she's warm.

This ass of hers was meant for me.

Every piece of her was meant for me.

"I'll make it up to you, Kentlee. I'm sorry," I apologize.

I wait for that bitter taste to flood my taste buds from actually apologizing, something I never do—but it doesn't. It feels okay to apologize to Kentlee when I've truthfully done wrong. It doesn't feel bitter or bad, it just feels good, *normal*.

"Make me come and I might forgive you," she breathes huskily. I reach down between her legs to find that she's already wet.

Fuck, this bitch is too good to me.

"I'll make you scream my name, and you'll ache from my cock all day long, baby girl. Then tonight, I'll eat that pussy until you can't take another second. Until you're screaming for me to stop," I murmur into her ear as she arches her hips closer to me, tipping herself, searching for my cock.

I place a kiss behind her ear before gently pushing her down over my desk. Then I plunge deep inside of her.

I fuck her body the way we both like it.

Hard and fast.

Her whimpers fill my office space, along with the sound of my skin slapping against her ass. Fuck, she's always so good. Her cunt is tight and wet, *every time.* I order her to play with her clit. I'm close, I can feel my back begin to tingle with awareness, and I'm going to come soon.

"Make that pussy squeeze me tight, baby girl," I demand, trying to hold myself off.

She's too much, her noises too loud, her body too tight, and all mine.

The combination is more than I can handle and when I feel the first pulsing wave of her pussy clamp down around my cock, I let myself go. I piston in and out of her with a fever I didn't think possible, and she screams while I grunt and empty inside of her.

This pussy is mine, only mine.

Every time she tries to get mad at me and throws attitude, I'll need to show her who owns this—who owns *her.*

"You okay?" I ask leaning over her body as I continue to fuck her at half-mast. She's so warm and wet, I could live buried inside her all day—every day.

"Yeah." She sighs and I know that, *for now*, she's forgiven me and all is well.

I wonder how many times I can make up for fucking up with sex?

Kentlee

I sit down at my desk and feel the soreness Fury left behind just minutes ago. I was so pissed off and hurt this morning when I drove to the clubhouse. I was hell bent on chewing him a new asshole. Then he looked at me, and like an idiot, I melted.

I am so weak when it comes to him, *already*.

This can't be good.

When he apologized, he looked as shocked as I felt at the words. I wonder if he has ever said them before. *I'm sorry.* I don't think that he has. The man he is, in the position he is in, I don't think he is a one who admits mistakes often, if at all—let alone verbally apologizing.

I sigh, shaking my head out of my daydreams. Pierce is going to be a challenge. My feelings for him are already too strong.

I've done the unthinkable.

I've instantly fallen in love with a rough and dangerous man—a rowdy man.

I've fallen for a man who drinks, smokes, and rides a Harley.

A man who is an outlaw and does what he wants, *consequences be damned.*

I've given up my family to give life to a child we created. I am under no illusion that Pierce is tamable, or that this road I am now traveling down will be easy, but I hope with all my heart that it will all be worth it in the end.

"You look pale," Marcy remarks as she hands me a contract.

"I uh… I'm not feeling well," I scramble in my omission.

"What's up?" she asks. I know her and I know she won't stop asking me questions until she's satisfied with the answers.

"I had a fight with the guy I'm dating. We're moving in together," I say, hoping it's enough to pacify her.

"That's why you're getting a bigger place?" she asks as her head dips down at the contract she just wrote up for me.

"It is," I admit. She smiles almost wickedly.

"The hot as fuck biker. Please tell me you let that fine piece of man put his dick inside of you?" she giggles.

"Yes. Pierce," I confess. She jumps up and down, clapping. That's how our boss finds us.

"My office Johnson," he barks, looking at me with annoyance. *I wasn't even the one jumping around.* I sigh as I walk into his office, closing the door behind me.

"What was that all about?" he asks, lacing his fingers together as he places them behind his head.

"Well, Mr. Walker, I'm pregnant," I blurt out.

I can't keep it from him. I wish I could, but he needs to know. I then watch as his brows shoot up in surprise.

"Oh, yeah? Well, congratulations, I suppose," he says, looking unsure of how he is to remark to my situation.

"Pierce Duhart and I are going to rent the house on Maple together. Marcy was bringing the contract to my desk to sign," I say. His mouth opens slightly before he shakes his head.

"You're with the president of the Notorious Devils?" he asks in surprise.

"I am," I nod.

"The one who just signed that contract to open the titty bar downtown?" he asks.

I actually feel the blood draining from my face at his

words.

"The *what*?" I ask breathlessly.

"Titty bar. That's what he said it was going to be," he says, and with the audacity to look sorry for telling me.

"I – uh – he never told me what he was doing with it. I never thought to ask," I mumble, more to myself then to Mr. Walker.

"You look sick. Why don't you take today off. You can make up for it on Saturday. There's already a list of ten people long who have appointments," he offers kindly. While he's not really being *that* kind, I take him up on his offer.

Titty bar.

The words ring over and over in my head as I drive home. I shouldn't care that that's what he's doing, I really *shouldn't*; but I'm hormonal, and pregnant, and a *fucking woman,* so of course I goddamn fucking care.

I slam my hand against my steering wheel before I get out of my car, slamming the door shut; then I go inside of my house, slamming that door, too.

I am so pissed and angry as hell.

I take out my cell phone and call the person with whom I'm so furious.

"Fury," he says distractedly into the phone.

I should be praising Jesus he actually *answered* this time, but I'm so pissed I can't even think about that.

"*You're opening a titty bar?*" I scream into the phone.

I hear him grumble something and a few seconds later he's back.

"Yeah, babe, you gave me the contract for the bar yourself," he says, unbelievably calm.

"I thought you were opening a bar, not a strip club," I

grind out. He laughs. *Laughs.*

"Bars make money, yeah, babe, but they don't make the kind of money I want. Strip clubs are where it's at. What's got you so hot under the collar about it?"

The man is crazy—totally and completely crazy—if he can't see why it's pissing me off.

"All those naked women, all the time? While I'm here, obliviously waiting for you to grace me with your presence. Gee, Pierce, I don't know why I would be upset about that," I say sarcastically.

"Cut the sarcastic shit, baby girl. The bitches at the club-house are a lot skankier than the strippers I'd hire, but you don't get pissed about them," he points out.

He's wrong.

I do get pissed about them, especially Katie *fucking* Powell and her disgusting ass.

"I hate all of it—the club whores *and* the strippers," I admit.

I hear his curse under his breath.

"You think I'm going to go out and get some easy pussy, that's what this is about? Or do you just not like the idea of me seeing all that skin? What's the real deal?" he asks.

It sounds like he's smoking. I tuck that away and try to stay on task.

"All of it," I say, pressing my lips together, even though he can't see me.

"You gotta let that shit slide, baby girl. Am I in your bed?" he asks.

"Last night you weren't," I snap back bitchily.

"You need me right now, sugar? I'll be wherever you are," he whispers.

I know he's trying to keep other people from hearing him.

"I was sent home from work for being emotionally insane, but I have to work all day Saturday," I admit.

He chuckles.

"Give me five, babe, I'll be right there. I'll show you exactly where I need to be, and exactly *why* I only want you," he murmurs.

I tell him goodbye before we both disconnect. I am completely irrational. *Holy hormone insanity.*

I run into the bathroom and quickly shower before I put on my sexiest bra and panty set. If he's coming over here to comfort his emotionally insane girlfriend—I better look hot while he's doing it.

The door bursts open and I am standing in my bedroom with my red pushup bra and red lace panties, my hair long and wavy.

"Fuckin' gorgeous, every single part of you, sugar," he mutters. He pounces on me and I fall back onto the bed.

"I'm sorry. I'm crazy," I whisper.

Pierce throws his head back laughing before his eyes roam over my face.

"I love it. I love all your crazy shit you throw at me. I didn't do right by you yesterday, baby girl. I can understand why after that you'd blow your top at the titty bar. I get it," he murmurs as he kisses down my jaw to the top of my breast.

"You're crazy if you love my insanity," I giggle. He slides my panties to the side before he traces my center with his finger.

"It's hot, the fact you give half a shit, sugar." He moans as he slides his finger inside of me and finds me wet.

I'm always wet for him. *Always.*

"Pierce," I call out. He looks up at me, his gray eyes dark and stormy.

"Yeah?"

"I need you to make love to me right now," I whisper. He nods.

"Whatever you need, babe, you get," he groans as he pulls my panties down. Then his mouth covers my clit and his tongue gently strokes me.

Pierce does as I need—as I ask. He makes love to me for hours.

It is gentle and it is slow.

He shows my body the attention it desires and it fills my heart with love.

This man is all hard edges and gruffness, but he's soft and sweet, too. When he's with me—he's exactly what I need.

chapter twelve

Kentlee

"We need food," Pierce says as his fingers gently stroke my ass.

I'm lying across his chest, snuggled into his hard body, and loving the attention he's showing me. Soft and sweet.

"I don't want to leave this spot," I shamelessly admit.

"I know, baby girl," he murmurs. "You find a place yesterday for us?" he asks, reminding me of the signed contract that's in my purse.

"I did. I signed the contract this morning," I smile.

I then proceed to tell him all about it.

I make sure to include that it has an attached, two-car garage and a nice sized backyard.

"When can we get in there?" he asks.

It surprises me that he's so calm. I keep waiting for him to freak out and run away; for him to tell me that he's not ready, or to just disappear, but aside from his moments of unavailability, he's been there for me.

"On the first," I say, chewing my lip and raising my head to look up at him.

"A week," he murmurs before he blows my mind adding, "*nice*."

"You're excited, then?" I ask. His hand cups my cheek.

"Yeah, baby girl, I'm fuckin' excited. Can't wait to get in a place where we can start setting up for the future. Would make me a fuckin' dick if I didn't want this. You're good for me. *This* is good. Feels *right*," he grins before taking my lips in a sweet, fast, hard kiss.

"Food," I mutter hazily.

"Food," he agrees, with a nod.

I roll off of him to search for something to wear for the rest of the afternoon.

"Can't put you on the bike being knocked up. We'll go grab something in your ride," he announces.

I knit my brows together in confusion.

"Why can't I go on the bike?" I ask.

I like riding on the back of his bike, being pressed against him, holding onto his hard middle.

"Not gonna have you back there and then have to lay it down. Not putting our baby in danger like that, babe," he explains. It makes me fall a little harder for him. This man warms my heart in a way I didn't think was even possible.

"Okay," I whisper as tears shine in my eyes.

"Put some clothes on, I'm fuckin' starved," he grumbles.

I dash the unshed tears away with my fingers and root

around in my drawer to find some panties and a bra. Then, I grab a pair of cutoff shorts and an oversized, cropped shirt that hangs off of my shoulder and shows off my stomach. I'm not going to have this flat stomach much longer. I want to show it while I got it.

Once I'm dressed, I throw my hair up into a messy bun and slide my feet into a pair of flat canvas shoes. I'm going for an *I-don't-give-a-shit-messy-look* today. Pretty sure I've succeeded, because the only person that I give a shit if he likes what he sees is Pierce. I watch him, but his eyes are trained on my bare stomach, and they're heated.

"Ready?" I ask, taking my purse and throwing it over my shoulder.

Pierce just stares at me, his eyes dark and cloudy and his nostrils flaring.

"Fuck no," he growls.

I blink up at him in shock.

"What?" I ask.

"You can't wear that shit out in public," he grunts.

I blink again, not believing this conversation.

"Loose cut off shorts and an oversized shirt? I'm not even showing cleavage," I obviously point out.

"You're showing leg and stomach. Too much fuckin' skin, baby girl," he grumbles.

I throw my head back laughing.

"My pussy aches from you being inside of it just an hour ago. I've got stubble rash all over my body from your beard, and my hair is a hot fucking mess. Yet, you're worried about a little stomach and my legs showing? You can't be serious," I laugh. He shakes his head before grabbing a handful of my ass and pulling me into his chest.

"Dead fuckin' serious, Kentlee. This body is *mine*. Mine to touch, mine to fuck, and only mine to look at," he grumbles before his lips press hard against mine in a bruising kiss.

"I'm hungry, baby," I mutter breathlessly.

"I'll feed you, but know that in the future, you don't show any fuckin' skin unless I'm with you," he orders, slipping his hand beneath my hair, at the nape of my neck.

He bends down to brush his lips across mine in a brief touch before he steps away and holds his hand out. I put my hand in his but he shakes his head with a grin on his perfect lips, instead.

"Keys, baby girl," he murmurs.

I gape up at him.

"To my car? Uh, no," I say, shaking my head.

"I'm the man," he points out, quickly taking the keys from my hand.

"What's that mean?" I ask, following him out of the house, pausing only to watch him lock the front door behind me.

"Means if I'm in a car, unless I'm fuckin' dying—and probably even then—I'm fuckin' driving," he states.

I stop in my tracks and just stare.

"Are you being serous, or are you fucking with me?" I ask in surprise.

"Dead fuckin' serious," he says as he folds his big body into the driver's side of my car.

"You're a crazy alpha-male, aren't you? I mean, I know you're a man's man, but I didn't expect you'd be at quite this level," I point out, putting my seatbelt on as we head toward whatever restaurant Pierce decides we'll be dining in this afternoon.

Obviously, women don't get choices with him in charge.

"Don't get bitchy and crazy on me when I can't fuck it out of you right now," he mumbles. His response causes me to burst out laughing. "And don't get cute," he grins, stopping at a red light.

"I'm happy," I smile, taking his hand in mine.

He doesn't say anything else, just puts our combined hands on his thigh. We ride to the restaurant in silence, comfortable silence, and I can't help but daydream a bit about what is going to become of our future together.

Babies. A house. Tons of delectable sex.

I can't wait.

Fury

Kentlee hasn't said much at lunch, but it doesn't bother me. *She's happy.* I'm making her happy, and that's all that matters. I take my phone out of my pocket when it begins to ring and almost groan.

My dad.

I called him yesterday but he was busy, which was his subtle way of telling me he was knee deep in pussy. I should be disgusted, but I'm not. When my mom died, my dad started fucking every piece of tail he could.

I would get pissed at first. I thought that he was happy my mom was gone, that he was reveling in being free. Now that I'm older, I understand that it wasn't because he was going wild with his newfound freedom, it was because he was trying to forget. He loved my mom, loved everything about her and the life they shared.

"Pops," I say, answering the phone.

I listen to him take a drag off of his smoke and almost laugh when I think about Kentlee's words about *me* being too old to smoke pot.

"You called," he grumbles into the phone.

My eyes catch Kentlee's, whose eyes are wide and staring at me, a fry hanging limply in her fingers.

"I did. Met someone," I mumble.

"Old Lady material?" he asks. I can tell he's grinning.

"Not quite," I admit. My dad chuckles.

"Too sweet for that, then? You always did have a weakness for the sweet ones," he says.

"Yeah, exactly that. We're having a baby though, Pops," I inform him.

The phone remains silent.

"Pops?"

"Yeah. I... you're going to have a baby?" he asks.

I can tell he's getting choked up.

"I am," I say, taking Kentlee's hand in mine as I smirk at her. She returns my smirk with a bright, beautiful smile, and I feel my heart flip at the sight.

"My son is going to have a baby with a sweet girl," he breathes.

It almost makes me blush.

"Yeah."

"When do I meet her?" he asks.

"Got some shit to take care of up north, but after that, we'll take a little road trip out to you," I explain, hoping it's enough for my dad to understand.

My dad knows what's going down with the Aryan's and the Cartel. This isn't something that I can brush under the

133

rug. I need to deal with it, and probably sooner rather than later.

"Sounds good. And son?"

"Yeah?"

"I'm happy for you. Treat her right, if she's the sweet you want," he advises. I grin.

"Plannin' on it, Pops," I say before I end the call.

"Your dad?" Kentlee asks, knowing damn well it was him.

"He can't wait to meet you. Kinda pissed I have to put it off until I handle some club shit," I say. She smiles sweetly.

Perfection.

Kentlee and I spend the day together. I take her to the home improvement store and load up on boxes to pack up her little house. I grab bubble wrap, tape, and packing paper.

I probably won't pack a fuckin' thing for her, but I want her to have everything she needs. I'll be the muscle, loading the shit up, and I'll help in any way she wants me to—but packing? *Nope.*

"I guess I'll get started tonight," she says as I finish unloading the packing shit from her car.

"I gotta head to the club for a few hours. I got a meeting with a contractor for the new bar at five, and then some work I need to do at the clubhouse. You'll be all right here alone?" I ask, not wanting to leave her.

Something is calling me to stay, but I can't. I have so much shit to catch up on. Shit with the *Bastards*, and the new strip club. I can't spend any more time playing hookie with my woman.

"I'm good, baby, just going to start packing the kitchen. I can eat takeout and microwave stuff until I move. Not that I cook much for just myself, anyway," she shrugs.

I wrap my arm around her thin waist, bringing her close to my body.

"Can't wait for you to cook for your man, baby girl," I murmur, kissing just behind her ear, where I know she loves it. I trail my lips down her slim neck.

"Yeah?" she asks breathlessly on a moan.

"Fuck yeah. Filling my belly before I fill you with my cock? Sounds like an epic fuckin' night," I tell her. She presses her tits against my chest. I can feel her nipples through her thin shirt and I go from half-mast to hard as steel. "I don't have time, Kentlee."

"Please, I'm so damn horny," she whimpers. *Fuck me.*

"Hands and knees. It's going to be fast, baby girl," I warn.

I watch in amazement as she strips, fast as lightning, and falls to her knees, spreading her thighs and tipping her ass for me.

"Gorgeous," I mutter, stripping my own clothes before I fall to my knees behind her.

I grab her ass with my hands and spread her cheeks apart, groaning at the sight of her tight little asshole.

Fuck, I want in there.

I want to claim every part of her as mine. But not right now, not while she's got my baby inside of her.

I don't say another word before I glide my cock between her pussy lips, watching as I slowly sink inside of her. Kentlee moans beneath me and throws her head back as he arches her ass even more, causing me to slide even deeper inside of her tight cunt.

Fucking epic, every damn time.

"Pierce," she whimpers. Her voice fuels me—fuels my fire to fuck her harder, to make her whimper, and whine, and moan for me.

I wrap my hands around her hips and dig my fingers into her flesh, fucking her hard, listening to my skin slap against hers. It's like music filling the room, her whimpers and my grunts.

Fuck.

I wrap my hand in the knot of her messy, piled up hair and wrench her back as one of my hands goes to her clit. She needs to come, because I'm hanging on by a fuckin' thread.

"Come on my cock, Kentlee. Show your man how much you love his cock inside of you," I urge.

She shivers before I feel her pussy clamp down around me and I roar in her ear with my own release. It came on with a vengeance I hadn't expected, but fuck it was hard, and so fucking good.

I wish I could do it again.

"Pierce," she moans as her whole body begins to shake.

Slowly she slides to the floor, her legs and arms too weak to hold her own body weight. I pull out of her before releasing her hair, and then lie down next to her on the floor.

"You a happy girl now?" I ask, gliding my fingers through her wet pussy. Her come mixed with mine feels so good on my fingers.

"Mmmm," she moans.

"Can I leave for a while and get some shit done so that I can come home at a decent time and fuck you again?" I murmur against her shoulder as I slowly fuck her with my fingers.

"Yeah," she sighs as her hips lift to meet my fingers.

"Do you need to come again?" I ask. She opens one eye to look at me.

"No, I'm okay. That just feels really good," she confesses.

I pump into her a few more times before I remove my hand from her body and find my clothes.

"Get some packing done and I'll be home a bit later," I say, not thinking about my word choice. I watch her lips form a lazy smile.

"Okay, Pierce, I'll see you later tonight," she mutters, making me smile.

She's so fuckin' cute when she's sated like this, and I find that it kills me to fuckin' leave her. I do, though. I have contractors to meet, plans for the *Bastards* to make, and I have to check on our latest shipment to Canada.

I walk away from her, from the place I want to be, so that I can get some work done. I have to keep a presence at the club, even if all of my brothers know that I'm fuckin' some town pussy. I narrow my eyes on the road and leave where I want to be most without looking back.

chapter thirteen

Kentlee

The next week goes by so quickly, my head is spinning. I spend my days at work, my evenings packing, and my nights—my nights I spend with Pierce inside of me before we both pass out. He hasn't been around other than to fuck and sleep, but he's been busy with the new strip club, something I'm trying very hard to accept as a reality, even though I hate it. He claims one of the other guys will be managing the club, but he wants to make sure all of the construction goes as planned. I don't know if I believe him. I can imagine that holding auditions would be very exciting for a man, and he wouldn't want to miss it.

I'm trying to keep my hormonal crazy in check, but it isn't easy.

Now, it's moving day.

I was hoping we could wait another week, but Pierce needs to do it this weekend. Apparently, he has something to do out of town next weekend, though he won't tell me what it is.

I hate that he's keeping things from me, but we aren't at a place where I feel like I can demand answers. He's in my bed every single night, *so far*, and he always tells me where he's going, texting me throughout the day.

I don't think he's really hiding anything, just omitting his exact whereabouts, because it's something to do with the club. He says that they don't tell anybody anything; they keep it to themselves and run everything they do secretly. I can't help but wonder how illegal it all really is.

My cell rings as I finish packing the last box and I am surprised to see Brentlee's name flash on the screen.

"Hello?" I ask in confusion.

"Hey," she says, sounding small—tired, maybe.

"What's up?"

"You aren't mad at me, are you?" she asks.

I sigh heavily at the question. I *should* be mad at her. She let me walk home alone, and she didn't stand up for me. But I can't be upset with her. She's always been the overachieving, perfect daughter. I wouldn't expect her to buck our parents—ever.

"No, Brent," I concede.

"You're moving in with him, then?" she asks timidly.

I hate that she seems scared.

"Yeah. Today, actually. My entire house is packed and he should be here any minute to take the first load to the new place," I admit, trying to hold back my smile. I can't, though.

I'm too flipping excited.

"Scotty says that Fury is bad news, that the whole club is dangerous. He, uh, he doesn't want me talking with you anymore. I'm so sorry, Kent. This sucks so bad," she whispers. I can hear the tears in her voice.

I want to tell her that it's okay. I understand. But I hate it. I want my sister in my life.

I've already lost my parents, isn't that enough?

I hate Scotty.

He's such a pretentious asshole, and he's so fucking controlling, it's unbelievable. Not that I don't have my own controlling ass of a man, but unlike Scotty, I can't imagine Pierce ever telling me I'm not *allowed* to talk to my own family.

"I'm always just a drive and a phone call away, Brent. I'll always be here, and I'm always your sister, no matter what," I tell her.

I hear her hiccup as she sobs into the phone.

"I love you, Kentlee. I know we haven't always been on the same page, but you're my big sister, and I love you so much," she murmurs between her sobs.

It kills me.

I want to hug her, I want to watch her walk down the aisle in her gorgeous wedding dress, and I want her to be part of my baby's life.

Unfortunately, we don't always get what we want.

I sit down on the couch and I have a good cry. *I need it.* I mourn the loss of my parents and my sister.

While I don't have them, at least I still have Connellee. My brother. My supporter.

I hold hope that one day my family will reunite and mend all the wounds we've inflicted on each other, but for now I have to accept what's happening.

"What the fuck?" Pierce growls as soon as he walks through the door and sees me crying on the sofa.

"Nothing," I mumble, putting on a fake as shit smile.

"You sure? Who do I need to fuck up?" he asks, taking the few steps he needs to be right in front of me. He shocks me by dropping to his haunches to look me in the eyes.

"I'm sure, baby," I whisper, wrapping my arms around his neck and bringing his mouth closer before I kiss him.

"Right," he grunts before he pulls me closer to him, spreading my lips with his tongue.

"Fuck, my *eyes*," Bates yells from the doorway.

"*Bates*," I cry out, surprised to see him standing in my living room.

"Here to help you move, darlin'," he mumbles.

My shitty mood disappears because Bates' is here, and he's helping us. Just when I think my circle is doing nothing but shrinking, a silver lining appears.

Today, that silver lining is Bates.

"Stop lookin' at my woman and start moving shit," Pierce barks.

Bates just grins before giving him a mock salute.

Between the three of us, it only takes a couple hours to completely move my stuff into the new place, which looks empty as hell with only my furniture in it. Pierce only moves his clothes over, leaving all of his furniture in the small room of his at the clubhouse.

I look around and try to envision where I'm going to put things; then I make a list of what I can buy to make it a bit homier. I can't paint the walls, but I can add big framed prints. Soon, I'll be able to add pictures of our little family—

our baby—all over the walls. I have a feeling I'll be filling the space up like crazy.

"You like it?" Pierce asks after Bates has left.

"Love it," I sigh. He wraps his arms around me from behind, his lips sweetly touching my neck.

"Glad my baby girl is happy," he murmurs.

"When do you leave? How long will you be gone?" I ask.

I have a doctor's appointment in a week and I want him there.

"No more than a week," he says as his lips skim my skin, sending chills over my whole body.

"I have a doctor's appointment next Friday. Do you think you could try and make it back for that?" I whimper as his hand pops the buttons of my shorts and dives into my panties.

His finger skims my center and I push my ass into his hips, giving him room and silently begging for more. I cry out when his fingers pinch my clit.

"I'll be here, baby girl. I'll be here when you need me, sugar," he vows as he slides two fingers inside of me, teasing me, barely entering my pussy.

I want to grind down on him, and I even grit my teeth to keep from doing so. He's in a mood, a slow mood, and no amount of begging will change the way he plans on fucking me. I've learned a lot this past week about how Pierce fucks. It's never the same, and he comes home in moods.

"Thank you," I sigh as his fingers, finally, plunge all the way inside of me.

"Need this pussy, baby girl," he says as he kisses down my neck.

He can have it.

He can have whatever he wants.

As long as he keeps touching and kissing me—*I'm his to do with as he pleases.*

"Take it," I moan.

Pierce moves his fingers, using them to shove my shorts down before he fills be from behind. His hand on my back pushes me down, and I use my own hands to brace myself on the coffee table. I cry out when he slides out of me and then slams back inside. *Fucking perfect.*

"I'll hold you up, sugar, just relax," he commands. I do just that, waiting for him to fuck me, hard and fast from behind. Maybe I read his mood wrong a few moments ago.

My head hangs down as he begins to slowly fuck me.

Nope. I read him just fine. He just wanted to torture me.

My legs shake with each plunge of his cock inside of me. It's hard to keep myself standing, but it's what Pierce wants, so it's what I'll do for him. I feel one of his hands leave my hip before he wraps his fingers around my nipple, pinching and pulling on the sensitive bud. I throw my head back with a surprised moan.

"*Pierce*," I cry out.

"Fuck, yeah. So wet for me," he mutters as his hips begin to slam a little more forcefully into the backs of my legs. His cock burns; it hits me so deep at this angle, stretching and filling me with each thrust.

"I need to come, Pierce, *please*," I shamelessly beg.

At my words, his hand slides from my breast, down to my clit where he begins to pinch and rub firm circles. It's too much, and it's sublime all at once. My body feels like it's strung up tight, wound and ready to explode.

"Come, baby girl. Come around me," he grunts.

It doesn't take much more persuasion. Pierce bites down on my shoulder and I scream his name while my whole body begins to shake with my climax.

"Fuck. Yes," he grunts as I feel his cock grow and then twitch inside of me, filling me with his release.

I sigh at the full feeling.

My heart is full, and so is my pussy.

This man fills me in any way I can imagine, and every way I could dream up.

"You need to rest," he murmurs, pulling out of me before he picks me up and carries me to our bed.

Ours.

I can't believe he's going to be living with me one hundred percent—full time. I feel giddy and excited and happy - *so blissfully happy.*

"I should clean up," I murmur as my eyes begin to droop.

I'm tired and sated. *It's been a long Saturday.* Pierce chuckles from somewhere in the bedroom, and a moment later, I feel something warm between my thighs. I open my eyes and look down to see him cleaning my body of the left-over evidence of our lovemaking.

"Pierce?" I question.

This is the first time he's done this, and I can't believe how caring he's being.

"Sleep," he whispers before his lips touch my lower belly. Its a little rounder now, looking like I've eaten a big cheese-burger and am bloated, but he and I know that there's a baby inside of there.

The next morning, I wake up and I instantly know that I am alone. The house is just a bit colder, completely silent, and sad without Pierce milling around. I look to my nightstand to reach out and grab my phone to check the time. I find an envelope sitting there, instead. My name is written on the outside in sharp, manly writing. I open it and find a pile of cash and a note.

Kentlee –
Gonna be gone a week so here's some cash.
Get whatever the fuck you need. House shit, food, whatever.
    I won't be around much but I'll text you every night.
    Take care of my baby and take care of you.
-Pierce

I run my fingers over the note, and can't stop the smile that spreads across my face.

Then, I take the cash out and count it. *Three thousand dollars.* I count it a second time, just to make sure, and then I stare at it in surprise.

Pierce already paid the deposit and the first month's rent on the house. He paid all the fees for opening utilities, too. There's no way I can spend this much on food for just me.

I decide that I can buy some maternity clothes, which I desperately need, and I want to look at prints to decorate the walls with.

I grin to myself.

I take half of the money and put it in the nightstand. No way do I need the full amount in clothes or pictures for the house.

I spend the day shopping. Buying maternity clothes for work, and then for around the house. My clothing options

145

have become slim lately, nothing is fitting, and rubber bands holding my jeans closed can only work for so long.

Once I have bought some basics, I decide to look at the home decor store. As much as I want to go wild, I decide to stick with necessities. The whole trip only eats up seven hundred of the fifteen hundred I took with me.

I go to the grocery store and spend another two hundred dollars, and then put the rest of the cash back in the envelope to join the half from this morning.

Later that evening, my phone rings. I surprised to see that Pierce is calling me instead of texting.

"Hello," I answer excitedly.

"Baby girl, how was your day?" he asks.

His voice is low but the background noise is loud, like a party.

"I went shopping, bought some maternity clothes. But Pierce, you left me way too much money," I scold. He chuckles.

"Sugar, spend it all. I have plenty. Miss you," he murmurs.

I hear a girl's high pitch giggle in the background.

"Pierce, where are you?" I ask. He doesn't say anything.

"Just campin' at another club for the night, and then onward tomorrow morning. Having a few beers before I hit the sack, baby girl," he grumbles.

It makes my stomach flip, and not in a good way. I can hear the loud voices, male and female, in the background, along with loud music. He's partying. I need to trust him, though. It's hard, and I might have to force myself, but I need to do it.

"Okay, Pierce," I whisper, trying to keep my tears at bay.

"Remember what I promised you, Kentlee?" he asks.

I don't say anything. *I can't.* He's promised me a lot, and so far, I think he's delivered. Now, I'm not so sure.

"Only cunt I want is yours, baby girl. Nobody else's," he vows. I nod like he can see me.

"Only you, Kentlee," he says again.

"Only me," I finally whisper.

"There's my good girl," he says. I can tell that he's smiling.

"Okay, I'm okay," I promise. I hear him laugh.

"Get some sleep, sugar. I'll call you tomorrow," he promises.

I hang up, feeling his promise is true; yet I can't stop that sinking feeling in the pit of my stomach that's telling me – *something is not right.*

Fury

Last night's party was insane. Pussy everywhere—naked and waiting. My brothers know how to party, no matter what chapter we visit, and these Canadians are no different. I stayed true to Kentlee. I promised her I wouldn't fuck any whores, and I didn't.

That doesn't mean I kept my eyes shut, though. I grin, thinking about all the little shows those whores put on for us last night. *Fucking epic shit.* Girl on girl is always a favorite view of mine, and those bitches did not disappoint.

Now, I'm in work mode.

This shipment has to make it to the Aryan's or we'll be out, not only a fuckton of cash, but also a client. I, personally, wouldn't give a fuck about being out a client like these racist bastards; but at this point, it wouldn't be an amicable split. The last thing we need are more enemies. We have our hands full with the Bastards as it is.

We make our way just back over the US/Canadian border and wait for the truck full of guns and ammo. If protection is what this truck wants, it's going to get it. There are twenty-five of us waiting to ride this fucker from the border to Calgary. Five of my brothers and me, then twenty of our Canadian club brothers.

I take over driving the truck.

Letting the paid-off driver leave, I take matters into my own hands.

The roads are clear and it seems like we're going to get the shipment where it needs to be, on time, and unharmed.

It all seems way too easy.

I watch as my brothers start peeling off from behind me, the bikes disappearing one by one. Suddenly, I am surrounded by cops.

I slam on the truck's breaks and come to a stop.

Fuck.

Fucking Shit.

I watch as they step out of their police cars and draw on me. I look around and notice that I'm alone.

Guns are drawn, and I'm alone.

Just a whole truck full of illegal guns and ammo trying to cross the border from the US into Canada, and me.

Numbly, I follow the police officers barked orders, but my thoughts aren't on them.

My heart starts racing and images flash through my mind.

I can't stop myself from thinking about Kentlee and our

baby.

This is *it* for us.

I am so fucking fucked.

I narrow my eyes as I lift my hands at the officer's commands.

How in the fuck did they know I was transporting illegal guns? Unless they were tipped off somehow, a plain truck shouldn't have drawn attention. I sit in the back of a patrol car, my mind moving from Kentlee to exactly what's happening to me. Finally breaking out of my shock, the only conclusion I can come up with is that someone is in on it from the inside.

Problem is, I don't know who. My club or the Canadian club?

Someone is dirty and I plan on smoking the fucking rat out.

This isn't the first time in my thirty-five years that I have been arrested, but this is the first time I give half a shit.

This is the first time I have someone waiting for me.

This is the first time I know I'm not going to just skate on by.

This is also the first time I have been in serious fucking shit.

I close my eyes and curse to myself as I am read my rights, as they march me toward a police cruiser. It doesn't even matter. I'm fucked no matter what I do. I don't say a word as I'm hauled to jail. My next step won't be bail. I already know this.

My next fucking step is goddamn fucking prison.

Hours later, I am told to make a phone call, and as much as I want to call Kentlee, I can't. I need my attorney. Not just our decent attorney in Idaho, but I need my Pops' federal attorney.

This isn't just a slap on the wrist.

The local cops have already informed me that the Feds are on their way to drag me to their own turf.

Fucking Feds.

I am so fucking fucked.

My attorney tells me to sit tight, don't say shit, and wait. He agrees I won't be given bail and says he'll get started on my case immediately. Luckily, my dad has given the guy enough money over the years that he considers me an urgent case.

I can't think about anything, though, except for the woman who is waiting for me back at home.

Kentlee and my baby.

I try not to think about the fact that I didn't make her my Old Lady. She's not going to have the support of the club for our baby, and I just moved her into a place that she can't afford on her own.

I'm such a piece of shit.

I should declare her immediately, but I can't.

Declaring her my Old Lady makes her a prime target for the *Bastards*.

Without me there to protect her, I'll have to lean on my brothers. I could do it, but do I think that they'll protect her as good as I will? *Nope.*

I have to bank on the fact that she's a big girl and can take care of herself. She will. Hopefully, she'll understand. I don't want her to be a target. I have to protect her the only way I know how from here, and that's to *not* claim her.

The only hope I have is that Bates knows she's mine.

He'll take care of her.

chapter fourteen

Kentlee

I want to believe in Pierce and I want to trust him, but he makes it so damn hard—all of the time. I only heard from him that first night he was gone. I've been trying to fill my time with working as many hours as Mr. Walker will allow.

It's Friday now, and I'm sitting in my doctor's office, lifting my shirt while he rubs cold goop on my belly. The little wand he uses presses against my stomach and then the quiet room is filled with the sounds of my baby's heartbeat. It's gorgeous and miraculous all at once.

I am so pissed that Pierce isn't here to witness it.

Once I am finished at the doctors, after I answer all of his questions—yes, I feel okay; morning sickness isn't too bad; yes, I'm drinking plenty of fluids; and yes, I'm taking my pre-natal vitamins—I go home.

I'm tired and I feel nervous.

I've tried calling Pierce since last night, worried that I hadn't heard from him and worried he wouldn't make it to-day, but there was no answer. *I had a right to worry. He never showed and he still hasn't called.*

I change into a pair of leggings and a tank that is too tight around my belly. I'm home alone; nobody is going to see me. I just need to breathe. Hours tick by with nothing—no texts and no calls.

I wonder if the pressure of this new life has gotten to him. *Has he run off, never to be heard from again?*

I don't think he would leave his club; the men there are like brothers to him. And he's their leader – their president.

A knock on my door around eleven in the evening star-tles me. I walk to the peephole and see none other than Bates Lukin standing on the other side. *I don't hesitate.* I open the door and he strolls right inside.

Once I have closed the door behind him, I look into his face and I gasp. He looks worried and stressed. I haven't seen him look this way since the day he left for boot camp all those years ago.

"Bates?" I question. He sighs.

"Sit down, babe," he mumbles as he sits on the corner of my sofa, his arm across the back and his legs spread out.

I do as he instructs, my body automatically moving. Something is so wrong, I can feel it in the room. It's so heavy, I can practically taste the doom swirling around us.

"It's Fury," he says. I shake my head.

"No, he's hurt? *Worse?*" the words fall from my trembling lips. Bates just shakes his head.

"Arrested. Don't look good, babe," he informs me with a blank stare.

I can't stop the tears from flowing.

"Where is he? When will he be out? What happened?" I rattle off.

Bates moves closer to me, wrapping his arm around my shoulders.

"Gun trafficking across the Canadian border means federal time, babe. He's being held in Boise without bail. Has a good lawyer, so hopefully he won't be in for too long," he mutters.

I look into his eyes. They're full of sympathy and pity and I hate it.

"When can I see him?"

"He didn't put you on the list of visitors," he grunts. *My breaking heart shatters.*

"Seriously?" I ask as the tears continue to fall from my eyes.

"I'm going tomorrow to see him. I'll try to talk him into putting you on the list, and I'll get more details about the whole thing then," he explains.

It fucking hurts.

The outright pity he's looking at me with *kills*.

"What am I going to do, Bates? I just moved in here and I can't afford the rent, let alone anything for the baby. I am so fucked," I whisper. Bates gives me a little shake.

"The baby?" he asks. I nod.

God, he doesn't know. Pierce never told him.

"Don't worry about any of that right now, babe. I'll help you figure something out," he says.

I want to believe him, I truly do, but I see nothing but

doom for my future. *Destitution and doom.* I have no familial support aside from Connellee, and Pierce is gone.

"You'll let me know more when you find out?" I ask through my sobs.

He just hums as he holds me close. It's friendly. He's my friend, and he's exactly what I need right now. Eventually, I feel my exhausted eyes begin to close. Then my body is being lifted and carried to my bed.

"Sleep. I'll contact you when I know more," he murmurs, placing a gentle kiss on my forehead before he leaves me alone.

So fucking alone.

I can't help myself.

I cry some more.

Bates Lukin - Sniper

That dickhead.

I get on my bike, leaving Kentlee alone and fucking broken.

I ride to the clubhouse for emergency church.

Drifter will take the gavel as acting president since Fury is gone. Drift is a good guy, but a total hothead.

I walk into the room for church, dead last. Usually, I would give a shit, but I don't today. Not after watching Kentlee fall apart in my arms.

"Nice of you to join us," Torch says.

I flip him the finger before I flop down in my chair.

"Okay, Fury's locked up," Drifter announces, as if we didn't already all know.

The few guys that were with him scattered as soon as they saw the cops, and I should be glad only one of us is caught, but I'm not. Brotherhood means watching your brother's back, not abandoning him as soon as you see trouble. And never fuckin' leave your president's dick blowin' in the wind.

"What's the lawyer say?" Buck asks. He's older, hard assed, potbellied, and an all-around decent guy.

"Trying to get him a deal. Plead out, three years of a five-year sentence and then a year of probation," Drifter informs.

I groan at the length of time. Three fuckin' years and his woman is pregnant, scared, and alone.

"Got another problem," I voice.

Everybody looks at me.

"The club?" Dirty Johnny asks, referring to the strip club that I'm in charge of managing.

It's supposed to open in three months and it'll be a shit-ton of income for us. We need it open, sooner rather than later.

"Nope," I say. This problem has nothing to do with the club and everything to do with Kentlee.

"Fury knocked up his piece," I say, trying to keep myself looking impartial.

"How in the fuck do we know if it's his?" Bull barks out laughing.

"It's his," Torch says quietly from the end of the table. Everyone looks at him.

"What, you were there or some shit?" Dirty Johnny cackles. I roll my eyes.

"Kentlee Johnson ain't a whore. The baby is his; he moved in with her last weekend on the DL. Promised to take care of her and the baby," I inform them, even though I know it would piss Fury off like nothing else. The whole room looks at me with shocked expressions.

"He never claimed her, and I've never even seen the bitch," Drifter points out.

I curse Fury in my head.

Fury and his need to keep Kentlee separate from the club.

"He was into her, he'd want his baby taken care of," Torch says. He's on the same path as I am, but that's only the two of us.

"We vote. Those in favor of financially helping the woman *claiming* to be knocked up by Fury?" Drifter asks.

Torch, Dirty Johnny, and I raise our hands.

"No's?" Drift asks. The rest of the room raises their hands.

Twenty to three.

Fuck.

"Tell you what? You want to employ her at the club once she pops the baby out? Feel free. That's about all we can offer her without Fury actually claiming her," Drifter says. I watch the other guys nod.

Kentlee Johnson working in a strip club?

The thought is almost comical. Fury is going to be fucking livid. Even if I put her as a cocktail waitress and not on the stage. He's going to flip the fuck out.

I decide I just won't tell him. What he doesn't know won't hurt.

I lie to myself.

The guy is going to be fuckin' pissed.

I saddle up for the eight hour ride to Boise. I have to get Fury's instructions on how he wants to deal with the *Bastards* at this point, and tell him about his baby mama—beg him to put her on his fucking list.

He should have claimed her and taken care of her, not hidden her like some prized possession he didn't want his brothers to know about.

Kentlee is a good girl, a sweet girl, but she's fuckin' strong, too. She deserves everything good in life, not to be someone's dirty fuckin' secret.

Fury

Visitor's day.

Fuckin' bullshit.

I dress in my trousers and brown tee, with a long sleeve shirt over the top and buttoned. I roll the sleeves just past my elbows and tuck the shirt in *neatly*. On my feet, old man white tennis shoes.

I hate the bullshit they make us wear, the regulations, and all of the fucking rules.

Everything is timed.

Breakfast at a certain time, lunch, labor, working out, and even leisure time is on a goddamned schedule. I line up with the rest of the men I now share a home with. Punks, assholes, creeps, gang members of all kinds, and then other brothers like myself—some enemies and some allies.

I walk into the big empty room and make my way toward my designated table, waiting for my visitor.

One of my only approved visitors, *Sniper*. He comes toward me, jeans, black tee, and boots. No cut and no chains hanging from his pockets. *Searched.*

"Brother," he says, dipping his head when I stand to greet

him with a handshake.

"How's things?" I ask.

I'm asking about everything, the *Bastards*, the Aryan's, Cartel, Canadians, and of course, Kentlee.

"Need to know the news on those guys with no fathers," he says, talking in code. He wants orders on how to deal with the *Bastards*.

"Should be smoked out," I instruct.

I want them gone, cleared out of our town.

"Will do, brother," he says with a nod.

"How's she?" I ask, needing to know.

I need to know she is okay and safe.

"Not good. Wants to see you," he says.

The air leaves my lungs. *Fuck no*. No way in hell would I let that pure creature step one foot into a federal penitentiary.

"Can't let her see me like this," I say, looking into his worried eyes.

"You guys have a baby coming, man," he remarks, as if I could fucking forget that I left my woman alone and pregnant to be locked up.

"Keep an eye out for her; get the brothers' help," I say. He shakes his head.

"Didn't claim her. They voted; they're not doing shit for her," he informs me.

It makes my stomach turn.

I didn't claim her for a reason. I didn't want her getting dragged into shit. I didn't want her seeing all the bad shit that comes our way.

I wanted to keep her clean, and pure, and fucking perfect. I should claim her now, but it won't matter. It's been voted and it won't be overturned.

Fucking useless.

"*Fuck*. You'll watch out for them?" I ask, knowing that Sniper has a soft spot for my girl. I'm going to use his obvious pining over her sister to keep my woman safe.

"I'll do what I can," he says. With that, our time is up.

I have a meeting with my lawyer next—plea deal.

I watch my brother leave and my slick suited attorney waltz in. He doesn't belong here in his thousand-dollar suit, but he's here and I hope he has good news for me.

"Three years, one-year probation," he says, cutting the bullshit.

"Time off for good behavior?" I ask hopefully.

"Nope. Three years, full sentence, and one-year probation. It's your first major offense, they're willing to work with you," he explains. My back stiffens.

"Three years, full sentence?" I ask, curling my lip in disgust.

"I'm advising you to take it. You never know the judge you'll get in court. You get a hard ass, it could be double that time, Pierce," he informs.

I sigh heavily before I take the paper from him and reluctantly sign the fucking piece of shit.

"There," I hiss, thinking about the fact that I won't be free for three fucking long ass years.

"Sucks, man. Wish I could get you out of this one, but being caught red handed leaves little to doubt," he murmurs.

I have to agree with him.

I was fucking caught driving the goddamned guns over the border, or at least trying to.

Once I'm back in my tiny as fuck cell, I lie on my cot and close my eyes. I think about Kentlee, how her body was already changing and how I won't see her fully develop.

I won't see her fat with my kid. I won't watch my kid come into this world. I won't hear its first words or see its first steps. All that shit that I was actually looking forward to.

Then I think about money. I made her move to a place she couldn't afford and she has the extra expense of a baby now. I hope that her parents will help her out. Maybe she can tell them what a fuck up I am and they'll take her back into the fold?

I'm a coward and a piece of shit for not making sure my shit was square. I was being a cocky asshole and now? *Now, my woman is alone, without family, and without the club at her back.*

I'm too much of a pussy to contact her, to let her see me in here, weak and locked up.

I hope that she'll forgive me when I'm out.

I hope that she'll give me a second chance.

I fuckin' love that girl and I never told her.

chapter fifteen

Kentlee

"*He doesn't want you to see him like that.*"

Bates' words play on a constant repeat inside of my head. It's been four long months and I haven't heard a word from Pierce. Not a letter or a phone call. I've been waiting by the phone and checking the mail religiously, in hopes of some form of communication from him.

I have received *nothing*.

I have cried and mourned his absence from my life.

Bates has been invaluable to me. He shows up weekly, like clockwork, to do whatever it is I need help with.

Last week, he built the baby's crib, a gift from my brother. A gift I needed too badly to send back. I thanked him from the bottom of my heart, with tears rolling down my cheeks.

"Proud to be an uncle, Kent. I'll do whatever I can. I wish I could do more. If I weren't so busy in school, I'd come there and help you," he says, his words hardly above a whisper. It's late and surely his roommate is sleeping close by.

"You've done more than I ever expected or could dream of, Conn. Thank you so much. When you get a break, will you come and meet him?" I ask. He agrees.

Him.

My baby is a him.

I found out last month that Pierce and I are having a beautiful boy, and he will be beautiful. Pierce is stunning, so I know that this baby will be blessed with good looks, too.

Only four months of his three-year sentence have passed, and already it feels as though it has been a lifetime.

I only had him for mere weeks, but I feel his loss fully. The knock on the door alerts me to the fact that it's time for my weekly visit from Bates.

I live for these moments.

"Hey," I say with a fake smile on my face.

"Hey, LeeLee. Fuck, little dude is growing like crazy," he says, placing his rough hand on my swollen belly.

It's true. It seems as though my stomach has doubled in size in just the last few weeks.

My smile softens, turning real at his gentle touch. I don't want Bates, not at all, but it feels nice to be around someone who is genuinely kind to me. I haven't had a lot of that lately.

When I told my parent's about Pierce being in prison, they said an *I-told-you-so* and ended the conversation. I don't know what I was hoping for but, that wasn't it.

Connellee is the only person in my entire family that I have talked to in seven months, and he's hundreds of miles away.

"I know. I'm going to have to evict him soon if he doesn't stop growing," I murmur.

Bates throws back his head in laughter.

"How are you doing financially?" he asks, just as he asks every single time he comes by.

I'm not doing too badly, but I'm not doing that great either. I sold my badass car and got a small four-door, used sedan, cutting my car payment in half.

I've been contemplating moving to a cheaper place, but I don't want to live on the bad side of town. Granted, there is no real bad side of town here; it's just that I want to feel safe, and this neighborhood does that for me.

Plus, there's the sick part of me that wants to stay here because of the memories of Pierce here. We only had a few days here together, but I can walk into a room and just picture him here.

"I'm okay now, but I'm going to have to get a different job or something after he gets here; something that pays better," I answer.

I hate admitting it.

Being broke is no laughing matter, especially when you have a baby on the way, and all the expenses that come with it.

"I'm managing the strip club, LeeLee. I didn't want to even suggest it, and I'll help you out as much as I can, but would you consider working there once the baby comes? You'd make a shit ton more cash," he suggests.

I burst out laughing. It's hilarious, really.

"Bates, I'm going to be fat and gross. I may never lose the baby weight, and you want me to strip?" I ask.

"Fuck no. Fury would kill me if I let his woman strip," he says.

I look down at my feet, trying to hide my tears.

Pierce's woman.

I wish I were.

I'm not.

It was made very clear to me that I am not Pierce's, by any means. Not only by him, but by the club. Bates explained that, usually, when a member gets locked up, the club helps his Old Lady out. Bills, babysitting, groceries, and whatever she needs, the club is there for her.

This gave me hope, maybe my situation wasn't as dire as I thought it was going to be. Then Bates hit me with the truth. I wasn't claimed by Pierce. He hadn't told anybody about me, or about the baby. They weren't convinced I was really pregnant with his child, and they all voted against helping me out.

I wish I could be mad at the whole lot of them— but I'm not. I completely understand their reasoning for why they did what they did. *The person I'm disappointed in is Pierce.* I'm not even angry anymore, just sad and disappointed.

"Then what's the plan?" I ask, shaking the negative thoughts out of my head.

"Cocktail waitress. You can work nights, be home with the baby during the day. The tips will be way more than what you make at Tommy Walker's office," he explains.

"Who would I ask to watch the baby? Who could I trust?"

"Drifter, the VP, his Old Lady would do it. She watches a bunch of the kids, and she'd be down to help out," he offers. I shake my head.

"No, I can't ask for club help. No way," I say. Bates just smiles sadly.

"What about Mary-Anne? She loves kids. Maybe she could rent the baby's room, you could move the crib in your room?"

Mary-Anne is Bates' little sister. She's about twenty now and she would probably be a great sitter. She was always such a sweet girl, and unless something has changed, she probably still is.

"Can I trust her, Bates? Can I seriously trust her? This is a baby we're talking about, it's not like pet sitting," I say, sounding bitchier than I want to sound—but this is *my* baby.

"Swear on my life, LeeLee, you can trust her. She wants out of my parent's place, but can't afford anywhere on her own. Bet she'd watch the baby in exchange for rent. Do you both a solid. She'd get out from under my father's relentless thumb and you'd get free sitting."

I shiver thinking about Bates' father. The man gives me the willies; he always has. He's a rigid, uptight asshole, worse than my own father. Beyond that, he's verbally abusive and manipulative. There was a reason Bates ran off to the Marine's the day he turned eighteen, and his father was that main reason.

"He bad with her, too?" I ask him. He knows what I mean; I don't need to explain.

"Not like he was with me, but she's ready to be gone," he confesses. I nod.

"Okay, yeah, she can move in. And in exchange for rent, she can watch the baby while I work. Thank you Bates. I really appreciate everything you're doing for us," I murmur.

I can't believe I'm going to work at a strip club with a baby at home. I cringe at the thought. But beggars can't be choosers and I'm not opposed to begging at this point.

"You'll be safe. I'll make sure I'm there during your shifts. You'll make a shit ton of money, plus it'll put you in with the club. At least I can offer some more protection if you're living with my sister and working there," he explains.

"Do I need protecting?" I ask, suddenly worried about his choice of words.

"Lots of shit is going down with the club. You're pretty far removed, I hope. But I'd rather be safe than sorry, you know?" he attempts to explain.

It doesn't ease my panic.

Suddenly, I want his sister here, like, now.

"Well, maybe you can help me move the crib into my room and stuff so Mary-Anne can move in whenever," I suggest.

He just smiles before he places a kiss on my forehead.

"You're going to be fine, LeeLee. I'd never let anything happen to you," he says with a grin, I shake my head, knowing he's telling the truth.

Bates would never purposely let something happen to me. He's always been a great friend, more like family. He's been my biggest supporter and ally during the past four months.

Without him, I'd be lost.

I wish that Brentlee could see all the wonderful inside of Bates. I wish that she could see past the smoke and glitter that Scotty offers and accept Bates the way he is. He's such a good man.

Four days later, Mary-Anne is moved in. She's just as sweet as I remembered, with her long dark hair and light green eyes.

Her body is lithe, but curvy where it counts. She hugs me like she's missed me these past years, and I hug her back.

"Thank you so much, LeeLee," she whispers in my ear. I take a step back to see tears shining in her eyes.

"Thank you, too, Mary-Anne. We're a team now," I say, smiling at her. She takes my hand and grins back.

"We are. The best team," she murmurs.

I can't help but feel happy in this moment.

Mary-Anne is in community college, studying graphic design. She wants to open an online business where she designs wedding invitations and cards.

One night over chocolate cake, *our very nutritious dinner,* she explains her dream to me. It sounds perfect. A business owner, her own boss.

"And the great thing is, if I decide I don't want to live here anymore, I can pick up and go and not even lose one client," she says. I nod.

"That's so awesome, Mary-Anne. I mean, not many people are able to do that kind of stuff. I'm so happy that you found what you wanted so early on in life," I sigh.

"What did you want to do?" she asks tentatively. I smile.

"I never had a plan. When we were little and we had to come up with an occupation for career day, my mother wouldn't hear of it. She hated those assignments. She told Brentlee and I that the best thing we could do for ourselves was to marry a man who could support and care for us. We were to be his wife, the mother of his children, his backbone. I wasn't ever really allowed to dream," I confess. Mary-Anne takes my hand in hers.

"You can dream now, LeeLee," she encourages. I scoff.

"Dreams are for people who have the capability to actually make their dreams a reality. I have a baby coming in just about a month. I have rent to pay, and apparently a new waitressing job as soon as my maternity leave is over. I have a man who won't claim me—a man who is in prison and refuses to see or speak to me; a man I am so head over heels in love with, I make myself sick; a man who doesn't feel the same way. No, Mary-Anne, I can't dream now," I lay it out. All of it, and Mary-Anne doesn't hide her sympathy for me.

"Its okay to dream, LeeLee. Your dream doesn't have to be something unattainable. It can be having a healthy and happy baby. It can be working shit out with Fury. It can be whatever you want it to be," she says. I take a deep breath, letting it cleanse me.

"I want that. A healthy, happy baby, and Fury. I want it all, marriage and happiness and a family," I whisper wiping the tears that begin to fall as I stand up to head to bed.

"Then you'll get it, babe," she says, standing to wrap her arms around my shoulders and pulling me in for a big hug. "You'll get it all, I just know it," she whispers before she lets me go.

We separate to our rooms and I lie down and think about Pierce. *Fury.* I think about how safe I felt in his arms, how right it all felt. Being with him, having him hold me, having him inside of me.

I shouldn't want him like I do. I should give up on him completely and move on with my life. He won't even call me on the phone. Something inside of me still wants him. Still needs him. He owns a piece of my heart and I'm afraid I'll never get it back. He'll always own it.

What we had for that short amount of time, *that* was my dream come true.

I pray that he'll come back, and when he does, that he'll still want me. But instead of hiding me, I hope he'll be proud to have me on his arm.

I want it all.

I want my little dream.

A family with a hard man, a rough man, a fucking rowdy man.

I lie back in my cot with my arms behind my head.

It's been a long fuckin' five months.

I close my eyes and wonder where Kentlee is right now. *Has she had the baby yet?* It's got to be getting close. I know she's having a boy. *Snipe shared.* I also know that Mary-Anne, his little sister, moved in with her. That news made me breathe a sigh of relief.

At least she isn't completely alone now. I almost came un-glued when he told me that her parent's wouldn't accept her back into their lives. If I could order a hit and get away with it, I would target those two jack holes.

Then, I remember that I've abandoned her as well. Sniper tries to get me to call her every time I see him, but I can't do it.

If I hear her voice, I'll fuckin' break.

I can't break in this hell hole. I have to stay strong. Only the strong survive. I'll make everything right once I get out. It's a vow I make every single night before I close my eyes.

I'll do right by her.

I'll earn her forgiveness.

I'll earn her trust.

I'll earn her heart.

Without her, my life would be worthless.

I close my eyes and I remember her sweet face, her long blonde hair, and her bright blue eyes. The way she looked up at me with awe and amazement every time I made her come. The way her curvy body melted for me, and into me, with a single touch. The way she tasted, from her lips, down to her perfect pink pussy. *Fuck*, that cunt—spectacular every single time I sank inside of it. She accepted me, no questions asked, and not much shit thrown my way.

I was a fool for trying to hide her.

I'll be a damned if I'll let her go.

chapter sixteen

Kentlee

*B*ear *Pierce Duhart Johnson* was born on a Tuesday at two o'clock in the morning. He came screaming into this world, ready to fight with two balled up fists, a tuft of blonde hair, and a strong set of lungs. He was twenty-one inches long and nine pounds.

I couldn't have him naturally. I tried. I tried no drugs and no surgery; but after twenty hours in labor, I was exhausted and he wasn't progressing. I had an emergency C-section. A few hours later, I held him to my bare skin. He was perfect.

Three months later, he's still perfect.

Being a mother has come fairly naturally to me. I have no clue what I'm doing, but each day we survive. I consider it a success. Bates and Mary-Anne are my saviors. Without them,

I don't think we would have survived this long together.

Tonight is my first night working at the strip club, aptly named *Devils*. Bates brought my *uniform,* or lack thereof, this morning.

It makes me cringe.

"This is gross," I say to myself as I look in the mirror.

I'm wearing a pair of super stretchy shorts, best described as hot pants. Lucky for me, they are high rise and come up to my belly button in the waist; plus, they're black so hopefully they are also slimming. On top, I wear a bra, *a sparkly gold little bra* that barely covers my breasts. I put my long blonde hair into a pony tail and slide bright red high heels onto my feet—another piece of my uniform.

I scrunch my nose at the sight of myself. I look skanky.

"Hot mama. Holy shit, your body is bangin'," Mary-Anne says after she whistles at me from the doorway of my bedroom.

"I look slutty," I mutter. She laughs.

"It's a strip club, babe. You're going to be the classiest dressed person there," she informs me, making me smile.

I so totally am—but I still look skanky.

"Are you sure you're cool for the whole night? My shift is from seven until three. I have to help clean up after it closes," I remind Mary-Anne.

"Puh-lease. That baby loves me. We'll be just fine, he and I," she says.

I know she will. I know that *they* will. I just don't want to leave him. I grab my purse off of the bed and a coat to cover my naked body. No way am I walking out of the house in this thing. I could only imagine what my neighbors would think.

I walk over to the swing, where Bear is blowing raspberries. I stop the swing and lift him out before I cuddle him close to me, inhaling his sweet baby scent.

I gave him a bath before I got dressed, so he's clean and ready for bed, which will be in fifteen minutes. He's on a routine. Seven in the evening until seven in the morning; twelve hours with, *usually*, only one wake up in between for a bottle and diaper change.

He's such a good baby, so calm and sweet.

He has gray eyes that rival his father's and leave me weak every single time he looks at me. I love that he inherited them, but I wish I had Pierce here with me, too. I miss him so much more than I should.

"Almost one year down. Two more to go, sweet boy," I murmur before I give him a kiss and strap him back into his swing.

I thank Mary-Anne again and let her know that I'll have my phone behind the bar, but if there's an emergency to call her brother. Then I walk out of the house and off to my first day of work…as a cocktail waitress—in a strip club.

Something I never thought I would ever do – in my life.

The club isn't open yet and Candy, *her real name*, teaches me the cash register and shows me where everything is located. She's tall and thin, bottle blonde hair and brown eyes. She's nice and seems sweet. She warns me away from the strippers. They're competitive and things can get nasty if they think you're trying to get their tip money.

"Just keep your head down and serve drinks, girl. Don't make friends with anybody," she advises.

"Including you?" I ask with a smirk. She giggles.

"We're on the same team. Sure we live for tips, but we're down here in the trenches working our asses off. Not up there shakin' 'em. Us girls gotta stick together." She grins and it eases my worry. I like her and I think that working with her could actually be fun.

"So you got a man?" she asks.

Isn't that the million dollar question? *Do I have a man?* I'm not sure.

I haven't heard from him in almost a year. Not a letter, not a phone call. Bates keeps me updated on how he's doing, but Fury doesn't even pass messages to me through him. Last time Bates went to see Pierce, I gave him a wallet sized hospital photograph of Bear and asked him to give it to Pierce. I never heard a word about it.

"You do," she says, breaking me out of my thoughts.

"I don't know if I do," I confess. She nods.

"Complicated. I get that. Boy o' boy, do I get that." She grins before the door opens and strippers start to shuffle through. I see Bates walk in a few moments later and he smiles widely before he makes his way toward me.

"Hey, LeeLee. You doin' okay? Candy gettin' you all set up?" he asks, wrapping me in a big bear hug.

"Yeah, I'm a lot less nervous than I was when I first got here," I confess. Bates chuckles.

"I'll be here the whole time. I'm staying on the floor tonight just to make sure you're doin' all right. Nobody's gonna mess with you, LeeLee," he murmurs. I rest my head on his shoulder for just a second before I straighten up and give him a wide smile.

"I got this," I say with determination.

"Yeah, you do," he grunts.

He tugs on the back of my ponytail before he walks off to do whatever it is managers of a strip club need to do before opening.

"You know Bates, then?" Candy asks. She looks confused.

"Yeah. Back in high school, he dated my little sister," I explain. She nods before she starts showing me exactly what tables will be mine for the night.

"So, do you know anything about the club then?"

"My complicated situation is the president," I admit. Her eyes widen in surprise.

"Drifter?" she whispers.

"No, Fury," I say. Her mouth drops open.

"I only met him once, right before we opened. They were holding interviews for staff; not dancers, but actual staff. He was intimidating as all hell, girl. How did a sweet thing like you end up with him?"

"It just happened. We have a baby together." I say.

She'll know about Bear soon enough. I can't help but boast to anyone who will listen about my little man.

"His kid?" she asks, her voice a mixture of awe and shock.

"Yeah, right before he went away," I say.

"Fuck. So you're on your own with a baby?"

"He's three months old," I reply with a nod. "Bates is always around, though, and his sister lives with me."

"That's gotta be rough, him being *gone*-gone," she says.

I nod.

I need to drop the subject. Luckily, the doors open and men start filing in, thirsty and ready to party.

I don't think about Pierce, or even Bear, the entire night.

I'm too busy, too distracted, and by the time I haul my ass home at three-thirty in the morning, I'm wrecked. I'm also three hundred dollars richer in tips.

I take a shower and pour myself into bed at four in the

morning. Bear wakes up at seven every morning; thankfully, Mary-Anne doesn't have classes until nine. She gets up with him and I sleep in until she has to leave.

I get a total of four and a half hours of sleep before I start my day all over again, then I have to work again the next night. Four days on and three days off. It's going to be exhausting, but it's going to pay the bills.

At this point, that is what I am truly thankful for.

Fury

I live for these visits. The one's where it's Sniper and he has something for me. A photograph of my little boy.

A boy.

Bear Pierce Duhart Johnson.

At first, I was pissed that the kid didn't have my last name, but Sniper explained to me that she tried to put my name on the birth certificate but they wouldn't let her.

There's some kind of form I would have had to sign. Since I wasn't fuckin' there to do it, he has her last name. My girl, though, she still gave him my name. It makes me love her even more. He's beautiful, too. Blonde hair and gray eyes that match my own.

He's perfect.

"Brother," Sniper says, pulling me in for a hug and slap on the back.

"Snipe," I nod. He watches me.

I've changed a little in here. My beard a little longer and my hair a fuck ton longer. I haven't cut it once. Right now, it's pulled back into a neat ponytail at the base of my neck.

"You doin' okay?" he asks, the exact same question he asked me months ago, the last time he was here.

"I'm survivin', brother. Almost halfway done, man. Can't complain about that shit one bit," I say. He nods.

"Little dude's nine months now. Fuck, is he cute, too," he chuckles.

I try not to hate him. It's my fault I'm here, not his; but it stings that he gets to see my son and I don't.

"Got a new picture?" I ask like a crackhead hurtin' for a hit.

Sniper nods, taking it out of his top pocket and sliding it across the table. I flip it over and my heart fucking pounds in my goddamned chest.

It isn't just a picture of Bear, like I've been getting.

It's a picture of Kentlee and Bear together.

My whole fuckin' world in one picture, staring right back at me.

I trace the side of her face and can almost feel her soft skin. She's kneeling on the floor in a low cut, plain white tank. I can see the swell of her larger breasts peeking out—*fuck, they look good*. She's got her hands out and he's standing, holding onto her for dear life, with a huge slobbery smile on his face and four teeth in his mouth—two on top and two on bottom.

"She needs to hear from you," he says.

I shake my head, placing the picture in my pocket, unable to look at the glowing perfection of that fucking image and all that I'm missing for a second longer.

"Not while I'm here," I adamantly state.

"Brother, she's workin' her tail off, taking care of your kid, and she doesn't even know if you still want her. If you still want *them*. Bitches need reassurance. She's gone through a ton of shit since you been locked up. You need to *call* her," he urges.

I feel my fists clench at his words.

"What shit's she been through? I thought you were watching out for her, for them?" I bark. He sighs before leaning back in his chair.

"The fatherless sons haven't been a problem. They're lying low these days, if that's what you're worried about. I just mean she went through labor, brought your son into this world, went back to work, and she's lonely. Her family still won't have nothin' to do with her, aside from the brother, who calls her every couple of weeks. She has me and Mary-Anne, but that's it," he says.

It fuckin' breaks my heart. Kentlee is sweet, loving, and so fuckin' perfect. She should be surrounded by people who love her.

"Where's her head at?" I ask.

"She's strong as fuck; stronger than any Old Lady I've ever known. Always got a smile on her face, no matter how fuckin' beat she is. At that baby's side if he makes a fuckin' whimper. She's there, man. You'd be proud of her. She's a good mom, a hard worker, and she's strong— so fuckin' strong."

I don't miss how many times he praises her strength. He wants me to know that claiming her as my Old Lady would be the smart thing to do. He just doesn't realize that I've never wanted one. Making her my Old Lady is a commitment I wouldn't and couldn't take lightly.

As opposed to making her the mother of my child?
Christ, I'm a fuck up.

"I'll think about calling her," I say, mostly to get him off of my back.

"You talk to your Pops?" he asks, changing the subject. I'm grateful for it.

"Yeah. Pissed as fuck he didn't meet Kentlee before the baby came. Wants to get out to Idaho, but there's trouble in his own neck of the woods with those racists," I tell him.

My Pops has been trying to cut club ties with the whole Aryan group. I'm fuckin' pleased as punch; hated those racist pricks from day one. But they're proving to be a problem. A problem that comes bearing bombs and shit. Total redneck bullshit, too.

"Yeah, troubles starting to leak down our way from them, too. We're all on alert though, brother. Keeping shit wrapped up tight," he informs me. I nod.

A few minutes later, visiting hour is over and it's time for me to go back to purgatory.

"She fuckin' anyone?" I ask, though I don't know why.

I shouldn't want to know.

What a woman does when her man is in prison for as long as I'm in shouldn't matter.

All I should give a fuck about is that she's taking care of my son.

"She'd never do you like that, brother," he says. His eyes stay firm with mine, never wavering. *Fucking full-fledged truth.*

"Had to ask," I say with a shrug before turning to walk away.

"Fury," he calls. I lift my head to look back at him.

"Call her. She loves you, brother," he says, and then leaves me standing there.

She loves me.

Does she?

I know the answer to that. I knew the answer before I was even locked up. Of course she loves me; and I fuckin' love the hell out of her.

Then *why?* Why can't I claim her and make her one hundred percent mine?

Why can't I think about having my name permanently marked on her body for the world to see?

Why does it scare me and make me nervous? I am a total goddamned failure.

If my father knew my turmoil, he'd probably punch me in the nose for being a pussy dickwad.

I'm not stepping up to my responsibilities.

I'm not being a man.

I'm a coward.

I don't call Kentlee, because of the coward I am. I can't hear her voice. I can't hear the tears I know that she will shed when she finally hears my voice on the line. I can't let her hear my own tears. Tears I will surely cry for her. Tears I have already cried for her, a thousand times over. *I'm a pussy.* A complete and total pussy.

One day, I'll be strong enough to call her. One day, I'll be strong enough to write to her. But for now, I just hold her picture in my hand and stare at it. The smile on her face, the happy yet tired look in her eyes. The extra curves to her beautiful body. If I thought that body was hot as fuck before, it has nothing on what carrying my kid gave her. Bigger tits, wider hips and her trim waist is still small, but softer. She looks good—*sexy as fuck*, gorgeous as ever, and tired too—but good.

Maybe Sniper is just trying to make me feel bad. She

doesn't look like she's suffering too much. I try to convince myself that I'm right, and Snipe is just feeding me bullshit, but I know the truth. I see it in her pretty eyes. She's exhausted. I close my eyes, counting down the end of another day.

Twenty-two more months and I'll be back home. Back to my woman and my kid, where I belong.

Twenty-two more months until I can take leadership back in my own club.

Twenty-two more months of hell and it'll all be over.

I'll be flying on easy street—just twenty-two more months.

chapter seventeen

Kentlee

Two years to the day.

That is how long Pierce has been gone.

It has been two years and four days since I have heard his voice. I should move on. I should try dating and finding someone else who will love me. Someone who will be there at night, not only for me, but for Bear as well. *I should – but I can't.*

My heart aches for one person, and one person only – *Pierce "Fury" Duhart.*

The selfish bastard.

If I could make myself forget him, I would – in a heart-beat.

If I could make myself forget the way I felt when he

touched me, when he looked at me – I would do it without looking back.

But I can't.

I still dream of him.

I dream about being held in his arms.

I dream about the way he would groan my name when he was inside of me.

I'm past the point of sadness. Now I'm angry.

So fucking angry.

I feel a hand on my ass and then it slaps me. I look down to see a man from a bachelor party. He's completely wasted and he's smiling like an idiot. I roll my eyes and keep walking. It happens every night I work.

I'm pinched, slapped, yanked on, and yanked down.

I stopped wearing my hair in a ponytail on day two, when a man yanked on it to get me to sit on his lap. Now, for the past year, I've been wearing it in a high bun on top of my head.

I've lost weight since working here. Not just baby weight, either. I've legitimately lost weight. I'm smaller than I've ever been, My legs are looking fan-fucking-tastic, but I'm *tired*.

Running around the club, serving drinks, and then running after an active toddler when I'm off—it takes a lot out of a girl.

Mary-Anne has been a godsend, but she's finishing up school and she's ready to go somewhere else. I can see it in her eyes. She has the itch to ditch this town, and I don't blame her one bit.

Tomorrow, I'm going to tell her to go. She's making money on her business venture and she's young; she needs to see the world. What she doesn't need is the responsibility of a baby that isn't hers. Bear is mine, he's all mine, and I can't rely on her or anybody else a minute longer.

"How you doing tonight?" Candy asks as she inputs an order into the cash register.

"Tired," I admit. She smirks.

"Your nights about to get even busier," she says. I furrow my brow in question.

"Club's doing a patch-in. You didn't know? It's *your* private room they rented," I groan.

I hate patch-in parties.

I wish they did them at the clubhouse and not here. This means that after my shift, I have to stay at least two more hours, if not longer, and serve drinks while they *watch* strippers, *fuck* strippers, and *fuck* clubhouse whores.

It's complete debauchery and it means Katie Powell, otherwise known as *Kitty,* will be here.

I can't stand that little bitch.

I grab my phone out from behind the bar and make a phone call to Mary-Anne, explaining that I most likely won't be home until after six in the morning. Luckily, she doesn't have classes tomorrow, so she's happy to get up with Bear and watch him during the day while I try and catch up on sleep.

"Mary okay with watching the little man?" Candy asks. I nod as I take the lined up shots and beers for the ass-slapping bachelor party.

"Yeah, but I'm going to have to let her be free. I'm going to encourage her to travel. She can't hang around and be my babysitter forever," I say with a sad smile.

"She can't, but she would," Candy point out. I nod.

"That's why she can't stay," I say sadly as I take my tray and turn to leave. I can feel Candy's pity burning a hole into my back.

I've been saving my tips like crazy, spending as little money as I need to, so that, hopefully, I can go back to work during the day somewhere without taking a huge hit to my savings. I have one year left until Pierce is released, but I have no idea if he'll come back to me or be done with me. At this point, I have a feeling that he's done. No man sits in prison for two full years without contact, still wanting the woman he left behind.

My heart aches, not only for myself, but for Bear.

Will he ever know his daddy?

Once the club closes down, I take a deep breath and watch as the members of the Notorious Devils MC waltz through the doors. Girls in barely-there outfits hang off of the men as they head toward their designated room. Candy chews on the bottom of her lip and gives me a worried look.

"You sure you don't want me to stay and help?" she asks. I shake my head. Candy has a teenager at home, she doesn't need to hang around here.

"Go home, girl. I got this," I say with a lift of my chin. She squeezes my shoulder before she heads out the door.

I take a deep breath outside of the closed party room door and pray that this night of debauchery isn't too traumatizing.

I plaster on my fake, bright smile and make my way inside. I hear the men shout my name as soon as I walk in. I like most of them. They're dirty assholes, but they're fun bastards, and I wonder why it was that Pierce tried to keep me hidden from them.

I spend the evening serving booze to a bunch of raunchy bikers, and by the end of the late night/early morning, I feel the need to bleach my eyeballs. Watching Bates fuck Kitty up on the stage while she ate out a stripper was just too freaking much for me to take.

Once I walk inside of my house, everything else melts away. The sight of my little man toddling around with a snack cup full of cheerios and a slobbery smile on his face makes everything worth it. He makes the late nights, the hard work, and the miles I walk in high heels all worth it. He is my life, my light, and there is absolutely nothing I wouldn't do for him.

"How was it? You look beat to shit," Mary-Anne says as soon as I collapse on the couch and bring my little man with me for a quick snuggle.

"Lechery at its finest. You really don't want to know," I say, laughing.

"They're gross aren't they?" she asks, wrinkling her nose.

"They really, *really* are," I confess. "I wanted to talk to you before I fall into a comatose sleep."

"Yeah?" she asks, looking confused.

"I don't want you to stay here just because you think I need you. You have dreams, you have plans, you need to do them now," I instruct, hoping that I'm not hurting her feelings. She can't stay here, and I can't be dependent on her.

"You know I'll stay for as long as you need me. Living here has been fantastic; it's been nothing like the life I had with my parents," she says.

I know this. I know how bad her home life was. She's told me more than Bates ever did. It's sad and it's horrible all at once.

"*Go*. Seriously, you only have this one life, Mary-Anne. Make the best of it," I murmur, trying to keep my tears at bay.

Tears slip down my cheeks anyway. Mary-Anne wraps

her arms around me and we embrace. She's like a sister to me. I haven't had Brentlee all this time, but I've had a sister in Mary-Anne, when I needed one most.

"Okay, I'll figure stuff out this week. Will you help me pick a place to go?" she asks, looking so hopeful.

"Yeah. Somewhere sunny or somewhere wintery?"

"Sunny and beautiful," she whispers.

I grin. *California* it is, then. I don't tell her that. Instead, I place a kiss on her forehead before I pepper kisses all over my baby's sweet cheeks, and then I go and pass out from complete exhaustion.

Later that evening, I make dinner for Mary-Anne, Bates, Bear, and myself. Tonight, Mary-Anne and I are going to tell Bates the plan. I'm sure he's going to get all big brother protective about her leaving, but he knows what's best for her. She needs her freedom and she needs to fly.

"You're leaving, right?" he asks, shoving a bite of lasagna into his mouth.

"Yeah," Mary-Anne confesses. I wonder how in the ever-loving hell he figured it out.

"Where to?" he asks around his food, not seeming pissed at all.

"California. I want the beach." She grins widely and he nods once.

"I'll set you up with cash to get you there. Only thing I ask is I get a call from you once a day, every day—that way I know you're okay," he informs her. My mouth drops open in surprise.

"Seriously?" she squeals. I can't help but giggle at her elation.

"Yup. Now, what're you gonna do?" he asks, pointing his

fork at me.

"No clue." I blow out a breath and he nods.

"Hows about I move into Mary-Anne's room? That way you have a man around the house and help with Bear when I'm around?" he suggests.

I blink once before I grin. My heart skips a beat at this man. He's so good, so kind, and so damn sweet. I can't believe the lengths he's willing to go to take care of me—of *us*. It is as if a switch is flipped inside of my head and I suddenly see him in a different light.

Bates, my one constant these past few years. *Bates*, the man that is here, watching over me, helping me, and taking care of me. He's smiling with straight white teeth, his dark hair messy and his eyes bright with his usual wicked gleam.

"I don't want to cramp your style with the ladies, Bates," I murmur. He grins back at me.

"Ain't gonna cramp shit, babe. Got a clubhouse full o' whores to suck and fuck, don't need to wine and dine those bitches," he says. Mary-Anne starts making gagging noises while I feel as though my stomach has completely dropped.

"Yeah, I know how you work, too. I was at that patch-in party last night," I remind him.

At the time, I just ignored it; but today, now that I'm seeing him in this whole new light, it makes me sick. He's a man and he's here He's kind and caring, helpful and sweet, even if he is screwing around like a whore. I caught Fury seconds from getting his dick sucked by Katie Powell, would it be so bad to want Bates for my own? Am I tricking myself into feeling more for him because he's here, right here in front of me when Pierce can't be? It doesn't make me want him less. I'm confused. So confused.

"I do not want to know," Mary-Anne says, holding her hands up in mock surrender.

"You really don't," I admit, shivering in fake disgust.

Bates just shrugs and continues to eat. *This is family*. This is what I envisioned when Pierce and I moved into this place. Now I'm sharing it with somebody else. I should be missing Pierce, but right now, I don't. I have Bates, his smiles and his jokes, his love and his devotion—even if it's not romantic.

This is what life is all about.

Loving, teasing, joking, and laughing.

I wish that my table could be complete with Pierce, Brentlee and Connellee, but would it? Would Pierce even be here if he were out of jail? I've lost faith in him, in the us that he painted a picture of in my head. I have my sweet baby boy, Mary-Anne, and Bates here with me, along with phone calls from Connellee touching base with me.

They are my family now.

I have to push everything and everybody else out of my mind. I have to focus on the present, not the *what-ifs*, or *could-bes*.

Bates Lukin -Sniper

I take a deep hit off of the joint in my hand before I let it out and chase it with some whiskey.

We lost brothers today.

Not just a couple, a whole fuckin' charter. Our brothers in Calgary, Canada are just gone. Fuckin' obliterated.

Blown the fuck up.

It has those Aryan's stink all over it. *Those bomb happy*

pieces of shit. I was never so happy than when MadDog decided to finally cut ties with them. I hated being associated to them at all whatsoever. I'm not one hundred percent pure white, so they pretended I didn't even exist when we had to make contact. Half Russian, a quarter African American, and a quarter Cherokee Indian was too mixed for their taste. *Fuck 'em.* I ever see another one of those racist assholes again I'm going to put a bullet in their head.

"You doin' okay?" Vault asks me as he slides up next to me. He's our treasurer, our money guy.

"Yeah, just angry as fuck those assholes got the best of us," I admit, downing another shot.

"You gonna tell Fury?" he asks, worry etched in his features.

I shake my head once.

No tellin' what Fury would do being locked up the way he is. He'd be liable to find someone with Aryan tats and kill them, adding more time to his sentence. No, that surly bastard needs to come back as soon as possible.

"He don't need to know a fuckin' thing until he's back on free ground," I murmur.

"Fuckin' truth," Vault agrees, slapping my back.

"Need some company?" Kitty asks as Vault stands up to leave me to my drinking. I sigh and look away for a moment before I feel her hand slide up my thigh and cup my cock.

"Get another girl and I'm in," I grunt. I turn to look at her and watch as her eyes light up. I think this bitch likes eating snatch more than any guy I've ever met.

Kitty runs off to find a willing victim and I take two more shots. I need to get drunk to fuck this dirty bitch. I need to get drunk to get my brothers off my mind. I need to get drunk to get the desire I have to take Kentlee as my own off of my mind. I can't go there, not only is she lonely, she's my friend. Nothing more.

I try telling my cock and my heart that, but they don't fuckin' listen. Every time she walks past me in her skimpy as shit little sleep shorts and tank, sans bra. Her fat tits and ass are typically not something I'm attracted to but fuck do I want all of her—or at least my cock does. My heart loves her for a completely different reason, she's soft and gentle, I love that about her.

"Ready, baby," Kitty says shaking my thoughts away. I look over and see a pretty redhead standing next to her.

Oh yeah, I'm fuckin' this new little bitch tonight.

#

Twelve months.

Twelve measly months.

That's all the time I have left in this hell.

I know one thing. I ain't never coming back here again. Fuck this shit.

I can't wait to be free. To eat, do, go, and fuck what I want, when I want, and where I want. Although, maybe not the fucking part. I still only dream of one pussy I want to fuck each night, and that's Kentlee's.

I close my eyes and try to remember the way she smelled. Light and fruity, some bullshit girlie lotion she bought that smelled like cherry blossoms or some shit, but it was her. I miss the way she smiled at me, the way her eyes would light up when I would pull her close to me. The way she moaned and whimpered while she was around my cock. Fuck, her whimpers were my undoing.

I wonder what she's doing right this minute. Late on a Friday night. She's probably home from work with Bear. Giggling and cuddling with the little man. Little guy can already walk, apparently. He can say a few words, too.

I'm missing so much, but it's a sacrifice I need to make. No way am I going to meet my kid for the first time in lock up. *Fucking hell.* I want to be able to hold him in my arms without somebody telling me *not too close, not too tight, and keep your hands where we can see them.*

Fuck that.

An involuntary tear slips from my eye, and I'm glad that I'm alone. Prison is not the place to cry. I can't help myself, though.

Thinking about everything that's waiting for me when I get back, thinking about my woman and my boy—makes me an emotional fucker.

Twelve months.

Twelve measly months.

That's all I have left.

If I tell myself that enough, then maybe I'll feel like it isn't such a long time.

chapter eighteen

Kentlee

"We can't," he whispers as his hand cups my cheek.

"We shouldn't, because we can," I murmur into the dark, feeling the warmth of his hand against my skin.

It's been so long since a man has touched me. My thighs quiver as the thought of his hand sliding down my body.

"He's my brother, Kentlee," he mutters as the heat from his breath fans my face.

Fuck. He smells like whiskey and it makes me groan. I imagine what his whiskey laced tongue tastes like in this exact moment.

"He doesn't even want me, Bates, what does it matter?" I reason. I need someone to want me. I need to know that I'm not completely broken, not completely undesirable.

"Kentlee," he moans before his lips brush mine in a soft kiss.

Bates burps loudly from the kitchen, breaking me of my daydreaming. I know what he's doing. He's drinking straight from the milk carton, *again.*

Our one shared kiss proved that we were not really into each other. I was just lonely. I still think he's beautifully built and sexy as shit, but there's no sexual connection between us. When his tongue slipped between my lips, there was nothing. I felt absolutely nothing. All desire was just—gone.

I hear him rustling around in the kitchen, burping again. If I could choke him, I would. Six months. That's how long we've been roommates, and it has been five months too long. I love him, like a brother, but the guy is a pig—*a totally slob.* I wonder how he was even in the military.

I thought they were supposed to beat the sloppiness out of these guys?

"You're disgusting," I say, wrinkling my nose as I walk into the kitchen to make breakfast for Bear.

"You love me," he responds, wagging his eyebrows. It's always how he responds.

"I don't love your pigness or your crudeness," I point out. He laughs.

"Without me, you'd be bored to death," he says with a grin. I want to yank on his thick, dark beard and pull. He's annoying as shit.

We danced around possibly having feelings for each other, when he moved in and we found ourselves alone together. Flirty comments turned into flirty touches, which turned into our one and only kiss. I'm glad we got it out of the way, otherwise I may have wondered forever if pining over Pierce was a mistake or not. There is no denying the way my body reacts to Pierce. It's nothing short of sexual dynamite. Too bad he's a fucking piece of shit asshole. I'm still angry with him. I probably will be until the day I die at this point.

"Without you my house would always be clean, and it wouldn't smell like disgusting man. Oh, yeah, I'd be bored." I roll my eyes and Bates laughs before I hear him scoop Bear into his arms and blow a raspberry on his tummy.

"Us men gotta stick together, dude," he rumbles.

It makes me smile. One thing that made me more attracted to Bates than I should have been was the way he is with Bear.

Bear giggles his little boy laugh and I wish I could keep him this way forever. Though, so far, I've said that about every stage of his life.

"Is Tammy coming over tonight to babysit?" he asks, taking the plate of eggs and toast from my hands and snapping Bear into his highchair to eat.

"Yeah," I say with a sigh, sitting down with my morning cup of coffee.

"Good. Before your shift, you're gonna come with me to the clubhouse. Party tonight and you need to show up," he informs me. I almost laugh.

"What the hell am I going to do there, Bates?" I ask on a laugh.

I haven't been there since the day I stormed in, pissed off at Pierce, almost three years ago.

"You need to make appearances when you can. He'll be out in six months, LeeLee. He'll want to claim you, and those guys need to already respect you," he announces. I can't help myself, I burst out laughing.

"I'm a half-naked cocktail waitress that brings them shots

and beer during their fuck parties. I could walk in there wearing a nun's habit and they *still* wouldn't respect me, Bates," I inform him.

"They will when you're the president's Old Lady—when you're his, and you walk in there at his side with his baby in your arms. They'll respect you."

"These are all *if's*, Bates. I haven't heard from him in two and a half years. I don't know that he'll want me. In fact, I'm assuming he doesn't." I lower my head and take another sip of my coffee. It's so depressing to think about the future, about what will happen six months from now.

"He wants you, LeeLee. He loves you," Bates says. I can't help the snort that comes out of my mouth at his words.

Loves me.

That's fucking hilarious.

If he loved me, he wouldn't have abandoned me for two and a half years. He wouldn't refuse to see me, refuse to talk to me, and refuse to write to me. He wouldn't refuse to see our child, either.

I've been a mix of emotions since he left. Angry, disappointed, and sad. Disappointment and sadness have won out in my overall feelings on the subject. Disappointment not only in Pierce but in myself. I've let him rule my life these past few years. Rule how I live my life. Not moving on, sitting around in limbo for a man that doesn't even recognize me. That can't even call me.

Now the disappointment is gone and I'm just tired.

"Sure, whatever," I respond, trying to hold back my tears.

I've cried so much in the past two and a half years; I don't know how I can have any tears left to cry. But every night, more tears come. Like clock-work. Like a bad dream. Like a record on repeat.

"Okay, then its something that will happen when he's out," Bates murmurs.

I try not to roll my eyes at his words. He doesn't know shit. Pierce is going to do whatever the hell he wants, and if that means he doesn't want Bear and me, he won't think twice about cutting us loose.

"I'm going to take Bear to the park today, wanna join?" I ask as I stand up to clear Bear's dishes and my coffee cup.

"I got shit to do. Keep an eye out, yeah?" he warns. I nod.

I'm used to the warning, he always says that when I go out in public alone. Like he's worried something will happen to me. I doubt any of the club's enemies even know I exist.

Bear and I spend the morning and early afternoon in the park together. I love the warmer weather and the fact that we're the only people here.

I watch my son play, and I push him on the swings for over an hour, because it's his favorite part. It makes me think of his father. The wind whipping his blonde hair around, his little arms up in the air, and his voice, giggling with delight…

Freedom.

The way Pierce feels on his motorcycle.

Though I haven't known Pierce for long, or all that well, I can see so much of him in Bear. The way Bear always runs through life, barreling head first. I wonder if that's the way Pierce was as a child.

I was the most cautious of children, always afraid I would get hurt.

Bear is nothing like that.

He's stubborn and headstrong and fiercely protective of me. He hates to have anybody take my attention away from him, and the only man he doesn't get pissed off at if he's near me is Bates.

The mailman shook my hand once, and I swear I thought Bear was going to take him out at the knees.

Totally Pierce's genes on that one.

Once we're done at the park, I take Bear home and put him down for a nap. I spend that quiet time cleaning the house before Tammy arrives, and I have to do the dreadful and go to work.

Tammy is a fifty-something empty-nester who lives down the street. I've known her for two years and she's the sweetest woman. She has four grown children and two grandchildren. They are all spread out and she's lonely. She used to offer to watch Bear all of the time, but I had Mary-Anne living with me, so I never took her up on it.

When Mary-Anne moved to San Diego, I needed someone to stay with Bear at night. Bates ran a background check on Tammy and said she was clean as a whistle. So I finally took Tammy up on her offer, on a trial-basis, and she's been my rock ever since. I pay her, and she enjoys the little extra spending cash. She usually spends it on her grandbabies, which makes me like her even more.

"Knock-knock," Tammy says as she walks through my door.

I'm just wrapping my thin coat over my horrendous work uniform.

"Hey, Tam, I'm just about ready," I call out from my bedroom as I grab my purse and throw it over my shoulder.

Just then, Bear comes toddling toward me and throws his arms up, his signal that he wants me to pick him up.

I scoop him up and carry him into the living room. Once

he sees Tammy he smiles widely and says *Hi.*

"Hello, sweet boy. Are you ready for your Auntie Tammy cuddles?" she asks, holding her arms out for Bear. He quickly wiggles from my grasp and toddles over to her waiting open arms.

I love that he has her. I love that he has a grandmother-ly figure to cuddle, since he doesn't have my parents. I don't know what ever happened to Pierce's father, but I wasn't ever able to meet him, and I haven't heard a word about him since Pierce went away.

I thank Tammy for watching Bear, like I do every time she does, and I quickly make my way toward the *Devils* Club.

Candy is waiting for me with wide eyes when I walk up to the bar and stow my purse.

"What?" I ask, knowing full well she has some kind of gossip for me. Just the look on her face says it all.

"He didn't tell you?" she asks. I narrow my eyes on her.

"What was Bates supposed to tell me this time?" I ask.

Bates has the worst habit of neglecting to tell me things, like patch-in after parties, and basically anything to do with the Notorious Devils club.

"The whole place is closed to the public tonight," she chews on her bottom lip for a minute before she continues, "Notorious Devils charter club is here, and they're going to have a big party."

I nod, taking in all of her words, and then I pale. *Charter club.* That sounds familiar. Then I remember what Pierce told me when we first got together. His father is the President of the Charter, which means he could be here tonight. I panic.

"He wanted me to come to the clubhouse before work tonight. He never said a damn thing about this," I practically growl. *"That ass."*

Candy knows it all. She knows about Pierce and she knows a bit about the club, and she definitely knows that Pierce's father is part of the original club in California. I can't think. It's too much.

"Pierce's father is going to see me tonight, *like this*," I motion to my sparkly bra and hot pants with five inch, red high heels that finish off my whore outfit.

"Maybe he won't realize it's you," she says with a shrug.

"Yeah, maybe he doesn't know I work here? Maybe the floor will open me up and swallow me whole?" I murmur to myself. Candy grins widely at me.

A few hours later, I'm slammed. I'm so busy serving these completely disgusting assholes shots and beers, I don't have time to worry about Pierce's father, whom I recognized the second he walked through the door. He's tall, like Pierce, with the same shade of blond hair, and those fucking gorgeous gray eyes.

They could be twins.

Initially, he made my knees weak. But now, I see the subtle differences in him. His voice is scratchier than Pierces, his eyes have crinkles that Pierce's don't have yet, and there's a darkness behind his eyes that gives me chills. He's seen shit, he's *done* shit that Pierce hasn't; or at least, hadn't before he went away.

"Over here, darlin'," Pierce's father calls.

I let out a shaky breath before I make my way toward him. He hasn't called me over once yet, and I'm dreading this.

"Can I help you?" I ask, trying not to make eye contact. I learned early on, with this bunch of men, the less eye contact, the better.

"Need another shot of whiskey," he murmurs.

I quickly go get that for him. I don't want him to meet me like this the first time. I don't want him to think I'm some whore. I don't want to see the disappointment in his eyes that his son knocked up some girl that had to resort to *this* to feed her baby.

"You know of a girl 'round these parts named Kentlee?" he asks when I drop his shot off a few moments later.

My eyes fly to his but he's staring at me as if he knows the answer already. His knowing gaze ruffles me, but I'm too ashamed to admit the truth.

"N-No sir," I stutter. He grins.

"Call me *MadDog*. I didn't think so. You ever find her, you make sure you tell Sniper I want to talk to her. She's got my grandson, and as soon as my son gets back, I'll be wantin' to meet them. My son's been an idiot for almost three years now, and I'm just about fuckin' done with his shit. I'm giving him 'til about one week after his release to straighten himself out, and then I'll be back," he announces.

I press my lips together tightly before I open my big fat mouth.

"You know she had a boy, then?" I ask. His hand snakes out, taking mine in his grasp.

"Know a lot more than anyone else. Know sometimes you gotta shovel shit when life gets hard. Ain't gonna hold dick over her head for what she done the past two and a half years. My son's been a fuckin' moron with this girl. Should have claimed her, given her protection and money, at least made sure the club would take care of her. Fuck, I woulda gone above his ass and done it myself if I could at the time," he mutters. I gasp.

201

"Please, I-I don't want to meet like this," I whisper as tears form in my eyes. He gives me a look of pity and squeezes my hand before he lets it fall.

"Don't know what you're talkin' about, darlin'. You come across that Kentlee girl in town, you pass the message, yeah?" he asks. I nod without speaking before I turn and run behind the bar. I need a minute—*I need a fucking year* to process everything he's said to me.

All I know is his road name is MadDog and he's Pierce's father—and he knows exactly who I am.

Later that night, after I send Tammy home, I take a shower and crawl into bed.

I let my evening replay in my mind.

I didn't see MadDog do anything unseemly. He behaved himself completely. He drank and he smoked, but he observed. He observed the men around him, the shows on stage with the strippers, and then the ones with the men and the strippers or club whores. He didn't touch anybody, and his dick stayed firmly in his pants.

I don't know if it was for my benefit, or if he just doesn't do that shit out in public like the other guys. I grin to myself. I have a feeling it was just for my benefit. Pierce would undoubtedly participate in a full evening of free flowing pussy if he was single and had the chance.

I call my father.

I don't call him often, but I try to check in.

"You're a fuck up," he mumbles into the phone before I can even tell him hello.

"Hey, Pops," I grumble. He sighs.

"Laid eyes on her, son, and you're a fuckin' fuck up if I ever knew one," he barks.

I want to flinch, but I don't—not where anybody can catch me.

"On who?" I ask, even though I know exactly who he means.

"Went to Idaho to check shit out about a month ago. The whole charter went. Wanted to make sure Drifter was keeping shit in line. Met the girl. Gorgeous, though I wouldn't expect you to sink yourself bare inside anyone that wasn't. She's sweet, too—innocent, shy, so I get it. One thing she ain't that you said she was—*is weak*. She'd make a fine Old Lady," he informs me.

It makes my defenses go up.

"You don't know her," I bark into the phone, pissed and fucking angry.

I'm not mad at him. Not really. I'm fucking jealous. He laid eyes on my woman, on Kentlee, and I haven't seen her in over two and a half years.

"Don't need to know her, son. I saw her with my own eyes. She's strong as fuck. You don't claim her the fuckin' minute you pass those walls, I'll give her my protection and bring my grandson to California with her," he warns. I feel my blood pump, really pump through my veins as rage quickly follows.

"You won't do a damn thing, old man," I growl so the guards don't overhear my anger.

"Get your shit together, or that's exactly what I'll do," he informs me before he gives me a low fucking blow. "I'll give her my protection, my patch, and my bed, Pierce. Don't test me. Get your fuckin' act together.," he says.

Then the old fuck hangs up on me.

My father is not only threatening to take them out of Idaho, he's also threatening to take her as his woman. His Old Lady. It makes my head spin and my stomach ache to think about Kentlee being in any man's bed other than mine. I won't let him do a fuckin' thing.

I wonder though, does that mean that it's obvious she's over me? Have I fucked up past the point of being able to make it up to her? Will she accept me back? Maybe she wants another man, maybe that's what this is about? Maybe she wants my fuckin' dad?

I try to push everything from my mind.

I thank whatever god is up there that it's time for leisure. I make my way toward the gym and I work out until dinner. I eat and shit and go to bed, all while eyes are on me. I'm so sick of guards fuckin' watching me. I can't breathe without someone's eyes plastered on me.

I close my eyes when I'm in my cot and grind my teeth.

My own fucking father is threatening me, and I know the bastard will come through, too. It isn't an idle threat, it's a goddamned promise. He'll do it. He'll come in and take them from me if I don't step up.

After spending two and a half years in here, away from her and away from my child, I'm not sure I deserve them when I get out.

Maybe I should let my father swoop in and take them away.

They'd be better off *without* me at this point.

I'm a *worthless* fuck.

I don't *deserve* them.

But I *want* them.

Fuck that. I'm not letting anybody take my family from me. She's mine. Her cunt's mine and her heart's mine. Everybody else can pack sand. I'll slit the throat of any man that tries to take them away, father or not.

My father is the second man to tell me that Kentlee is strong. Sniper has been saying it this entire time, but he has a soft spot for her—always has.

Is she strong enough for me?

For this life?

I open my eyes and stare into the darkness.

For the first time, I hope that she *is* strong enough.

God knows I'm not going to be easy to put up with after I get out. I'm probably going to break her.

No matter what Sniper and my Pops say, I don't trust that she can handle me, handle the life, and handle the role of Old Lady.

Fuck, I think I want her to be strong enough.

For the first time in my life, I'm hoping that Sniper and my Pops are right—that she's Old Lady material—because fuck me, I think I might want to publicly claim her, stamp her, and brand her as *mine*.

If for no other reason than another man knows she's fuckin' mine. Since they're all so fuckin' hot to try and take her from me.

chapter nineteen

Kentlee

Today is the day.

Pierce is being released.

There's a huge party and Bates is insisting that Bear and I be there. I'm not sure that it's appropriate, though. I don't know the emotions Pierce will have at seeing his son for the first time, and I don't want him to be embarrassed or angry.

"LeeLee," Bates sighs.

"No, Bates. He'll need a few days to decompress. You guys do your party thing. Besides, I have to work tonight," I say. He narrows his eyes on me.

"You don't. You weren't scheduled," he says wrapping his arm around me and pulling me into his side. I smile as I rest my head on his chest.

"Candy is down with the flu. She called me an hour ago. She feels horrible, but I heard her puking her guts out. It's Friday night, it's going to be busy, and you need a waitress. Pierce will be happy to spend the evening with his brothers. I don't want to throw too much at him at once," I explain. Bates growls.

"You are being a chicken shit," he announces giving me a little shake. I nod in agreement. "He'll be happy to see you LeeLee, trust me. He'll *want* to see you. Don't hide away the way he's been doing all this time."

I am such a chicken shit. I've had this image of Pierce in my head for three long years. This image that he'll see me and fall to his knees with such joy and jubilation at the sight of me in front of him. It's all complete fanasty.

Then, there is the image I have of his complete rejection. Of him taking one look at me and being disgusted with me. I'm not the same twenty-three year-old girl I was the day he left. I'm twenty-six. I've had a baby and I've had countless sleepless nights. I've worked my ass off and I'm fucking exhausted.

I had hope that he wanted me, that he loved me. I held onto that hope for so fucking long, but what if he doesn't want me. If a man wants you, he'll do anything to have you, to keep you, to make sure you and everybody else in the world knows you're his. Pierce has done none of this, in fact he's pretended I don't exist.

I'm too confused to see him. Too confused with my own wants and desires, with my own feelings. I honestly thought that this day wouldn't come. That I would just forever live in limbo. Now that it's here, I need more time. For me. For my head. To figure out exactly where my head is at.

So I tell Bates a little of what I'm thinking, but not every-thing. He thinks I'm so fucking *strong*. He doesn't realize how weak I really am.

"I am a total chicken shit. I can admit it. He hasn't wanted anything to do with me for three years, Bates. Do you blame me for being scared? I'm petrified. What if he really doesn't want me? What if I'm standing there waiting for him to hold me and confess his love for me, and he doesn't even remem-ber me?" I ramble.

Do I even love him? Truly? We had weeks together that resulted in Bear. Maybe all of this is just me having misplaced feelings because he's the father of my baby. I don't want to look at him and feel nothing; I don't want what happened be-tween Bates and me to happen to Pierce and me. I don't want to kiss him and feel no desire for him. I want to keep that time we had together wrapped up in a perfect little memory, never to be destroyed, forever to feel like perfection.

Bates holds his hand up to shut me up.

"He ain't gonna forget you, babe. Trust me on that."

"It's better this way. He can party with the boys and then come around when he's ready. Bear and I are a package, and we're an intimidating package at that," I say.

I should demand he comes home immediately, and I should kick his stupid ass. But my insecurities are too high. I'm too scared and nervous and all around—*weak*.

"I don't know how to convince you LeeLee, I don't know what else I can tell you other than I know he wants you, and he wants to see you. You guys have some serious shit to work though. I love you Lee, I really do, but this is so far over my head, I don't know how to help you." Bates stomps off, mut-tering to himself just as Tammy walks through the door.

"He got a problem?" she asks, watching him storm off to his bike.

"Pierce gets out of prison today. Bates thinks I should be waiting at the clubhouse for him with Bear. I don't want to overwhelm him, and Candy called in sick, so I need to work anyway. Bates doesn't agree," I explain before I shrug. Tammy nods.

"You must be terrified," she says softly. My eyes meet hers.

"I am. It's truth time. Does he want us, or do we continue not to exist to him? If he ignores us now, it's not because he's in prison and doesn't want to put us through all that crap, like he claimed—it's because he really just doesn't want us," I confess. Tammy wraps me in her arms.

"If he doesn't want you, then he's a fucking fool," she whispers into my hair. I shake a little with laughter. I have never heard Tammy curse, ever.

"If he doesn't want us, then we move on. Three years is a long time to wait for someone, but for him I'd wait forever if I had to. *Jesus, I'm such a mess, I don't even know what I'm saying anymore*," I say, giving her a watery smile and she cups my cheek.

"Because you are a girl who falls in love and she's forever in love. I understand it. I'm the same kind of girl. I got lucky. My husband fell in love and it stuck with him, too. I hope that your Pierce is the same," she whispers.

I don't miss the doubt shining behind her eyes. She can see the heartbreak writing on the wall, and it makes my heart ache with self-pity.

I thank Tammy for watching Bear on such short notice, and she brushes me off. I'm glad I have to work tonight. Hopefully it will keep my mind off of Pierce, off of what he's doing down at that clubhouse.

I know Kitty is still there. She graces me with her presence every single time they close down the strip club and have a club party.

I close my eyes in the parking lot of the Devils Club and I try to calm down. I try not to picture him fucking some nameless, faceless, club whore while I'm working my ass off. I try not to picture him at all, because if I do, I'll lose my shit completely.

I walk inside and begin to set up for the evening. Friday nights are always crazy here, and tonight promises to be the exact same. I watch quietly as strippers begin to file in, followed by the bartenders.

A few moments later, the doors open and we are officially open for business. I hope that it is one of those insane nights where I forget to take a break because we're so swamped, that way I won't be able to think about Pierce and *what* or *who* he's doing.

Freedom.

Fuck.

Finally.

I grin when I see Sniper, Dirty Johnny, Drifter, and some recruit waiting outside of the gates of hell for me. There's a truck with my bike on the back and I grin as the recruit walks it down a ramp. My fuckin' bike. *Finally.*

"Brother," Drifter says. He takes my hand before hugging

me, slapping me on the back.

"Good to be fuckin' outta there," I murmur, stepping away from him, clasping hands with Dirty Johnny and then Sniper.

They all tell me they're glad to have me back.

Then, Drift hands me my cut and I slide it on.

Fucking hell.

So good.

"Let's get the fuck outta here and get you home, brother," Drifter says.

I can't agree more. I climb onto my bike and start her up. She rumbles between my thighs and I take off.

Freedom.

Fuck.

Finally.

It's a fuckin' trek home back to Bonners Ferry, Idaho. Eight hours, but we make it in seven, hauling ass and not giving a shit because I am finally free. When we arrive at the clubhouse, I'm not shocked to see a party already in full force. There's pussy and brothers everywhere.

I'm welcomed by the entire club, and a beer is immediately thrust into my hand. Someone tries to give me a joint, but I don't take it. I'm on parole for twelve months, including random drug tests.

Beer is one thing, green in my system? *Nope.*

"Where's she at?" I ask Sniper when he slides up to me at the bar.

"Didn't want to be rejected or some shit. Scared to be here waiting for you. Said she'd see you once you'd settled in," he informs me. I nod.

Kentlee is nervous, scared even, and I don't blame her. Three years is a long time to go without contact, and she's been completely on her own. Sniper tells me her brother has only come to town once, and it was a complete clusterfuck.

Apparently, her parents tried to sway him to their side. It didn't go over too well. Now, he stays away from town, but calls her regularly to check in.

My conscious is telling me to go and find my woman—to fuck her into the mattress, to remind her who owns her.

Remind her who her man is.

But I need to calm my ass down a little. I can't run to her. If I do, what kind of weak ass bitch do I look like in front of my men?

"Well, then—let's fuckin' party," I say with a wide smile, pretending like it isn't killing me to stay away from her.

Sniper shakes his head, shooting me a look of sheer disappointment.

Yeah, well he can shove his disappointment up his fuckin' ass.

"Hey, lets go down to *Devils*, show the Prez the club," Bull cries out.

Everybody cheers. I've had updates on the club from Sniper. It's making a fuckin' mint, and it's a great place to have parties. *Tits and Ass?* I'm down. There's only one body I want my hands on, but I'm not fuckin' blind, and I need to look as though I'm single for my boys. Until I decide what exactly I'm going to do with Kentlee. If I'm going to make her my Old Lady or continue to keep her separate from the life.

"Sure you don't want to go back home?" Sniper asks. I shake my head.

"I want a clear head for Kentlee. I'll see her in the morning," I say.

I should want to go over there to see her, and I do, but

this, *my brothers*, this is what I need right now. It's late, and Kentlee is no doubt asleep. *So is Bear, I'm sure.* I don't want to disrupt their routine. God knows my presence alone will probably cause my feisty Kentlee to come out, and we'll end up in some kind of fight.

I also don't want to see the look of disgust and disappointment on her face, aimed straight at me. I know she probably hates me. I know she's probably going to tell me to go fuck myself. I can't have that tonight. I can't handle it.

"You should see this one cocktail waitress. Fuck, she's stacked, and the ass on her makes me fuckin' weep. Been beggin' her to dance, but she refuses. I'll wear her ass down one of these days, though," Bull rambles as we make our way inside of the club.

It's fucking insane.

It's crowded, and there are three stages with dancers all around, plus waitresses and dancers on the floor. It's everything I pictured when I rented the space. A feeling of pride and gratitude wash over me at seeing my idea come to fruition. I can't keep the smile off of my face. Sniper outdid himself. Without him, this wouldn't be what it is. My vision has come to light and, thanks to him, it didn't just vanish and rot away with me in prison.

I follow my brothers over to a table that's marked *reserved* in front and center. Bull informs me that it's always reserved for *Notorious Devils.*

Sniper wanted to make sure any member that wanted a seat always had the best one in the house. I laugh, shaking my head, and my long hair hangs in my face. It's buggin' the shit out of me, so I quickly put it in a bun at the top of my head. I haven't got around to cutting it. It was my little bit of rebellion in hell.

"Where's that hot bitch you were tellin' me about?" I ask Bull. He nudges me, lifting his chin behind me.

I turn around and my eyes scan the figure walking toward me. She's got on bright red, fuck me high heels and bare, long lean legs. She's wearing tiny little black shorts that are high on her slim waist, hips— holy fuck, her hips are curvy. My mouth waters. My eyes continue to her tits, and fuck me, my dick hardens at the sight of them in the little bra she's wearing as a top. Then I scan her face and I—see—*red*.

Kentlee.

Kentlee is a fucking cocktail waitress.

In a strip club.

In *MY* strip club.

She walks closer, and as I stand, her eyes stop on me and her step falters.

I watch as the color drains from her gorgeous face and she freezes. The guys are whooping and hollering for her, but she's frozen in place, staring at me.

I can't look away.

I'm so fucking pissed, but I'm so fucking turned on all at the same time.

I thought my attraction might have dwindled, like maybe I imagined her being prettier, sexier, and hotter than she really was. I figured I built her up in my mind. Sure I had pictures of her, but nothing compares to the woman standing across from me.

After three years, she's standing in front of me, and she looks like a goddamn wet dream. She looks tough, badass, and like a dirty little slut; but still manages to ooze sweet innocence.

A dirtied up angel.

"Fury," Sniper grunts behind me. I don't acknowledge him.

I can't take my eyes off of her.

Oh, I'll be having words with Sniper later. I'll be beating the shit out of him for allowing the mother of my child to work here, wearing what she's wearing. But right now, my cock is so fucking hard for her, I can't think of anything else but burying myself inside of her perfect pussy.

"I need your office," I grind out. He places a key in my hand with a chuckle.

I take the four strides that I need to plant myself in front of Kentlee. I can smell her cherry blossom scent I'm so close, but I don't say a word.

Instead, I bend down and stick my shoulder in her stomach before I lift her, and carry her away.

"Pierce," she gasps. It goes straight to my dick.

Lucky for me, the office isn't too far away.

I unlock the door before setting her down inside. I kick it closed with my boot before I turn to lock us in. Kentlee is standing where I dropped her, on her *come fuck me,* red high heels, her hands twisted in each other, and her eyes downcast. She's scared and she fucking should be.

"The fuck you think you're doin' here?" I bark.

I watch as her back straightens and her head snaps up.

"Working," she snorts with pure attitude dripping off of her.

"See that, but that don't answer my question. Why in *the fuck* are you working in a place like this?" I yell, meaner and louder than I intend.

"The only way your club would help me was to employ

me here. It was either dance, or waitress. I chose waitress," she says, crossing her arms.

It pushes her perfect tits up, almost spilling them out of the nonexistent top she's wearing.

"Why here? Why not your job at Walker's office?" I ask, trying to focus on the conversation and not my straining cock.

"I can't support a baby—by myself—working minimum wage, Pierce. I wouldn't have been able to afford daycare for full-time work; let alone all the overtime I would have had to work. Bates helped me out by giving me this job. Without it, I wouldn't have been able to stay in our house. *Without it, I wouldn't have been able to afford diapers*," she says softly. It pisses me off.

It's my fault she's showing off her tits and ass for money.

I hate it.

"Sniper could have floated you until I got out. I assumed that's what he was doin', anyway. He knew I was good for it. All my club earnings have just been sittin' in the safe. Why're you out here looking like a whore?" I ask.

Her eyes widen before they narrow on me. I'm being an asshole, but this is my sweet Kentlee, she isn't some club whore.

"Your club didn't know who the fuck I was, Pierce. They wouldn't take care of me, and I'm not going to take any hand-outs from anybody. I'm an adult Pierce, I had to take responsibility for myself and for my baby. *I had nobody*. Bates helped me; he gave me this job, a job I work my ass off for, and earn my own money at.

"You think I want to dress like this and have guys grab my ass every night? You think this is how I saw my life going?

You think I wanted to wonder where we stood for three fucking years? You think I wanted to raise a baby all on my own? Give birth to him by myself? Don't you dare chastise me for putting food on the table, for paying rent, and for taking care of *our* baby," she screams, her face going bright red.

I take a step toward her, unable to stop myself.

I wrap my hands around her waist and pull her to me. My lips crash down onto hers and I take them roughly.

I'm taking.

I'm not giving *shit* right now, and she's going to fuckin' accept it, too. I feel her small fists pound on my chest, for about a second, her body stiff until my tongue slides out and traces the seam of her lips. Then —she melts.

She melts for me like she did three years ago. Her hands slide up my chest and tangle in the nape of my hair. Her soft breasts press against my chest, and she moans.

I'm done for.

This woman is mine.

chapter twenty

Kentlee

Pierce is kissing me.

The fucking asshole is kissing me and I love it.

I missed it.

I need it.

Words can't describe how I felt the moment my eyes landed on him. I could see the shock, surprise, and then the fury cross over his face. This is the last place he expected me to be, and I couldn't give a shit.

The attraction I feared was a figment of my imagination—was not.

My whole body ignited the second my eyes took in his face. I still want him, crave him. He's bigger and his hair, sweet heavens, it's long and messy and wild and absolutely superb.

Admittedly, in the beginning, I felt ashamed to work in the *Devils Club*; but at this point, I've come to accept that it's my life.

How can I feel shame for putting food in my baby's belly?

How can I feel shame for putting a roof over his head?

I can't.

I'm not doing anything illegal, and I keep my barely-there clothes fully in place—or at least I did until Pierce walked through the door. Now I wish they would disintegrate.

I moan into his mouth once his tongue invades mine. *Firm, warm, and wet.* My whole body feels as though it's going to explode.

I press myself closer to him, needing more, needing everything he can give me. It's been so long since I've been touched. *Three years and one week almost to the day.*

Pierce wrenches his mouth from mine as he trails hot kisses down the side of my throat, his tongue snaking out to taste my skin over the top of my breast.

"Pierce," I gasp when I feel his teeth bite down on the flesh of my breast.

"Strip for me, I want to see what I've been dreaming about for three long years," he orders as he takes a step back from me.

I exhale a breath and slowly shimmy my little hot pants down my legs before I untie the strings of my top. I'm completely naked, except for my high heels. I'm not a fool. The heels do wonders for my legs, and the rest of me isn't as tight and sexy as it used to be, so I need all the help I can get.

I should be screaming at him, so pissed off at how he handled the past three years. How he abandoned us, refusing to communicate at all whatsoever. But my body is too turned on to give an ounce of a fuck right now. All I can think about is how good his cock is going to be when it fills me full.

Pierce's eyes scan my body and freeze on my scar, my C-section scar. I move to cover it with my hands, hating how my belly isn't flat there. It will probably never be. I've done crunches, and yoga, and pilates, but it's not flat.

I gasp when his hands pull mine away and his finger traces the scar. It's hairline thin, but it feels tingly when he touches it—a weird sensation that doesn't seem like it will ever go away.

"Sniper didn't tell me how the birth went," he murmurs before he looks up at me. I see his eyes are shining with unshed tears.

"He was big and my body couldn't deliver him. After twenty hours, he needed to come out. It was the only way," I admit, trying to keep my own tears at bay.

Pierce drops to his knees and kisses the middle of my scar, right above my pussy.

"Should have been there for you. I fucked up, baby girl. Can you forgive me?" he asks as he presses his forehead against my stomach.

I *should* tell him no.

I *should* tell him to fuck off.

I *should* tell him a lot of things.

What I *shouldn't* do is wrap my fingers in his hair and gently pull his head back so that our eyes connect. His gray eyes own me. One glance and I'm his, always and forever. I know this, so I *shouldn't* look at him. I really *shouldn't* take his hand and place it above my breast, near my heart. Then, the last thing I *should* do is bare my soul to him.

But I do it anyway—I do it all.

"I've been sad, depressed, fucking angry, and disappointed over the past three years. But you own me. You own my heart. I'm yours, *always. I'll always forgive you, but don't ever leave me like that again.*" I whisper the end because I can barely speak past the knot of emotions in my throat.

Pierce stands and lifts me by the backs of my thighs before he carries me to the sofa in the office. He lays me down and nestles his jean clad hips between my thighs.

"Never leaving you again, baby girl. *You're mine.* Fuckin' torture without you at my side," he exhales.

Pierce's nose skims the side of mine, then moves down my neck to my breast. I moan when his lips wrap around my nipple and his teeth graze the tightened bud. I cry out when he sucks my breast into his mouth, and then it is as if a beast has been unleased.

Pierce grabs the insides of my thighs roughly and yanks them apart.

I cry out when his mouth covers my pussy and his tongue presses against my clit. His fingers dig into the flesh of my legs, and I arch closer to him. He feels good.

God, his tongue feels like absolute heaven.

Pierce slides his tongue down through my core and inside of me. He fucks me with his glorious mouth. My hands fly to his hair and I pull the tie out so that I can sink my fingers into his long, dark blonde locks.

When he closes his lips around my clit, and sucks while he slides two fingers inside of me, I tighten my own fingers in his hair and pull him closer to me.

"*Pierce*," I moan, loud and unabashedly.

I've missed him, his touch, and the way he makes me feel.

"Need inside," he murmurs as he kisses up my stomach.

My pussy is pulsing. I need him inside, too. I'm so close to exploding. I feel his hands fumbling with his pants as I lick myself from his lips. He groans before he slams inside of me. I wince at the intrusion. It's been three years since I've had sex, and it fucking burns.

"Pierce," I grind through my teeth. He looks down at me, his eyes a mix of lust and need.

"You okay?" he asks, his breathing heavy and uneven.

"You need to go slow for a minute," I beg as tears leak from my eyes.

I feel his chest shake against me, but he doesn't say a word. He slowly slides from my body before coming back inside. I can see his restraint with every move he makes above me, and it causes me to fall in love with him just a little bit more.

I lift up my head and take his lips with mine. He doesn't stop the slow push and pull. When he grinds against my clit as he fully seats himself inside of me, I whimper. His tongue invades my mouth in firm strokes, mimicking the way his cock glides in and out of me.

The pain is gone and now—now he feels *so* good.

God, I had forgotten. How I could have forgotten *this*—I don't know. I lift one of my legs and he slides his arm underneath my knee to spread me wider for him. I roll my hips up to meet his downward thrust and he rips his lips from mine, letting out a low moan.

"*Harder*, Pierce," I beg. He doesn't ask me if I'm sure. He doesn't second guess me. He does exactly what I beg of him.

He fucks me – hard.

My fingernails claw his back as my body climbs higher and higher toward my release. It's too good —*so fucking good*. I scream as his hips slam into mine, his pelvis grinding against my clit. Every single sweaty inch of his body that touches mine is blazing hot.

"Say my name," he grunts as sweat drips from his face onto my chest.

"Pierce," I cry as I come.

My arms pull him closer to me, wrapping myself around him, and my pussy clamps down on his hard cock.

"Fuck," he growls as his cock twitches and his come fills me.

We don't say a word.

Pierce is lying on top of me, still fully dressed with his pants around his ass, and I'm completely naked. I should care that he didn't take the time to shed his own clothing. I don't. I needed his touch; I needed to know he still wants me.

"Love you, baby girl," he murmurs in my ear, shocking the shit out of me.

"You do?" I ask cupping his bearded cheek. His eyes bore into mine as he leans into my touch.

"Always have. Since the moment I saw you strut toward your badass car, in your little secretary getup. Knew I had to have you, knew you would be it for me right there," he says in a hushed tone.

My heart swells at his words.

I knew he was trouble the moment I saw him, but I wanted him just the same. I should regret ever meeting him. The way he had stolen moments of time before he was ripped from my life, leaving me alone with a baby, and refusing to contact me—I should regret everything about him. I should hate him, but I don't—I can't.

"Why wouldn't you see me these past three years?" I ask.

Pierce immediately pulls out of me and I instantly miss

the feel of him. I watch as he yanks his pants over his hips and falls back against the sofa, closing his eyes. For a moment, I don't think he's going to answer me. Then, he opens his mouth and begins to speak.

"That place was fuckin' hell. They tell you what to do, and how to do it. You have eyes on you every goddamn second of every goddamn day. You're told when to eat, shit, shower, and fucking breathe. I didn't want you there. I didn't want you to see me like that. But most of all, I didn't want my beautiful, innocent Kentlee, pregnant with my baby, walking through the gates of hell. I'm a bastard for cutting off all contact. I know." He opens his eyes and finally turns to me, and I see the anguish clearly written on his face before he continues.

He reaches for me and pulls me onto his lap before he buries his face in my neck, inhaling my scent. Breathing me in. I feel his body trembling beneath me and it causes my heart to break for him. What it must have been like in that awful place, I have no idea.

"If I had heard your voice, I would have begged you to come. If I would have read one word of your letters, I would have begged you to come. For me, I had to cut it all off, baby girl. I needed you so badly. I wanted you worse. A second didn't go by that you and Bear weren't on my mind. I thought about you constantly. Snipe would give me pictures of the two of you, and updates, but more than that and I would have broken," he says into my neck, unable to lift his face. Then I feel wetness hit my skin and I know that he's crying.

"You couldn't show weakness in there, right?" I ask, understanding what I knew all along.

Knowing and *accepting* are two different things, though, and I still don't *accept* the way he handled the situation. Even if I *know* it was for the best for him.

"No. *Fuck no*," he grinds out. I touch his shoulder, which makes him jump and lift his head to face me.

"Never again, Pierce. Don't you ever, *ever* ignore me like that again. I won't accept it. I'm willing to forgive you, even though I probably shouldn't, but I can't live like that again. You may have needed to keep me at bay, but I needed support, emotional support. I needed *your* emotional support and I had nothing," I begin to cry. I can't hold back and Pierce is looking at me like I have two heads.

"You *wanted* to come there?" he asks. "I mean Sniper told me you wanted to see me, but in there? I didn't think you actually wanted to walk through those doors."

"I understand why you didn't want me there. I wanted to be able to talk to you, write to you instead of telling Bates to pass along a *goddamn message*," I growl. He takes my shoulders in his hands before he crushes me to his chest.

"I've fucked up so much, sugar," he admits.

I completely agree.

He sure as shit has.

"Now, you have to make up for lost time," I murmur. He looks down at me. I'm nestled against his chest, my face splotchy from crying.

"Yeah?"

"Shit, yeah. And I want to be your Old Lady," I announce bravely.

"One step at a time, baby girl. Now, let's get your ass home. Today was your last day," he says harshly.

I standup, dressing quickly.

"I don't think so," I counter as I fix my top after sliding my shorts up my legs.

"Uh, yeah, it sure as fuck is. I'm home now, which means I take care of you and Bear," he says, fixing his own pants.

"I'm not going to be left penniless and alone again, Pierce. I'm going to continue working. Sorry if you don't like that, but I really don't care," I say as I slip my feet back into my heels.

"Watch yourself, Kentlee," he warns. He wraps his hand around my bicep and pulls me into his chest, my back colliding with his hard body.

I'm ready to end this conversation. It doesn't matter what he tries to tell me, I'm not quitting my job.

"You don't get to come back and start controlling my life," I hiss, trying to break free of his grasp.

Instead, he wraps one of his arms around my chest, the other moving from my wrist to wrap around my hips.

"I'm your man, Kentlee. You ain't showin' off your tits and ass to a bunch of horny assholes every night. I'm puttin' my foot down on that shit right fuckin' now. Had Sniper told me about it in the first place, I would have put it down then, too. You can find something else," he growls directly in my ear. A shiver runs down my spine.

"You have no right," I say, struggling in his grasp. Eventually, he lets me go.

"Uh, yeah. I fuckin' do," he says, crossing his arms over his broad chest.

"No, you really don't. I've been taking care of Bear and me, *me*—by *myself*. You don't get to come in here and start making demands on how I live. I refuse to allow that," I say, my voice rising to a yell by the end of my rant.

"This is exactly the homecoming I wanted, Kentlee. *Fucking thanks.* Thanks for reiterating that I fucked up, 'preciate that. Thanks for informing me that you've been doing everything because I couldn't do anything for you, fucking great. Get your ass home, we'll finish this after I've cooled off," he says.

The look in his eye is void of all emotion. I feel like a bitch. I let my emotions rule my mouth and I've hurt him. I've pissed him off. I've de-maned him. But I'm pissed, too. I have a right to be just as angry as him. Maybe angrier. I don't know.

"Pierce," I whisper. He shakes his head.

"Get your shit and I'll walk you out," he orders with finality.

I shut up, walk to the bar, grab my purse and coat, and walk toward the exit. I can feel Pierce at my back. He's close, but not touching me. I already miss his touch. I've only had him back for minutes and I've messed things up.

"Where's your car?" he grumbles from behind me.

I exhale before pointing at my little sedan that's parked right under the parking lot's street light. I get to work early every night so I can have the safest parking spot in the whole lot.

"What's that?" he asks, looking at my car like it's the most disgusting thing he's ever seen.

Granted, it's not the prettiest car in the world, but it's clean, it runs great, and it's sort of newish. It isn't an eye sore by any means, and I feel blessed that it's as nice as it is.

"My car," I say with a shrug.

I continue to walk toward the driver side and take my keys out. Pierce is on me and has my back slammed against the door before I realize what's happened.

"Where the fuck is your Camaro?" he roars, his nose touching mine.

"I- I had to sell it," I mutter as tears well in my eyes again.

"*The fuck?*" he rasps. I close my eyes tightly before I open them and speak.

"I couldn't afford it with the house when you were first gone. I had to choose. I was working so much overtime, and all I was doing was keeping my head barely afloat. I sold it the week after you were sentenced. I could have the car or I could pay rent. I had bills piling up and only more coming regularly. It's no big deal," I shrug, my voice wavering with each word.

"You loved that car," he says, taking a step back and running his hand through his messy hair.

"Love my baby and having a house for you to return to more," I confess. His eyes shoot to mine, the anger gone from earlier and sadness in its place.

"Baby girl," he grunts, cupping my cheek with his rough hand.

"We have a lot to work through, Pierce," I murmur, unable to look away from his gray eyes. They are so focused on me, it's almost unnerving.

"Yeah, we do," he admits. His lips gently touch mine as his hand slips around to cradle the back of my head.

"I want us to work. I want more of us," I whisper against his lips. I want my dream dammit. I want my happy family. Pierce's hand dives inside of my coat and grabs my waist, pulling me closer to him.

"Ain't no way we won't work, baby girl. It's you and me. You can try to fight me on shit all you want, don't matter. I'll fight back, and you ain't goin' nowhere," he explains, pressing his hard length against my stomach.

"Pierce," I gasp, surprised that he's hard again.

"Can't help it. You make me hard all the time," he grunts, pressing his lips to mine.

He pulls the hair at the nape of my neck down and my mouth opens, my face tilting up before his tongue invades me. I lift my hands to tangle in his overly long hair and grip him tightly, pressing my body even closer to his.

"Fuck," he hisses harshly.

His lips trail down my neck and to the top of my chest, licking my collar before he sucks the skin softly.

"Please," I shamelessly beg. I want more, *again*. I need it.

"Not gonna fuck you in a strip club parking lot, sugar," he murmurs against my neck as he kisses his way back up to my lips.

"Come home, Pierce," I do my best to cajole.

"Home," he sighs.

"*Home*," I reiterate.

"Yeah, baby girl, I'll come home," he agrees before he steps back and opens my door for me.

Once I slide inside, he gently closes the door and I watch as he walks over to his bike and straddles the machine. I grin to myself as I drive away from the parking lot.

I'm happy—not blissfully so, but I'm happy.

Pierce is back, and he's coming *home*.

We have so much to work through, but he's coming home, and that's what is important right now. All of the other crap can wait. Tomorrow morning, he'll meet his son; but tonight, I have him to myself. I plan on worshiping the body I have been missing for three long years.

Fury

I follow behind Kentlee's cheap as fuck car, still angry that she sold her badass ride. I'm not angry at *her*, though. *No, I'm fucking furious at myself.* Why can't I just claim her as my Old Lady, stamp my brand on her, and be done with it? She even asked me to claim her, said she wanted to be mine.

Something is holding me back, though, and I can't figure out what it is. Wish to fuck I knew, because I can't leave her unprotected again. I fucked up this time, but I'm not fool enough to think she'll be waiting around for me if it happens again.

Pulling into the garage, I park next to her car and turn off my bike. I'm nervous. I'm nervous to go inside of my own house. Granted, I only spent a few nights here, but it's still mine. I watch as she walks up to me and takes my hand in hers before she goes inside.

There's a lady sitting on the couch, reading. It dawns on me that she must be who Kentlee leaves Bear with. She looks up smiling before she looks at me with nothing but pure shock on her face.

"Tammy, this is Pierce, Bear's father," Kentlee announces.

It pisses me off that she just states I'm Bear's father and not her man. I grind my teeth together and try not to go off on her for it. I shouldn't get pissed off over every little thing. I feel so on edge.

The woman is older, around my Pops' age, and she holds out her hand for me to shake. I do so and try to smile at her, but I'm not feeling very friendly. I'm a mixture of pissed off and horny, which isn't this lady's fault at all.

"Nice to meet you, Pierce. Well, Kentlee, I better be going

now. Bear was an angel, as always. You let me know when you need me again, all right?" she says, wrapping her arms around Kentlee in a hug.

I want to tell her *never*—she'll never be needing her again because she ain't working at that place another second—but I refrain.

I feel like a goddamn saint for as much as I've held my tongue in the past ten minutes.

"I'm just Bear's father then?" I ask Kentlee. Her eyes widen after I hear her lock the front door.

"It was the easiest way to explain. Tammy knows who you are and where you've been," she hisses in a loud whisper.

I ignore her bullshit and walk straight to the bedroom. I look around and it's like a completely different space, except it isn't. It's decorated now—a black comforter with beige pillows and blood red pictures on the walls. I don't pay attention to what they are, I'm too fuckin' horny and irritated.

"Pierce," she murmurs as she closes and locks the bedroom door behind her.

"I don't want to talk anymore. I'm just gonna piss you off and you're just gonna piss me off. Let's fuck and sleep. Tomorrow, you can piss me off all over again," I announce as I begin to strip my clothes off.

I'm fuckin' exhausted. The long ass bike ride, and the adrenaline that's been spiking through my body off and on all day long, has finally taken its toll on me.

"Fine," she snaps as she takes her bullshit outfit off.

"Hands and knees," I order.

With a huff and narrowed eyes, she does exactly as I demand. She climbs onto the center of the bed and slides down to her hands. There's one more thing I have to know before

I fuck her. I'm stupid to even ask, but I won't be able to sleep without knowing.

"You fuck anyone else while I was gone?" I mutter, my voice low.

I don't want to say the words, but I need to know the answer. She rises to her knees and turns around to face me.

"You're seriously asking me that, Pierce?" Fuck, she looks wounded, and it kills me.

"Unwritten rule in my world, baby girl. When your man's locked up, you're somewhat of a free agent," I grunt. She takes my bearded cheeks in her hands, her eyes focused on mine.

"Never. I couldn't ever be with another man. I'm yours, Pierce. Only yours," she whispers.

She moves her cool fingers to tangle in my hair, something she's made a bit of a habit of, something I love.

"We weren't together long and you had needs. I would try to be understanding," I say. She snorts.

"Right, okay," she huffs before her lips brush mine. "I'm a big girl, Pierce. I know how to keep my urges at bay. Besides, I didn't have much time for men when I was working and being a mom," she grins, tipping her lips in a half smile.

Suddenly, I have images of her touching herself fill my mind. This, I gotta see.

"Show me," I grunt.

"Show you?" she asks.

"Yeah, baby girl. Show me how you kept those urges at bay?" I grin, wrapping my hands around her fantastic ass and squeezing.

"You want me to masturbate for you?" she asks, her eyes wide and innocent looking. *Kill-ing me.*

"Yeah. Touch that pussy for me, baby girl. Get yourself

off," I softly demand. She shivers in my arms before she plants a kiss on my jaw and then wiggles out of my grasp to lie down on the bed.

Kentlee gives me a show, too. She touches herself for me—her tits, her pussy, and her clit. Fuck me, I almost explode before I even make it inside of her, it's so hot. Her little whimpers fill the room until I slam my cock in her wet pussy, and then her cries fill the space around us. I exhaust us until we pass out.

In the early morning, before the sun even comes up, I startle awake with a nightmare. I slide my cock inside of her pussy and fuck her gently, making her come again, before I fall back asleep, my cock still inside of her.

It's fucking heaven.

A dream I never want to wake up from.

Kentlee.

chapter twenty-one

Kentlee

I roll out of Pierce's arms and grab my phone to check the time. Its five-thirty, which means I have about five minutes before Bear is up and going for the day. I quickly go into the bathroom and clean up from the night before.

Pierce was insatiable and the aching between my thighs proves it. I grin as I get a pair of sleep shorts and a tank top to change into. I quietly slip out of the bedroom so that he can sleep.

Once I am in the kitchen, I start a cup of coffee and wait for the slapping of little boy feet along the floor to alert me that my little monster is awake. I grab my coffee and sit down at the kitchen table. One sip into my delicious brew, I hear the tale tell signs that Bear has risen.

I hear his feet slapping against the floor before I see him. His eyes light up as soon as they connect with mine and then he flings himself into my waiting arms. I pull him onto my lap as he snuggles against my chest and sticks his thumb in his mouth.

Our morning ritual. I love it.

"Morning, baby Bear," I murmur against his blonde hair.

"Hi, mama," he says before he lifts his head and looks at me with his puppy dog eyes.

"Milt peeaaseee," he begs. My heart melts. Milk. My little man loves his milk.

"Sure, angel," I murmur, standing and setting him down in my chair while I grab a cup and his milk.

Once I have him settled with his milk in my lap again, I hear a deep throat clear from across the room. I look up to see Pierce standing at the kitchen's entrance, looking concerned. He shouldn't be concerned. I've made him out to be a legend in Bear's eyes. I've talked him up so much. I was afraid that Pierce wouldn't want us and then I would have to explain that to Bear. Maybe I was stupid for trying to build him up into some almost mythical figure, but I wanted him to welcome Pierce in case he came home to us.

"Baby Bear, look who's here." I squeeze his thigh and direct him to across the room.

Bear stays silent for a second before I hear his breath hitch. Then he says the word I have been practicing with him since the day he was born. The word that I have paired with a photo of him, a shitty picture Bates gave me from a party a few years ago.

"Daddy," he cries.

Bear scrambles off of me to run toward Pierce before he

launches his little body into Pierce's waiting arms.

Pierce picks him up and Bear wraps his arms around him, burying his face in his neck. I can't stop myself—I turn into a blubbering mess at the sight. It's so beautiful and simple and wonderful all at the same time. Pierce's eyes meet mine over Bear's head and he mouths – *thank you* – to me.

I don't think. I stand and I wrap my arms around him and Bear. I shove my face in the other side of his neck and my lips go directly to his ear.

"No, thank you, Pierce. You gave him to me," I whisper through my sobs.

We stay like that, the three of us, for the next five straight minutes. Then, Bear's head pops up and he announces his hunger.

I take Bear and deposit him in his high chair before I start to gather items from the refrigerator and pantry for breakfast.

"Eggs, toast, and bacon all right?" I ask Pierce as he sits down across from Bear at the kitchen table.

"Yeah, baby girl, sounds great," he says, his voice gentle and soft.

I go about making breakfast, giving eggs and toast to Bear while I fry bacon.

"You are fuckin' spectacular," Pierce whispers in my ear as his hands wrap around my waist.

"I'm really not," I chuckle as I turn some bacon over in the pan.

"Baby girl, you really are. He's so fuckin' perfect," he murmurs.

I turn my head slightly to kiss the underside of his jaw.

"He is, isn't he? It's because he's the best parts of both of us, Pierce," I mutter.

"Fuck yeah, he is," he grunts, placing a kiss on my shoulder before he grabs the plate of bacon from the counter and sets it down on the table. I take everything else over to the table and sit down next to him, between my two guys.

"Marry me," Pierce blurts out as I'm taking my first bite of bacon.

"What?" I ask, turning to him in shock.

"Marry me, be my Old Lady, wear my ring and my brand on your skin," he says.

I stare at him in shock.

Last night, he ignored my asking him if I could be his Old Lady.

Last night, he didn't seem like he wanted to make us official in public.

Last night, he was so pissed off at me, he couldn't even talk to me.

"Seriously?" I ask. "*Why*?" I add.

"This is the way it's supposed to be. This is right. You, me, and Bear. It didn't feel right before, something was holding me back, but I didn't know what it was. Now, with Bear and you right here next to me, I know this is right," he says before he takes a bite of his toast.

It's as if Pierce is offering me my dream on a silver platter. *Marriage, a family, and love.* All wrapped neatly with a bow on top. How can I turn this opportunity down? Does it make me a spineless halfwit to accept after everything that has happened the past three years?

However, if I turn him down, I'll lose him. I'll lose the dream come true that he's offering me. He isn't a man that will accept no and stay at my side. There is no way I can ask him to give me any time. His pride won't allow him to stay. The man's pride is downright annoying.

"You really want me?" I ask through trembling lips.

Don't I deserve to be happy? To have my dreams come true too? I've stayed true to him, held onto threads of hope that this is exactly where we would end up. Even if it is sooner than I ever anticipated, how can I chance losing all of that?

"Always wanted you, sugar," he murmurs. I shake my head. There is one more thing I need to ask him.

"But not publicly. Now you want me to be yours, in front of your club, and in front of the world?" I ask.

"Fuck yeah. I want everyone knowin' you're mine," he growls.

I stand up and throw my arms around his neck while I plop my ass on his thigh. I can't not say yes. Even if it ends in complete disaster, at least I'll have had a taste of my dream.

"I love you, Pierce. Yes, I'll marry you, and yes, I'll be your Old Lady," I say, grinning at him with watery eyes.

"Fuck yeah, you will." He smiles and it's genuine, big, and beautiful. "Light up the room with this smile, sugar," he says, running his thumb over my bottom lip.

"I'm glad you don't want me to be your dirty little secret anymore," I murmur. His eyes narrow and his jaw clenches before he opens his mouth to speak.

"Get one thing straight, Kentlee. You were never, *ever* a dirty secret to me. I've always been pleased as fuck you were in my bed. I didn't want you immersed in the club life as an Old Lady because I didn't think you were strong enough. Takes a strong as fuck woman to be at the side of a man like me for life. That's what it was going to be, too—life. I wasn't sure I wanted any woman there forever, baby girl," he admits as his thumb continues to trace my bottom lip.

"You think I'm strong enough now?" I ask in a whisper.

"Know you are. Dealt with a shit ton while I was away. Did it effortlessly," he says. I snort.

"Not effortlessly," I murmur.

"You didn't fall apart. You got your shit straight and you took care of business. You didn't go out and whore around. Fucking effortlessly," he points out.

"You want me forever?" I shift the subject slightly and he grins.

"For-fuckin'-ever, baby girl," he murmurs as his lips gently brush mine.

Bear starts banging his plate on his high chair and I giggle against Pierce's lips before I slide out of his lap and get Bear to clean him up.

"What's your agenda today?" I ask while I'm wiping Bear's face and hands from his messy breakfast.

"Need to do some shit at the club, but that can wait for tomorrow. Gonna spend the day with my family," he says.

I couldn't wipe the huge smile off of my face even if I wanted to. The ring that he'll put on my finger, being his woman, the security of being his wife and having him at my side also give me guarantee of his club being at my back if he goes away again. I'm not stupid, he could easily go at any time. Being his Old Lady and having his last name guarantee's a place in the club for me if he isn't around.

It takes care of myself and Bear in a way that we didn't have the past three years. It is the only way I can give him what he wants, me leaving my job, and get what I want in return too—security.

"Yeah?" I ask. He grins.

I hear the front door slam and Pierce stands up, his fists

balled and clenched tightly as Bates walks through the kitchen and then stops. His eyes go to Pierce and they widen.

"The fuck you doin' walkin' into my woman's house like you own the place?" he barks.

It's then that I realize that he doesn't know that Bates lives here. How could he not know? How could Bates not have *told* him?

"You didn't tell him?" I blurt out.

Pierce's angry gaze leaves Bates to crash with mine. I'm holding Bear in my arms and my eyes leave Pierce's to collide with Bates'.

"Uh… no," he stammers.

"Someone better tell me somethin' pretty fuckin' fast," Pierce growls.

"Bates moved in after Mary-Anne moved to California. He offered to help with rent and protect us. He said it was better than us living alone," I confess.

My eyes scan back to Pierce, who is now focused on Bates. His jaw is so clenched, its ticking.

"You been livin' here with my woman and kid?" Pierce asks.

"Nothing's ever happened, Fury. Roommates, that's all," he says. It sounds like a plea.

"I know nothin' happened. I trust my woman. Who I don't trust is *you*—livin' in her house while I'm away, and you never mentioned it to me," he growls.

It scares me. He's on hundred percent Fury right now; no Pierce in sight.

"I was trying to help her," Bates says, squaring his shoulders.

"Get your shit and get the fuck out," Pierce roars, making

Bear jump in my arms.

"No problem, man," Bates says as he turns. Before he leaves, Pierce speaks.

"No matter what happened, what didn't happen, you laid your head down in the same house as my woman. It ain't right and it ain't respectful. I'm your fucking president, you disrespected me in my own home," he adds. I watch Bates' shoulders tense and his spine straighten before he turns back around to face Pierce.

"You didn't claim her, *brother*. You left her out swingin' with nothin'. I did nothing but help her, showing her and you more respect than any other man in the club. I sent Mary-Anne over here to help, I gave her a job, and when she needed it, I stepped in and helped pay *your* fuckin' rent. I didn't have to do shit. I could have treated her like the rest of the brothers— gave her a job and then slapped her ass when she walked by at the club, suggested she ride my cock, too, while she served me drinks. That's what you want? That more respectful than what I did?"

I watch as red literally climbs up Pierce's chest and to his face.

"Just go," Pierce says through a clenched jaw.

I watch as Bates leaves the house. I'm sure he'll be back later for his stuff, but right now, he's pissed.

"Where was Bear last night? He sure as fuck wasn't in our room," he growls, turning his anger onto me.

"Bates is hardly here. I have a little bed that I move back and forth. When I work, Bates doesn't come home, so Bear sleeps in his room. When I'm home, Bear is with me," I answer. Pierce nods once. I hope he's satisfied with that answer.

"What about women?" Pierce's nostrils flare and I shake

my head.

"He's never brought anybody over here, man or woman. Honestly, Pierce, he's been nothing but a gentleman. *He's never even tried to touch me.*" I whisper the last sentence, hoping he'll believe me. I don't want their relationship to deteriorate over this—over me. I don't want him to know about our one failed attempt at a kiss. It wasn't anything, neither he or I *felt* anything.

"The other guys, they do that shit?" he asks, refusing to comment on my statement about Bates.

"They're men, Pierce, and they were drunk," I say. He nods.

"Never again, baby girl. One of them even looks at you funny, I'll kill 'em," he announces.

I take a step back. He's so angry, so fucking furious.

"Pierce," I say hesitantly.

"Serious as fuck, baby girl. Didn't ever want you around them, that's why. They're dirty fucks. Now, they'll be dead dirty fucks they try anything with you again," he growls. He stalks quickly toward me before he pulls both Bear and me into his arms.

"Okay," I murmur, looking up and into his gray eyes.

"Go get dressed. Little man and I'll hang out, then we can all go do something together." He grins and, just like that, his fury is gone.

I'm not sure what to think about his rage and blow up, but I understand where he was coming from. I thought that he knew Bates had been living here this whole time. I would have never wanted to anger him over something like that, something that didn't mean anything.

I shower and dress in a pair of skinny jeans and a black

tank top, leaving my hair down and my makeup light. I have no clue what we're going to do today, but I don't care. All I care about is that Pierce is going to be with me, and that's all that matters right now.

I walk into the living room to tell Pierce to go ahead and get dressed, but as soon as my eyes land on what is happening in the room, my breath hitches. Pierce is sitting on the floor with Bear across from him and they're playing with Bear's oversized toddler Legos. Pierce is sitting cross-legged, his long hair messy and tumbled around his shoulders, but he's laughing and it's the best thing I have ever seen in my life.

"Don't just stand there, sugar," Pierce murmurs. My feet quickly shuffle to my boys.

"You guys just looked so cute together," I say, placing a red block on top of a yellow one.

We don't say another word. We play with our son, and it's the best fifteen minutes I have ever experienced. Eventually, Pierce leaves to shower and change while I dress Bear for the day. I grab my cell phone, so I can capture the day in pictures. Bear's first full day with his father; his father's first full day with Bear. It is definitely a day to capture, if there ever was one.

We don't go far. First, we go to a park and play—as a family. I turn into crazy picture mom, making Pierce laugh. Then we go to lunch and Pierce is able to see the true joys of having a toddler. He doesn't seem to mind Bear's activity level, though; he has more patience then I thought possible with him.

Finally, he takes me to a car dealership and buys me a black Camaro—brand new. I try to protest, but he won't let me. He pays in cash and my eyes bug out at the wad of money he hands the man.

"Your car's crap, baby girl. This is what you should be driving. It's you. No convertible this time, though. They aren't very safe," he murmurs. I don't care about that.

"You bought me a car," I whisper, my eyes welling with tears.

"Yeah. Gonna buy you a ton of other shit, too, and you ain't gonna balk at none of it," he mutters.

"I'm not?"

"Fuck no. Got three years of fuck-ups to make up for and this is step one. Nice wheels for my Old Lady," he says, grinning. It makes me smile big and brightly.

This man is too much. He doesn't have to make up for shit. Loving me and loving Bear is more than enough; yet, for him, it's not nearly enough.

I understand it, so I don't say a word. I let him be a man; I let him take care of his family, and I do it all with a giant ass smile on my face. He's home and that's what's really important.

Best day of my life.

Never thought the best day of my life would be so calm, easy, and chill. I spent the day with my son and my woman.

Closing my eyes, I think back on my day, on the moment I met my son's gray eyes, eyes that are clearly identical to mine. I grin, recalling his first word to me. *Daddy.*

I never heard anything more beautiful in my life. I'm a

fuckin' pussy and I don't even give a shit. This woman and this boy have me wrapped around their fingers.

When we came home from our day, Sniper had his shit cleared out of the bedroom and I helped Kentlee move all of Bear's things into the room. His own room, something he should have had since the day he was born.

Another fuck up of mine.

"Pierce?" Kentlee's voice breaks me out of my thoughts and my mouth goes dry the second I lay my eyes on her.

She's standing at the doorway to the bathroom, the light spilling out of the room behind her, and she's so goddamned beautiful it makes me ache.

"Do I look okay?" she asks, fidgeting with the scrap of fabric that I assume is supposed to be some kind of night-gown.

It's short and tight, encasing her tits and showing them off. They're almost spilling out of the top, and it goes straight to my dick. But what makes my belly clench is the thigh highs she's got on, along with the highest heels I've ever seen. Her long blonde hair spills down around her elbows and it's too much. It's exactly what I've been dreaming of for years, except it's better than I could have ever imagined.

"C'mere, baby girl," I murmur as I sit up on the bed and turn to let my feet hang off.

I spread my legs wide as she walks between them, her hands going to rest on my shoulders, and my own hands immediately wrapping around her hips.

"You're perfect," I say softly, looking up into her downcast eyes. A smile tips her lips before her sweet tongue sneaks out and wets her bottom lip. I almost groan at the sight.

"So are you, Pierce. You're bigger than before you left.

Your hair is longer, and so is your beard. I love it. But most of all, I love how much more open you are, how you obviously adore Bear and how you want to take care of us. I didn't know how this would go, you coming back, but I'm so happy," she says. Her words break my heart before they mend it back together again.

"I'm happy here, with you and with Bear. Nothin' is gonna take me away again, sugar," I promise before my hands slide down the silk of her nightgown to wrap around her ass.

I squeeze the flesh, remembering that there used to be more there, and promising to add to it as the weeks go by. I love her tight body now, but I miss her curves, too.

"Take me, Pierce. Own me like only you can," she moans as my fingers dig into the globes of her ass.

I stand up, walking around her, and press my hand in the center of her back, bending her over the bed. She shivers with anticipation, but she's in for a surprise. I'm not going to fuck her with my cock just yet. I fall to my knees and tip her ass back with my hands before I swipe my tongue through her pussy lips, grateful this little outfit didn't include panties. I hear her gasp right before she sighs as I lap at her perfect cunt.

I eat my girl like I'm starving, because I am. I've been starving for her pussy for three years, and it's going to take me a fuck've a long time to get my fill.

After Kentlee comes on my tongue, she stands before she turns around and sinks to her knees in front of me. Her innocent eyes look up at me and my heart stops beating for a minute. I can feel her hot breath on my hard cock and I want to shove myself down her warm throat, but I don't.

This is her trusting me.

246

I shudder when her tongue licks the head of my cock and then slowly she swallows me. She's timid and shy and I fuckin' love it.

I cup her cheek and apply pressure to stop her but I don't let her pull away.

"I'm going to fuck that beautiful mouth, Kentlee," I murmur, my eyes focused on her widened ones. She nods slightly and I take my time.

I fuck that gorgeous mouth of hers slowly—so fucking slow that when I come, spilling down her throat, it's long and I can't help but groan loud and deep. She takes all of me, every single drop and it makes my whole body shiver.

chapter twenty-two

Kentlee

I roll over and reach for Pierce's warm body, but the sheets are cold. Cracking my eyes open, I grab my phone and sit straight up in a panic when I look at the time.

It's after eight o'clock in the morning.

I roll out of bed and grab Pierce's t-shirt from the night before, throwing it over my naked body as I make my way out of the bedroom.

The sounds of movement and Bear's sweet babble instantly relieve me. I walk into the kitchen to see Pierce sitting at the table, his long hair thrown up into a sexy-as-shit messy man bun, and Bear gnawing on a piece of toast.

"You up already?" Pierce asks, looking up from his phone.

"You let me sleep in," I murmur, unable to take my eyes

off of him, his hair, and his naked chest.

I clench my thighs together. I'm sore, but I still want more of him. Pierce's gaze heats as his eyes narrow on my legs.

"You deserve it," he states with a grin.

I know he's thinking about last night. He ate me until I came and then I sucked his cock until *he* came down my throat, something I had never done with him before. Without even taking a breath, he was between my legs again, bringing me to another orgasm with his mouth.

Then he fucked me until I screamed with my third climax of the night. It was spectacular.

"Mmmm, you did, too," I murmur as I sit on his thigh facing Bear, who is happily chomping on his toast.

"I got church at ten this morning, baby girl. I'll probably be down at the club all day," he informs me as his hand trails up my thigh, gently caressing my skin.

"I'll miss you, but I can catch up on housework, laundry, and grocery shopping," I say with a shrug.

"You get a sitter tonight, yeah?" he semi-asks. I look at him with confusion. "I'm going to claim you in front of the club tonight. It'll be a party."

"You're not going to… do me in front of your club are you?" I ask as panic creeps up my spine.

"Are you fuckin' crazy, woman? *Hell no.* Those assholes ain't seein' any part of you. It's a fuckin' announcement. *Holy shit*," he growls. I can't help but start to laugh. "Ain't funny. I'm getting older, and you gave me a mini heart attack just now," he says, letting out a breath before he pulls me closer to his body.

"I'm gonna spank your ass for that remark, sugar," he whispers in my ear, his breath heavy and hot.

HAYLEY FAIMAN

I stop laughing immediately and squirm on his lap. Being spanked by Pierce might be fun, and I can't help the throbbing between my legs at the thought.

"I'll be by at eight. Be ready," he groans, squeezing me once before he places a kiss on my cheek and begins to stand. I scramble from his lap and smile at him.

"You'll be the death of me, woman," he grunts as he walks into the bedroom.

I let him go and get ready while I clean up his attempt at breakfast. All he made was toast, but the kitchen is trashed—a butter knife lays on the counter with butter smeared everywhere, crumbs are all over the place, and the toaster is out and plugged in still. I almost laugh. He's worse than Bear. I have a feeling my future will be filled with cleaning up after the men in my life. For a man who likes to have everything in its place everywhere else, he's hell on my kitchen.

I let Bear down from his high chair and pour myself a cup of coffee as I watch him toddle into the living room to play with his toys. He grabs a bucket full of hot-wheels cars and dumps the whole thing out before he roots through the pile and grabs the one motorcycle he has.

Genetics flow true in this house.

"Okay, at eight I'll be back. Be ready to party. Is there anyway Tammy can stay all night?" he asks as he slides his cut over his shoulders.

"Is it going to be an all-nighter?" I arch my eyebrow in question. He grins.

"Gonna be drunk, babe. Don't want to put you on the back of my bike if I've been drinking," he announces. My heart beats a little faster for it.

Protection and safety.

I love it and I love him.

"I'll ask her," I say gently. He nods before bending over the sofa to press a kiss to my lips.

"Be a good girl while I'm gone," he murmurs before he winks. Then I watch him bend down to Bear's level and give him a hug and a kiss on his slobbery baby lips.

"Be good for mama, boy," he grunts. Bear giggles like it's the funniest thing in the world.

"Bye, babe," Pierce says from the doorway. I smile, looking up at him.

"Bye, Pierce. I love you," I call out. He grins widely.

"Love you."

Fury

Leaving them wasn't easy.

I wanted to stay and spend time with them.

I have missed so much, but the club needs me and I need to take the gavel back from Drifter. I need to take my club back, and I need to know about the state of affairs.

The Cartel, the Aryan's, the *Bastards*, and the financial state of the business, legit and not. It is bound to be a shit day, but I couldn't stop my smile even if I wanted to.

I am going to claim my Old Lady in front of the whole club, and this weekend she will be branded mine.

The table for church is full, so are the walls along the edges of the room. Everybody is in attendance and it feels good. Drifter slaps the gavel in my hand with a slam to my back with his fist.

"Good to have you back, brother," he murmurs. I grin before I rap the gavel down on the table.

"Hit me with three years of catch up," I say. Drifter chuckles before he begins.

"Where are the *Bastards*?" I ask, once I've been caught up on finances and club business. Now, it's time for the heavy shit.

"Smoke man. Fuckin' disappeared after you went down," Torch says from the end of the table.

"Nobody dug around to find them?" I ask to no one in particular.

"Tried. They fuckin' vanished. No clue where they went," Torch explains. I nod.

"So they just kill an Old Lady and vanish? That's not fuckin' right," I mumble, earning me grunts of agreement from around the room.

"The *Aryan's*?" I ask, leaving the *Bastards* on the back burner.

If Torch can't find them, nobody can. He's a fuckin' genius on the computer.

"Laying low. Your dad cut ties after you went down, too fuckin' dangerous—and they're assholes," Dirty Johnny says with a shrug.

"What about the club in Canada that was dealing with them?" I ask.

"Aryan's retaliated when your shipment was busted. They decided to burn the clubhouse down. Everyone was inside," Bull murmurs, shocking me.

"How come I didn't know about this?" I narrow my gaze on Sniper, but he doesn't even look at me when he answers.

"Club voted to keep it quiet so you wouldn't fuck up in

the pen," he says, all emotion out of his voice. He's so pissed at me, but I can't seem to muster a fuck to give.

"Fine. A vote, whatever. What the fuck happened for retribution?" I bark, wanting to know.

I'm so fucking pissed, not only at Sniper, but the whole goddamn club. I asked every time Sniper came in to visit me what was going on, and all he ever told me was that the Aryan's and the *Bastards* were lying low. I didn't know they had disappeared. *Fuck.* And then add blowing up a whole club. I'm not only pissed at them, I'm pissed at my old man, too.

How in the fuck did nobody tell me a goddamn thing for three fuckin' years?

"Your Pops didn't want to rock the boat after everything went down. ATF was up all our asses, eyes on the club nationwide. He severed ties and that was the end of that," Drifter states. It makes me question everything; it doesn't sound right to me.

"The Cartel?" I ask.

"In works with the charter club for running dope, huge profit," Drifter announces.

Now I know what's up. They want to give up the guns and become mules.

More money.

"More heat on us and more jail time if we get caught," I announce. They all look at their boots, except Sniper.

"Won't be driving big fuckin' trucks, so odds of getting caught are less. We only carry to the border and we pass it off," he says.

"Where we getting' it from?" I ask, looking right at him.

"Club members getting it down at the Mexican border, pass it off to the Vegas club, and they bring it to Salt Lake City.

The SLC club takes the shipment to Butte, Montana, where we meet up and take it to the Canadian border, where our club in Lethbridge will deliver it to the Cartel in Calgary," Sniper explains. It makes my fuckin' head spin.

"That's why too many hands in the cookie jar. That's too much passing off," I explain. Torch nods his head.

"I'm in agreement," he says before he bends down to bring out a map.

"If we can get the California club out of San Diego to meet us in SLC, that's halfway. That's only one exchange off here in the states. Then we hand it off at the border and be done with it. Less hands the dope passes through.

"I mean, it's going to be a hard run, but if we set up a schedule and are on a rotation, then it won't seem so bad. In the long run, I think this could work. Our numbers are growing and we'll probably each only have to go out once a month," Torch explains. I look at the route. It could definitely work, and it would only be three clubs involved instead of five.

"The cut would be more for us too, since we'd only be dividing it into thirds instead of fifths," I say. I hear the guys murmuring around us. Everybody likes more cash.

"Let's take a vote," I suggest.

We vote one hundred percent in favor, and that makes me feel a bit better. I have Drifter set up the first meet in SLC and get Torch on making up a schedule. I tell him that I want to be in on the first drop, but after that, he can make me back up in case something happens and a guy can't go. Normally, as the president, I wouldn't do shit— but I'm hands on, and I don't have a problem helping my brothers out.

"Before we adjourn, I have an announcement I want to

bring to you all before tonight, when I make it official." Everybody is quiet and I can't hold back my smile.

"I'm making Kentlee my Old Lady."

The room is silent and then, all of a sudden, it breaks out into cheers and laughter.

"Finally. *Fuck me*, I was gonna steal her away from you if you didn't. Hot piece of ass right there," Bull grins. I can't even get pissed off at the old dirty bastard, I'm too fuckin' happy.

"Hey, sorry we couldn't help her out more when you were inside," Drifter says, slapping me on the back. I shake my head.

"I were in your shoes, didn't know the girl or have any facts on the baby, I would'a done the same, brother," I admit, even though I don't want to.

I want to be pissed at them; but in the end, it was all my fuck up, not theirs. We have rules for a reason. I get it. I don't like it, but I get it.

"Your Pops is coming tonight," Torch says after he shakes my hand.

"Gotta make it official with the old man before he tries to take my girl. He already fuckin' warned me he would," I admit through a laugh.

"Seriously?" Torch asks. I nod.

"Old man threatened me to take care of my shit, or he'd take Kentlee and Bear to Cali and claim her himself. Apparently, we have the same taste in women." I chuckle and Torch shakes his head.

"Not hard to want a woman like Kentlee at your side, brother. I don't know her well, but I've seen her around the *Devils* Club. She's sweet, and pretty as all get out. Be nice to wake up next to that in the morning," he grins.

"You saw her before the *Devils* Club, Torch," I grumble.

"I did. She was sweet then, too. But she changed, grew up, and took life by the balls when she had to. Impressed the fuck outta all of us. Sniper would keep us updated, warn us off of her, too. Nothing makes a man want something more than being told she's off limits," he smiles. I give him a hard look.

"She's one hundred percent off limits now. She's a little sister," I growl. Torch stars laughing.

"Brother, I am not even trying to go there. She's yours—your baby mama and your Old Lady. Pleased as fuck you have that for yourself. You deserve it," he says before he walks away toward the bar.

I spend the day hanging out with my brothers, catching up on their lives and just enjoying my freedom. Next week, I have to check in with my parole officer; but tonight, it's just my brothers, my Pops, and my Old Lady. Nothing could dampen my fuckin' mood.

That is, until I feel sharp talons on my leg, digging into my jeans. I look down at the completely naked body and bleached blonde hair of a train wreck—*Kitty*.

"Can I help you, Kitty?" I ask, removing her hand from my thigh.

"Missed you while you were gone, Fury," she whines.

It grates on my nerves.

"Can't say the same about you," I shrug. I watch as she pouts like a baby.

"Anything you want today, any hole you want, it's yours," she smiles. I shake my head.

"Nope. I got my own woman, Kitty. Don't need all that from you."

"I know the rules, Fury. It's a don't ask, don't tell. You

know you want to fuck all the pussy you can since you didn't have any for so long," she whines some more.

"Bitch, I got a woman. I don't fuck around on her. I don't give a fuck what anyone else does, but I ain't doin' *you*," I growl. She takes a step back.

"You're seriously turning me down for that whore? That whore who worked the floor of a strip club and lived with one of your brothers?" she says.

Her words light a rage inside of me. I reach out and backhand her. I watch her fall to the floor and I don't even feel guilty about it. I should, she's a woman, but I don't.

"Your job here, Kitty, is to suck and be fucked. It isn't to talk men into sticking their dicks in your stretched out cunt. It sure as fuck isn't to talk shit about the Old Ladies of this club. Remember your place, or you'll be ass first out on the street. You can sell that used up cunt on the corner for all I care. One more outburst from you, and you're gone," I roar. The room goes silent.

I ignore everybody and step over her shaking body before walking into my office. That bitch thinks she can talk about Kentlee like that, insinuate that she was fuckin' Sniper and whoring because she waited tables in a strip club—she can go to hell.

I slam my office door shut and take a breath.

"She didn't say anything you hadn't already thought," Sniper says from the chair in my office. He'd been waiting for me.

"Yeah, difference—it's my right to think and question my Old Lady. It ain't her right to even think about her," I growl. Sniper nods.

"Nothing ever happened," he says.

257

"I know," I admit.

I knew all along, no way would Sniper do me like that. And Kentlee, she never could. She's mine, one hundred percent.

"You're a jealous bastard with her," Sniper says. I look up to see he's grinning.

"Fuckin' right, I am. Got a right to be. *She's a hot piece*," I grin, repeating Torch's words from earlier.

"She would be, if she didn't feel like my sister," he chuckles. I nod.

"We cool?" I ask. He shakes his head once.

"Brother, never weren't. I was pissed you thought I'd be fuckin' her behind your back, but it looked shady. I get it," he admits.

I agree.

Shady as fuck.

"Thank you," I grind out.

"For?"

"Keeping her safe. Keeping her working, and my baby healthy and happy," I express. Sniper wraps me in a hug and hits my back.

"Always, brother. But not just for you, for her, too. She's a good girl," he says.

"The best," I admit.

I spend the rest of the day pouring over paperwork and financial figures. I have three years to make up for. Three years of minutes to read from church meetings. It seemed like my life was on hold for those years, but life here didn't stop. It kept pushing along, and now it's time to play catch up. Then, I'm going to pick up my Old Lady and show her pretty ass off.

chapter twenty-three

Kentlee

I think that I must be lucky.

I would have never thought this three years ago, when I was left alone and pregnant, but since that initial fear, I've had nothing but wonderful hit my doorway.

Between Mary-Anne, Bates, and Tammy, how could I ask for better people at my back? Sure, I miss my family—Brentlee most of all—but I have Connellee, and that's better than having nobody.

I stand in front of the mirror as a wave of sadness rolls through me. I try not to think about Brentlee often, but when I do, it makes me mournful.

I was uninvited to her wedding, and I haven't seen her since the day my parent's and I had the massive fight over

Pierce and my pregnancy. Years have gone by since I have spoken to my own sister.

That's a lie. I did see her about a year ago, but she didn't see me. She was sitting in a restaurant and she looked depressed. Twenty-one years old and she was dressed in a pantsuit, her hair in a French twist, with pearls around her neck. She looked polished and sophisticated, but she looked older. She didn't look like my young and vibrant sister.

I watched her, just enjoying *seeing* her, even if she looked depressed as hell. I watched as Scotty walked up to her table and her whole body stiffened. I didn't know exactly what that meant, but I hated it. I couldn't watch once Scotty was there. That man is a snake, and I don't trust him one single bit. I hope that one day my sister will come back to me, that we can be friends again. *I would love for her to know her nephew.*

I shake the sadness and disappointment away and inspect my clothes. Tonight is something special for Pierce. He wants me at his side and that's where I'll be.

I turn to look at my profile and suck in my stomach a bit. It could be toned more, but I'm thinner these days then when I met him. The leggings I'm wearing are tight and are a pleather type material, but with the comfort and stretch of leggings, making my legs look fantastic with the bright red, *Devils* Club, high heels I'm sporting.

I look at my white tank, which covers to just above my ass, wishing it were about two inches longer. I've got on a red, lacy bra underneath. I'm wearing my long blonde hair straight and down, my makeup dark, and my lips red against my pale skin.

I feel sexy and pretty.

I feel like a biker babe.

I'm all jeans and t-shirts, except when I have to wear the horrible hot pants and sparkly bra top at the *Devils* Club. Tonight, I want to be sexy for my man and for myself. I haven't gone out since before Bear was born, and tonight I'm going to enjoy myself.

"Ready, baby girl?" Pierce's voice timbres through the house and I look at myself one last time.

Ready as I'll ever be.

"Yeah, coming," I call out as I turn the lights off in my bedroom and make my way toward the living room.

Pierce is standing with Bear in his giant arms and the sight makes my knees weak. I don't know that I'll ever get used to seeing this man with Bear in his arms. It's *so* beautiful.

"Babe," he grunts as his eyes scan my body.

I blush before looking over to Tammy, who is smiling so wide I think her face might actually crack.

I ignore Tammy's smile and Pierce's hot gaze and take Bear from his strong arms. I nuzzle his sweet baby neck and gently kiss his cheek, trying not to dye it red with my lipstick. I tell him to be a good boy and then give Tammy instructions she doesn't need—like how the phone numbers are on the fridge to the doctors, that my cell will be on and with me at all times, and the usual panicked *mother-leaving-her-child* worries.

"Go have fun, Kentlee, you deserve it," she whispers in my ear as she gives me a big hug.

I don't know if I deserve a night off from work and mommy-hood, but I'm honestly grateful and thankful for it all the same.

Pierce doesn't say a word as I follow him to his motorcycle. It's been so long since I've been on the back. It seems like a lifetime ago. I stand there, trying to decide just how I'm going to ride on this thing in heels, it's been so long since I've been on the back of his bike, as he straddles it and starts the engine.

My mouth waters at the sight of him, his strong legs hugging the black piece of metal, his hair in his man bun, *so fucking sexy*, his beard covering his face. I clench my thighs together, remembering just how good that beard felt against me when he was licking my pussy.

"C'mon, sugar," he shouts over the rumble of the engine.

I shake myself out of my dreamy haze and place my hand on his shoulder as I climb on behind him. I wrap my hands around his middle and hold on tight as he takes off toward his clubhouse.

The night air is crisp and clean, surely making my hair a hot mess of a disaster, but I don't care. I've got my man and I'm finally happy again. He's made me promises that I can only pray he keeps. I could hold the past against him, I could be angry and bitter, but what good would that do? It wouldn't be good for Bear or me.

The best thing I can do is let this man love us, show us, and hopefully *prove* to us that he's going to take care of us. I'm going to hold onto my slice of happiness for as long as I can have it.

The clubhouse gravel parking lot is completely full of bikes. I've only been here twice, yet I have never seen it so packed. Pierce parks right in front, in an empty spot that must be always designated for him. There are a few guys standing outside, and he lifts his chin to them before grabbing my hand. I quickly try to finger comb my once straight and sleek hair.

"Babe," he rumbles as I tug my hand out of his.

"I need to fix my hair. It's a disaster," I huff, continuing to run my fingers through it to try and untangle all the knots.

Pierce turns and takes a step toward me before he wraps his arm around my back and hauls me into his chest. I'm startled by the move and drop my arm, looking up into his big gray eyes. He buries his other hand into my hair, messing it up further and I narrow my eyes at him.

"You look fuckin' sexy as hell tonight, baby girl. I'm gonna have to keep your ass close, because every man in there is gonna want a piece of you. Your hair is fuckin' sin, your tits goddamn unbelievable, and your ass—swear to Christ, I almost wept when I saw it in those pants. Stop *worryin'*."

He slams his lips down on mine before I can say a word. His hand slides from my lower back to my ass and he squeezes roughly, causing me to moan into his mouth.

"Let's go," he grunts.

I take a moment to wipe my lipstick from his face as he cleans mine up as well. I can't stop the giant smile from forming on my lips, and Pierce grins as he shakes his head. He keeps his hand firmly planted on my ass as he guides me inside of his club.

We walk inside and it reminds me of the night I came to tell him I was pregnant, except times ten. There are naked women, barely dressed women, and women in jeans and tanks milling around. A few people look at us but keep doing what, or *who*, they were doing before.

My eyes crash with familiar gray ones and I try to hide my shock, but I really am bad at it. I watch as the man smiles before he makes his way toward us.

"Kentlee," he says, taking my hand in his warm one.

Pierce's fingers dig into my ass and I hear him grunt beside me.

"Pops," he grumbles. The man looks at his son—they look even more like twins standing right here in front of me, together.

"*MadDog*," I say as he smiles warmly at me.

"You do as I suggested?" MadDog asks.

Pierce narrows his eyes and grits his teeth as he stares down his father and then he moves his hand from my ass and whistles so loud that it feels like I've burst an eardrum.

"Listen up," he hollers.

The room goes silent.

The men stare at him and wait. He's in control of everyone here. He is completely in charge, and I swear, he looks even bigger in this moment.

"Three years away was a fuck've a long time. I missed a lot with the club and with my brothers. I'm happy as fuck to be back. I also missed a lot personally, that means this little girl standing next to me. This is Kentlee, she's the mother of my son, and she's agreed to be my Old Lady and my wife. Anybody so much as looks at her sideways, and I'll fucking kill you," he roars.

I swear, you could hear a pin drop.

Then, not more than thirty seconds later, there are cheers and the music goes back up.

"Fuckin' wonderful. Now, when do I meet my only grandson?" MadDog asks. I can't help myself—I giggle.

"Will you still be in town tomorrow?" I question.

"Be here for a few days, darlin'," MadDog grins.

"Then of course, come over tomorrow and I'll make dinner," I suggest as Pierce places his hand on my ass again. I look up to him, but his head is turned and he's talking to a man I don't recognize.

"Sounds good," MadDog says quietly.

"Do you have another name I can call you? You know, aside from *MadDog*?" I ask, wrinkling my nose. He chuckles.

"Call me Max," he winks.

"Gotta make rounds, babe. C'mon," Pierce orders. I look up to Max who just smiles.

"See you tomorrow afternoon, Kentlee," he says gently.

It shocks me a bit. He looks tough and hard, but like Pierce, he's gentle when he wants to be. I smile, liking that Bear will have such strong men in his life, but also men that will show him that it's okay to be gentle at times, too.

Pierce leads me over to the bar and asks for a bottle of tequila and two shot glasses from the barely dressed girl bartending. She quickly hands him what he asks for, and I watch as he pours two shots. He hands me one and I just look down at it.

I haven't had hard liquor since before I had Bear. My tolerance was shit before, now it's probably nonexistent. I watch as Pierce takes his shot and then raps on the bar and asks for a couple of beers. I'm still staring at mine like it's going to sprout horns and do a little dance for me.

"Drink up, babe. We're havin' fun tonight," Pierce murmurs as he places a hot kiss on my neck.

"I don't drink at all anymore. I haven't since I had Bear," I admit, still staring at the tequila.

"Let loose, baby girl. Celebrate with your man," he murmurs against the side of my neck. His tongue snakes out and he licks my skin up to my earlobe before taking the lobe in his mouth and gently sucking.

Fuck, it feels good, too.

I down the shot and then chase it with a swig of beer.

Fuck it.

I'm going to have some damn fun with my man.

Pierce pulls me to stand between his legs and I happily wrap my arms around his neck and rest my head on his chest. I feel his hand on my ass, rubbing and squeezing me as the tequila warms my body from the inside out. I take my beer and nurse it while I inhale his spicy scent. It's turning me on. The tequila, the beer, his smell, and his hot hand burning through my clothes.

"'Nother one, baby girl," he murmurs, handing me another shot.

This time, I don't think. I take it. I am quietly enjoying my second beer, cuddled up with my man while he talks to his buddies. I'm in fucking bliss and getting more turned on by the minute.

The sound of a loud moan interrupts my blissful cuddle and I peak over Pierce's shoulder to check out the noise. My eyes almost pop out of my head at what I see. Katie Powell is on her hands and knees on the edge of the pool table, completely naked. She's sucking on a guy's dick, while another guy is fucking her from behind.

"Holy crap," I murmur.

Pierce turns around to see what's going on and then turns back to me.

"That's what she's here for, Kent," he says with a shrug.

"I know that. I've seen these girls fuck before, Pierce. What do you think they do when they close the club down and have private parties?" I roll my eyes and his other hand buries in my hair, tangling and pulling it tight as his eyes pin mine in place.

"I hate that you were there for that shit. I hate that you saw any of it. Don't remind me of your time there. It's fuckin' over now," he growls.

Pierce slams his mouth down on mine and his tongue forces its way inside of my mouth. He tastes like a mix of tequila and beer. I should hate the way it tastes, but on him, it makes me want him. I press myself closer to his body and slide one of my hands from around his neck. I glide my hand down his chest, feeling each ripple of his abs. I bravely, cup his cock on the outside of his jeans. He's hard, so I gently squeeze, and he groans into my mouth.

"Want those red lips wrapped around my cock, baby girl," he murmurs after he breaks our kiss.

"Here?" I ask shyly.

"I can take you somewhere," he murmurs as his hand wraps around my neck.

"If you want that right here, I'll do that for you, Pierce," I whisper, surprised by my own words.

Maybe it's the liquor, maybe it's the fact that everybody around here is engaging in some kind of sex and couldn't give two shits about the other people in the room.

Maybe I just want to make him happy.

"I want all of you, Kentlee. I want your lips on my cock, I want your pussy, and I want that perfect fuckin' ass. I wasn't fuckin' around when I said nobody would see you like that. *They won't.* I know a blow job ain't like fuckin', but I don't want one asshole here to think they got a shot at you. I don't want them to even imagine it's them you're blowin'," he grunts, releasing me. He then pours himself another shot and downs it right in front of me. I blink up at him in surprise.

"Would you want that with me though?" I ask, nodding behind him to Katie, or Kitty, or whatever the fuck they call her.

"Sharing you? Are you for fuckin' real right now?" he growls.

"With another woman, Pierce, not a man," I huff. He studies me for a beat before he speaks. When he does, it's with his gentle voice.

"Fucked a lot of pussy in this lifetime, baby girl. I've had threesomes, yeah, with whores. You're mine, though. Don't give a fuck if it's another woman or another man, I ain't sharing you, any part of you, with somebody else," he murmurs before he brushes his lips against mine.

"I want you to be happy, Pierce. I know how often the threesome thing happens. I saw it all the time," I mutter, looking down at my red high heels.

"I'm so goddamned happy with you, Kentlee. Nothin' could change that," he says before he kisses the swell of my breast.

"I don't want you to feel like you're throwing anything away for me," I whisper with watery eyes.

Fuck, I hate it when I drink and cry. It's embarrassing as hell.

"I'm thirty-eight years old, sugar. I've done and seen a lot. I ain't throwin' a damn thing away by having you as mine. *I'm finally living*," he says.

Pierce then crashes his lips to mine as his hands wrap around the backs of my thighs before he picks me up. I instantly wrap my legs around his waist and hold on.

I hang on as he carries me to his bedroom and slams the door behind us before he removes my octopus arms and legs from his body. I don't pause, I don't think, I just let my alcohol daze guide me—*to my knees*. Without even looking up, I unbuckle, unzip, and shove Pierce's jeans down his thighs. He's going commando, and I whimper as his cock comes into view. I lick his slit and then the entire underside of his length.

"Fuck," he hisses as he buries his hands in my hair.

"Fuck my mouth, Pierce. Give it to me the way you want it," I whisper, looking into his eyes.

I watch as he closes them for a second and then he looks down on me before he grins.

"Open up, baby girl. Time for you to be fucked," he growls. I shiver before I open my mouth wide.

Pierce doesn't tease me. *No*, he holds my head still with his hands and slides his cock between my lips and down my throat in one smooth motion.

I keep my eyes on his as he pulls completely out of my mouth, slowly, inch by inch; then he guides himself back inside, going a little further. He repeats his slow motions until his entire cock is down my throat. It's hard to breath and my eyes water, but his clenched jaw and his eyes full of amazement are worth every second of pain and uncomfortableness.

"You're so good to me, sugar," he rasps as he pulls out a bit and then begins to make short, quick, strokes into my mouth. *He is focused*. His eyes have moved from mine and are now focused on my mouth, on his cock sliding in and out of my mouth specifically – then he stops and jerks back from me.

"Stay there," he grunts. I watch in awe as he completely strips his clothes before he drops to his own knees behind me.

Pierce grabs the waist of my skintight pants and wrenches them over my ass and halfway down my thighs before his hand presses against my back to push me down. I fall to my hands, but I hear him make a noise of protest before he press-es a little harder against my back.

"Chest on the floor, sugar," he murmurs. I do as he asks, feeling the cool floor against my cheek, not giving a shit how dirty it is.

My legs are close together, my pants hold little stretch to spread them farther, but I don't think Pierce minds. He licks from my clit to my ass and I moan as his tongue swirls against my back entrance. It's forbidden and dirty and so fucking good. I gasp when his hands grab both sides of my ass and he spreads my cheeks farther apart before he licks me, *there*, again.

"Pierce, *please*," I beg, knowing how much he loves it when I do.

"Yeah, whatever you want," he murmurs before he bites my ass hard.

I moan because, *shit*, it felt good, and I don't even care that he's chuckling behind me.

"Gonna fuck you now," he announces as he slides deep inside of me. His hand goes to the back of my neck—pinning me to the floor.

Fuck, he feels so big like this.

Pierce's fingers, on his other hand, wrap around my hip and dig into my flesh, bruising me. It feels delicious, too. He slowly pulls out of me before he slams back inside, hard and fast. I whimper at the feeling. My legs are practically togeth-er, my chest on the floor, and he's behind me with all of his strength. I feel weak, but it feels good all at the same time.

"Hands," he barks.

I don't move, not understanding his demand. A second later he removes his grip from my hip and wraps his hand around my wrist, wrenching it behind my body. I do the same with my other hand, and his long fingers wrap around both of my wrists, pinning them to my lower back. The hand around my neck slides down my spine and moves around to my clit, his fingers pressing against my hardened nub.

"It's gonna be hard, baby girl, and it's gonna be fast—but you can take it, can't you?" he purrs, his lips skimming my shoulder.

I don't question. I don't doubt—I want to please.

I want to take whatever he gives me right now.

"I can take it, baby; give me everything," I whine. He grunts before he pulls out slightly and starts to fuck me with slow strokes. He doesn't slam inside of me, like I imagined he would. No, he's drawing this out. Slowly and with even strokes, he fucks my body while I am completely immobile, while his fingers tease my clit, bringing me so close to the edge, yet unable to come.

"You're so fucking wet, Kentlee. My cock is fucking soaked. Wet and hot. Goddamn, I could stay inside this sweet pussy and never leave. Would you want that? My cock slowly fucking you non-stop? Never letting you come, leaving you teetering on the edge for fuckin' hours?" he asks.

Cruel bastard.

I let a sob out at the thought. If I stayed like this for five more minutes, I was going to freak out, let alone *hours*.

"I'm going to let your wrist go, baby girl. I want you to play with your pussy for me. Can you do that?" He asks gently.

It's too much. Too sweet. I need him rough and rowdy. I need him slamming inside of me and fucking me until I scream. *This* – this is too much.

Pierce released my wrists and without a thought I shove my hand beneath my body and begin to roughly rub my clit. I need to come so bad, I'm about to go insane.

"Do not come yet," he barks. It scares me. I whimper and slow my movements down as he continues to fuck me his pace quickening, sliding in and out of me with long, fast, even strokes.

I tense when I feel him press against my ass; then he begins to massage me, and the feeling is so sublime, I don't hold back my moan of pleasure. I gasp when I feel him push his finger inside of me. He doesn't say a word, he just continues to fuck me with his finger and his cock—filling me. I think I'm going to combust at any minute, as I continue to stroke my clit.

I want everything hard.

I want more.

"What a good girl I have," he murmurs above me. I swear I get wetter at his words.

"*Please*, Pierce," I whisper hoarsely.

"Do you need to come?" he chuckles behind me.

"Yeah," I say licking my dry lips.

"Do you like my finger in your ass, sugar?" he asks gruffly, ignoring my pleas to climax.

"*Yes*," I sigh, giving up on any chance of relief.

I gasp when I feel him slide a second finger inside of me, stretching me ever more.

Holy fuck, I'm going to come.

"Pierce," I cry. He begins to thrust his hips a little harder.

"Okay, baby girl, you can come," he grinds out.

It is as if he's given himself permission as well, because he begins to slam his hips and his cock inside of me with so much force, the air escapes from my lungs.

I continue to stroke my clit, but harder and faster as I chase my climax. Then, when I do, my whole body goes rigid and I can't hold in my scream of pleasure.

Pierce is close behind me, slamming his hips against my ass and fucking my ass with his finger, fast and rough, and hurting me so fucking good that tears are streaming down my face. Then I feel him explode inside of me with his own release.

Pierce almost immediately pulls out of me, everywhere, and picks me up, carrying me to the bed before he gently lays me down. I don't move a muscle as he quietly strips my clothes from my body. I'm still twitching and there's cum leaking out of me, but I don't even care. My body feels *that* good – *that* sated.

"Love you, baby girl," he murmurs, kissing my shoulder.

"Love you, too, Pierce," I sigh before I roll over in the bed to face him.

Fury

Kentlee is facing me—sweaty, her makeup a little runny, and her red lipstick smeared. She's never looked more beautiful to me then she does in this moment.

I run my finger down the side of her face and down her neck. *Fuck, she's young*. The thought had never really crossed my mind before. I saddled her alone with a baby, and she was only twenty-three. Now, at twenty-six, she's still so god-damned young.

I'm twelve years older than her, and for some reason, it hasn't bothered me until this moment. Maybe because she's talked about giving me the things she thinks I want, the threesomes and the parties; maybe that was her way of saying she wants them, too. I have to know. I have to make her happy, and I'll do whatever she wants to make that happen.

"All that talk about me being happy, threesomes and shit. That because you want them? Do you feel like you're missing out because you had Bear young?" I ask, blurting it out like a fuckin' idiot.

"What?" She looks at me, genuinely confused, and then she smiles softly, lazily, in that *I-just-got-fucked-and-I'm-too-happy-to-think-about-anything-else* kind of way.

"No way. I don't want to lick some other girl's vagina. No, thanks. I just know that you never wanted an Old Lady, a wife, yet here you are, asking me for those things. I don't want you to feel like I've trapped you or ruined your life. If you wanted something more, I'd do anything to give it to you," she confesses.

For some reason, it goes straight to my cock. I feel myself twitch at the thought of this beautiful woman willing to give me anything. If I were a bigger dick, I'd take advantage of it. I probably still will - to a certain extent.

"All I want is you, Kentlee. I want my ring on your finger, I want you to carry my name, I want you on the back of my bike, and I want all of you on my cock," I say with a smile, thinking about how I filled her up just minutes ago.

Fuck me, it was good, too.

"Sounds perfect," she murmurs, wrapping her arm around me and pressing her body against my side.

"Good. Want you happy, babe, cause I'm the last man

you're gonna fuck. You better like what I give you," I grunt. She throws back her head, laughing. I wrap my hand around her juicy ass and squeeze.

"Yeah, same goes for you, baby," she grins. I nip her bottom lip with my teeth.

"Couldn't have picked a sweeter cunt to fuck for eternity," I say, smiling. She narrows her eyes for a beat before she presses her lips to mine.

"I'm on birth control, by the way. We never talked about it, but I wanted to let you know," she admits. I grin at her.

"Wouldn't have given a fuck, babe. Not a hardship filling you full of my babies. You're obviously a fantastic mother and you make gorgeous kids," I say, captured by her eyes—her gorgeous fuckin' eyes.

"Think my old man could get it up again so I could enjoy a ride?" she asks, shocking the fuck out of me as her hand begins to gently stroke my stirring cock back to life. Her lips taste like tequila and her—*sweet, sweet Kentlee.*

I moan as I shift my hips into her hand.

"Yeah, sugar, get up here and ride me. Make a fuckin' show out of it, too. I'm ready to play with those sexy tits of yours," I grunt as she climbs over me.

I can feel her warm, wet pussy, still soaked from our mixed come as she straddles my waist, her hand behind her, gently stroking me.

"A show?" she asks, arching her brow.

"Yeah, babe. I want a full on, eye opening spectacular. I want to watch you play with your clit while you ride me; I want you to pinch those pretty nipples; and I want to see you take my cock in that sweet, wet cunt, over and over again," I describe, watching her body shake with chills.

275

Fuck yeah, my woman likes it when I talk dirty—when I tell her what to do.

I lie back and watch the show. *What a show it is, too.*

Kentlee is perfect.

She's sweet and soft when she needs to be.

Kinky and dirty when I need her to be.

And…

Tough as nails when the world requires it of her.

She's so fucking perfect, I couldn't have wished for anything more.

chapter twenty-four

Kentlee

I crack an eye open and take in my surroundings. The room is plain and bare, but decently clean. I try to lift my head but groan when the room starts to spin. Pierce must hear me because within seconds, his body is draped over the back of mine—his chest on my back, his knee between my thighs, his hard cock pressed against my hip.

"Mornin', sugar," he murmurs against my neck as his long hair tickles my skin.

"Too early," I moan. He just laughs at me.

"We gotta get up soon and go home to our boy," he whispers against my skin, sending chills down my body.

Our boy.

Home.

Such beautiful words to me.

"Yeah, okay," I sigh. I try to move, but he doesn't budge. "I have to get out of bed to go home, Pierce," I groan into the pillow.

Suddenly, I feel his fingers at my core, gently caressing me, so soft and light. I can't hold the moan inside at his tender touch.

"Is your pussy sore, baby girl?" he whispers. His lips trace down my spine, his hair dragging along my skin and turning me on with each sweep.

"Yeah, achingly," I moan as my pussy begins to pulse from his light touches.

"Just relax. Let me make it better," he mutters before I feel his hot tongue against my sore slit.

I'm sore, but now I'm turned on.

Pierce's lips kiss my clit before he gently laps at it and then back down to my core. I feel him slip his tongue inside of me and then I vibrate from his moan.

"*Pierce*," I hiss. Lifting my hips, giving him more access to my body.

"Gonna fuck this aching pussy, baby girl," he says, kissing the side of my thigh before he slides away from me and wraps me in his arms, pulling my back against his chest. I feel his cock against the cheeks of my ass and I groan at his hard length.

"Guide me in, baby," he murmurs with his face buried in my neck.

I wrap my hand around his hard cock as he holds my thigh up and out, his other arm wrapped around my chest; then I slowly slide down on him. It fucking burns and I can't hold back the hiss of pain that escapes.

Pierce kisses my neck but doesn't move inside of me, then I feel one of his hands glide down my stomach and his fingers begin to gently caress my clit again. I rest my head back against his shoulder and begin to slowly slide up and down on his cock while his other hand begins to manipulate my sensitive nipples.

"This is it for me, babe. You and me and *this*," he mumbles.

"Us fucking?" I ask on a sigh. He rolls a nipple between his fingers and gently plucks the bud.

"For fuckin' eternity. When I'm with you, the rest of the fuckin' world melts away. It's only us," he rumbles.

"Only us." I mimic his words as I reach around and bury my hand in his fantastic long hair.

"Love your hands on me," he grunts as he begins to fuck me a little harder, lifting his hips to meet mine. I wrap my other hand around his forearm.

"Don't ever cut this hair, or your beard," I announce. He laughs.

"My baby girl wants me to have long hair and a beard, that's what she gets. Whatever you want, you get," he says.

Though I've heard the words before, I'm not quite sure I truly believed them until this moment. My orgasm rushes through my body without warning, and Pierce follows shortly after, his cum filling me and his teeth sinking into my shoulder with a grunt.

Hours later, we're at home. We released Tammy and we're now at the grocery store to get food for dinner with Max. I can cook, but I'm not the absolute best, so I decide to make something simple, likeable, and filling – meatloaf and mashed potatoes.

Bear is riding in the cart and Pierce is pushing while I grab things off of the shelves. It's so fucking domestic, it's almost laughable. Pierce with his jeans, leather, and man-bun; me with my leggings and oversized tank; Bear all smiles and drool from his seat in the cart.

We're a real family.

I never thought this day would come.

I halt mid-stride when I hear my name and turn around to see Brentlee standing just a few feet away from me.

I know I am looking at her like a deer caught in headlights, but I can't *not* look. She's standing right in front of me, heavily pregnant, and her face is bruised.

"Brentlee," I whisper, taking a step closer to her. She does the same and, seconds later, we're wrapped in each other's arms.

"Is that your guy?" she hesitantly asks after we break away from our hug. I feel Pierce next to me and his hand goes around my waist.

"Pierce," he murmurs. I know he's staring at her bruised face.

"It's nice to finally meet you," she whispers.

It makes me sick.

She looks like a shell of her past self. Her eyes are dead and her smile is fake.

"I'll go get the meat and potatoes, babe. You catch up and I'll meet you in front, yeah?" Pierce asks.

I reluctantly drag my eyes away from my sister to meet his. With a simple kiss to my forehead he takes Bear and they go in search of groceries.

"You're happy," Brentlee observes.

"Finally," I agree.

"I'm glad. Someone deserves to be," she mutters. I take her hand in mine.

"I'm your sister. I will always love you, Brent. I'm not going to pretend to know your life, but I can see it probably isn't healthy. I'm not judging, but I want to offer you my love and support if you need it. My door is always open to you, always," I whisper, trying to keep my tears at bay.

Brentlee nods her head.

"I would do nothing but bring trouble to your door," she confesses. I shake my head.

"You see that big ass biker I'm with?" I ask. She nods with wide eyes. "That guy, he can handle whatever trouble you could dream up. If he couldn't handle it alone, he's got a whole club behind him for backup. He's the president. Nobody is going to fuck with you if he's at your back, Brent," I say, feeling braver than I am. I'm *so* scared for her; she looks so fragile.

"Okay," she drawls. Though, whatever demons she's fighting, she's not ready to let go; she's not ready to leave, and there's nothing I can do for her. I place my hand on her stomach.

"Boy or girl?" I ask with a watery smile.

"Girl," she says solemnly.

"A niece. I'm already in love," I say before I wrap her in a hug again. "Anytime, Brent, night or day, just come for me— call, whatever, and I'm there—*we're there*," I emphasize, whispering in her ear.

She gives me a whispered *okay* and I leave it at that. I turn and walk away from my obviously abused sister. There is nothing I can do until she's ready. I just hope that she's ready before it's too late.

"He's hittin' her," Pierce growls as I start to make dinner a few hours later. Bear is down for a nap and we're alone in the kitchen.

"He is. He has been for a while, I suspect," I reply.

"Need to get her outta there, baby girl. She's knocked up. He could kill her," Pierce says. I turn to him, surprised by his insistence.

"I told her I was here for her. I offered her your protection, though I should have asked you first. I'm sorry about that," I say softly. He shakes his head before taking a pull from his beer.

"Don't ever be sorry for offering my help in a situation like that, babe. I'd go over there right now and drag her out if I could," he grinds out.

"She wouldn't leave him if you did. Or she'd simply go back. She hasn't hit her rock bottom yet," I say as I set the pot of water on the stove and turn it on.

"I know. I hate to see it, though. Hate to see a sweet kid being beat down by an entitled douchebag," he barks. It makes me laugh.

"How do you know what Scotty's like?" I lift a brow and it's his turn to grin.

"Made Sniper get me the info on your family when I was locked up. Wanted to make sure you were gonna be okay," he says with a smile and a shrug.

"Well, you're right. He's an entitled douchebag. I hate him, always have. She deserves better," I whisper, staring off into space.

"Like Sniper?" he asks, lifting a brow.

"Bates was good to her and good *for* her. They were just kids when they were together, but he loved her. She wasn't a trophy or just some slut; she was his girl and he treated her like a princess," I say as I stir the sauce in the pot.

"Hope she wakes up before it's too late," he murmurs as he wraps his arms around my waist and rests his chin on my shoulder.

"Me too," I whisper.

Dinner with my dad was... well... *interesting.*

The old fucker spent the whole night flirting with my woman and playing with my son. The fucking kicker? *I liked it.* Well, I wanted to gut him for flirting with Kentlee, but I enjoyed how easily they got along and how much my son took to him immediately.

We eat and hang out with Bear before Kentlee shoos us outside while she puts him to bed. Keeping to his schedule, which she says is important. I'm not going to fight with her about it because in all honestly, I know jack fuckin' shit about kids.

Once we're outside, my dad gets serious, real serious.

"You got a good life now, son," Pops says as he takes a pull from his beer.

"The best," I agree.

"Wish you could have found it earlier, like me and your mom, but what you got—irreplaceable," he mutters. I stare into the night sky.

"Naw, I found it at the right time. Would've waited another thirty years to get it if I had to. What I got? Ain't nothin' in this life any better," I say, sounding like the goddamned bleeding vagina that I am anymore.

"That's good, son. Protect it, feed it, and for god's sake, make some more damn babies. That kid is beautiful and needs siblings. My only regret was that I didn't give your mother more children. She wanted them, you know?" he says. I nod.

I know. She told me once that she prayed to have more, but my dad was immersed in the club and didn't want more baggage than he had at the time. He loved my mom, and he loved me, but more babies meant more time at home and less time with his brothers.

I probably would have felt the same way ten years ago.

Now, though, my family's what I want. They come first.

"Shit storm's brewin', son. I want you to be vigilant," he says, staring off into the distance.

"*Bastards* or Aryans?" I ask. My dad shakes his head.

"No fuckin' clue which ones; but mark my words, they're fuckin' plannin', and waitin', and biding their time. Then they're gonna strike with a vengeance," he warns.

I agree.

The shit with the *Bastards* just disappearing is fucking concerning; and the Aryan's blowing up one clubhouse, and then that's it? *Unnerving*.

"I'll keep an eye out, Pops," I mutter. He slaps my back before we head back inside.

My dad doesn't stay much longer. He's got booze and pussy waiting for him at my clubhouse, so he's ready to rock and roll. He gives Kentlee a hug and thanks her for the evening, promising to make more trips here and spend more time with Bear.

I can almost see the wheels turning in his head. He's been slowing down lately. I wonder if he's ready for retirement. When he is, I bet dollars to donuts it's here with his grandson. Maybe it's just wishful thinking; having my dad back on a regular basis would be a sweet deal. *I miss the old bastard.*

I take Kentlee to bed, but I don't fuck her. I can't. She's been walking funny all day and I know that her pussy has to ache. I fucked her long and hard last night, more than once, and then again this morning. I'm going to give her a little break tonight. *I'm feeling generous.*

I wrap her in my arms and pull her back against my chest, taking in her soft body pressed against mine and her sweet scent that surrounds me.

"I like your dad a lot," she whispers into the dark room.

"He likes you a little too much," I grumble. She giggles.

"Well, he still looks damn good for his age," she says. I squeeze her body in warning.

"Kentlee," I grunt, which makes her giggle even more. She rolls over in my arms and puts her small hands on my cheeks.

"I love you, Pierce. You're the only man on this whole earth for me," she whispers before her lips caress mine in a kiss.

"Get to sleep, woman. I'm trying to be a gentleman and give your abused pussy a break. But if you kiss me, I can't be held responsible for my actions."

"My pussy is abused. *Fuck*, it hurt so bad all day long," she admits. It's my turn to laugh.

"I know, you walked funny. Couldn't help but watch. Felt pretty fuckin' proud about it, too." I grin into the dark room and she huffs out a breath of air.

"You're such a man," she complains. I throw back my head in full on laughter.

"No shit, babe. Got the dick and balls to prove it, too."

"Pierce," she hums. I grunt. "Go to sleep, you caveman," she orders.

I do go to sleep; but for the first time in my entire life, I do it smiling.

This woman is mine. Her heart is mine, as well as her body. She takes me as I am, expecting nothing in return, but my fidelity and faith in us. She has it. She owns me, too—heart, body, and soul. She is my fucking weakness. A weakness I never wanted and thought I didn't need. How wrong had I been?

The love of this woman is worth anything and everything life could throw my way.

chapter twenty-five

Kentlee

A routine.

It's amazing to think that in just a few weeks, Pierce and I have fallen into a routine. And it's a good one. A great one, actually. I've smiled more this past month than I have in three years. The loss of my family and then the loss of Pierce was a blow to my heart. It shattered it, really. But now I feel alive – *free and happy*.

Pierce has even taken me to the clubhouse for a few parties. I've been able to meet with other Old Ladies and get to know them. They are nothing like that whore Katie Powell. Most of them are rough, but they are genuine, and they tell it like it is. I like that. I don't mind knowing where I stand with people. It makes life easier.

One of the Old Ladies, Rosie, is coming over to have a playdate with her daughter and Bear this afternoon. I can't keep the huge smile off of my face as I make lunch for us and wait for them to arrive. Rosie's daughter is just over three years old, so she and Bear should have a great time together.

There's a knock on the door, and I know it must be Rosie, so I call out and tell her to come inside. Bear is still napping, but I know he'll be up any minute.

I hear the front door open, but I don't hear Rosie's voice. I walk out of the kitchen and stop dead in my tracks at the sight in front of me.

The living room is full of men.

I don't make a noise. My only thought is that whoever these men are, they cannot know Bear is in the house. I must protect my son.

"Ain't that a pretty little white girl?" one of the men drawls as his eyes roam over my body.

"She's fuckin' perfect," the voice of another man says.

Then they charge toward me.

I turn to run, but they're bigger, faster, and stronger than me.

An arm wraps around my middle just as another one wraps around my mouth. I pinch my eyes closed waiting for more to happen, but nothing does. Strong hands wrap around my ankles and I am carried away from the house, away from my baby, and thrown into the back of a van. I say a silent prayer for Bear, and hope that Rosie shows up soon so that she can get him and call Pierce.

I don't say a word as the van drives off. The two men who spoke in my living room are in front, and the three who were silent sit in back with me.

One of them sits right next to me, the side of his body pressing against mine. I take a moment to look around and notice that all of the men are bald and tattooed.

Their tattoos aren't anything like Pierce's, though.

The man next me has a swastikas tattooed on his arm. He has a three leaf clover with the number six in each leaf. Then he has the number 1488 on his forearm. The letters AB are also tattooed on his hand. I notice a renaissance looking shield and sword tattooed on his opposite forearm, with another AB right above it. My eyes slowly take in the rest of the men and notice that they all have the same tattoos as the man next to me, but in different places.

"Who are you?" I hesitantly ask the man at my side. His cold blue eyes stare down at me before he smiles. It's not a friendly smile. It's fucking terrifying.

"Your friendly Aryan's, princess," he says. My eyes widen. *Holy shit— white supremacists.*

"What do you want from me?" I ask, my voice wavering and trembling.

"Retribution," he says, cocking his head to the side and studying me. "I wouldn't worry too much, princess. You're nice and pale, all that blonde hair and blue eyes. We'll make sure we treat you right," he murmurs. It sends shivers up my body.

Creepy as shit shivers.

Vault calls me as I'm sliding off of my bike in the clubhouse

289

parking lot. I frown at my phone for a minute before answering it. I look around the lot and don't see his bike.

"Yeah," I say as I step inside of the bar.

It's fairly deserted, a few people milling around, but it's a normal Friday afternoon. I have some shit to look over and then finalize before the first run from SLC to Canada happens, which starts Monday.

"You need to get home, Prez," he says. I shove my office door open.

"What for?" I ask distractedly as I power on my computer.

"Rosie came over for a playdate with your woman and kid. When she got here, the front door was open, Bear was screaming in his bed, and your woman ain't nowhere. Her cars in the garage, though. I just checked," he says.

Suddenly, it's as if I've left my body and I'm on the outside looking in. I can see myself sitting rigid as stone, unable to move, unable to breathe, and unable to speak.

"Prez." Vault's raspy voice cuts through my haze and I shake my head to get my shit together.

"I'm in my office. I'll be there in two minutes." I hang up the phone before he gets a chance to speak and start to storm out of the clubhouse, almost running over Sniper.

"What's goin' on?" he asks, not missing a fuckin' thing.

"I want everybody at my house five minutes ago," I growl. He nods.

"Kentlee?" he asks quietly. My eyes cut to his.

"Fuckin' disappeared. She's fucking gone," I say unable to hide my emotion.

Snipe knows, he fuckin' knows my woman, and he knows how I feel about her. I watch as something crosses his face—

fear, anger, and rage mixed together. I feel the exact fuckin' same goddamned way.

Without another word, I leave.

I race home and find Rosie holding an inconsolable Bear while their daughter is wrapped in Vault's arms. As soon as my son hears my boots hit the living room, he cries out for me and wiggles out of Rosie's arms, launching himself in mine. I pick him up and wrap him tight without thought.

My boy, my baby, he's so fuckin' scared.

Vault hands his daughter to Rosie and asks her to go to the kitchen for a bit. She doesn't ask questions, just does it without a word. Old Lady to the core, and a good one at that. Vault levels me with a hard look before he speaks.

"Rosie was supposed to be here at noon. She was runnin' about ten minutes late. Says the door was left open, so she walked inside. Lunch is set out on the table for the kids and the girls. Bear was in his room screamin' his head off, but nothing else was amiss. There were no signs of struggle, and the car is in the garage." He tells me all he knows.

"It's Bear's naptime from ten to noon. Maybe there was a knock on the door and she yelled out, thinking it was Rosie, and whoever it was came inside. Kentlee isn't stupid. She probably went because she didn't want whoever it was to know Bear was in the house. I know her," I state. Vault nods in agreement. Though he doesn't know Kentlee all that well, it makes sense that she wouldn't want harm to come to our boy.

"Then we're on the same page, because nothing else makes sense. She wouldn't run. You're engaged. She had all the shit out for the playdate, and her car, keys, purse, and phone are here in the house," Vault confirms, ruling out any other questions I might have had.

"Retaliation," I mutter.

"Retribution," Vault mumbles before my house is filled with every single patched brother we have.

"Need to find her fast," I tell the room of men, my brothers.

I walk out of the room, still holding my boy, who has cried himself to sleep on my shoulder. I call my Pops. This smells like the *Bastards*, but I can't be sure. I don't want to go after the wrong group and chance not ever finding her, or finding her too late.

"Torch called me," my dad says as his answer. *I'm glad*. I didn't want to explain shit again.

"Who's good for it?" I ask, trying to stay calm. It's using everything I have inside of me to do so.

"I tried my contact with the *Bastards* and the Aryan's, no answer on either. My guess? They're in it together," he suggests.

I let out a breath. Makes sense. *Bastards* have been wanting our territory for fuckin' ever, then we cut ties with the Aryan's. All has been quiet because they've been planning.

"Together," I repeat.

"Massive takeover," my Pops offers.

I nod to myself.

Massive takeover.

They don't know what they've done. I'll gut every single one of those fuckers, one by one.

And slowly.

"I need backup," I demand. It's not a question and my father wouldn't turn me down even if it was.

"Already loading up. Be there tomorrow," he says before he hangs up the phone. I let out a breath.

"All women and children need to be on lockdown, *mandatory*," I tell Sniper, who is behind me. I can smell the rage pouring off of him in waves.

"Done," he says. I turn to face him.

"I want every man to stay here. We're in planning mode, but I don't want anybody overhearing us. How they figured out Kentlee was mine already, I don't know; but if there was a leak, I don't want to chance it," I say. Sniper nods before his eyes meet mine.

"What if the leak is a brother?" he asks.

"I'll kill him, *slowly—deliberately take my time*," I say.

Sniper grins before he turns around to give my directions to the men.

Seconds later, Rosie is tearing out of the house and running to her car. I should give her Bear, but I can't. The boy would just cry. He *needs* me. I might be able to leave him with Tammy, but I'm not leaving him in the clubhouse. I don't know how those racist fucks found out about Kentlee, but I do know that if it's a leak in the clubhouse, I don't want a soul knowing where my son is.

It's time to plan out some murders.

I grin at the thought.

I'm ready to kill some racist fucks.

Now.

Kentlee

I wish I could sleep, but there's no way I can drop my guard around these crazy assholes. They've pretty much been ignoring me the whole way, talking amongst themselves, and they are sickening. They are a shame to the human race, and they make me ill.

"Make the call," the one next to me orders.

I can't help but wonder if he's the leader. He's stayed quiet the entire time and has just looked straight ahead, at nothing but the wall of the van. *He's unnerving.*

I listen as a ringing noise takes over the sound in the van. The phone is on speakerphone, and I wonder just who in the hell they're calling, until the voice on the other end picks up. I don't have to wonder another second.

Pierce.

"Where the fuck did you take my woman?" he roars. It makes me jump. The man next to me looks down at me, expressionless, but studious.

"Your little blondie is perfectly safe, aren't you sweetheart?" one of the men in front says, his voice sticky sweet.

"Pierce," I whimper as my voice cracks.

"You touch one goddamned hair on her head and I'll gut every single one of you," he growls, his voice low and menacing.

"You'd have to find us first, and we aren't the type who will be found if we don't want to be."

"What do you want?" Pierce sighs.

It sounds as though he's resigned, that he's given up and will do whatever it is that they ask. However, I know Pierce. *He will make these men suffer.*

"We want our guns or our money. That bullshit from three years ago isn't forgotten."

"You blew up a club and killed everyone inside; you took your money in blood," Pierce says just as I start piecing things together.

Pierce went to jail delivering guns to these jackholes, and now they want the money they paid for them back.

"Blood doesn't pay the bills and doesn't supply us guns," the man in front says.

I kind of understand his reasoning, even if he's crazy as hell.

"I don't deal with guns anymore," Pierce announces. The man laughs.

"Yeah, you're dealing with those wetback fucks. We know all about it. Doesn't change a goddamned thing. Money or guns, Fury. Get those to me by Sunday at noon or I'll turn this little white bitch of yours out. Every man in my club loves to fuck pure white pussy, and that's exactly what she's got. She'll be used to her fullest potential here. Text me when you're ready, and I'll send you a meeting place," he says before he hangs up.

I feel myself grow short of breath. His words ring throughout my head, over and over again.

Every man in my club loves to fuck pure white pussy, and that's exactly what she's got.

She'll be used to her fullest potential here.

I close my eyes tightly and try to calm down before I completely and totally lose it.

We pull into a warehouse and the van turns off before the doors fly open and I am yanked out. I find myself surrounded by at least twenty more skinheads and a whole group of bikers.

Scary-as-shit bikers.

My eyes catch a patch and it says *Bastards*. Two groups are in this together; two groups against one. I can only hope that I survive this, but it doesn't seem likely anymore.

"This the cunt?" a gravelly voice asks. I look up to see a man with a long gray beard and a pot belly standing in front of me, wearing a *Bastards* cut.

"Yup. Fury is pissed," the quiet man announces.

"Of course, he is. His piece of ass is gone," the gray bearded man says before he laughs.

"You know how territorial these types are. You sure this is how you want to play this out?" the quiet man asks long-beard.

"Hit 'em where it hurts, their pride and their cocks. It's the only way they'll take anything serious, Mark," long-beard says, calling the quiet man Mark.

Well, at least I know one of their names now.

"Well, his pride is definitely on the line," Mark says with a nod. "I'll keep her with me. There's too many men around here," he offers. Long-beard grins.

"We could play for a bit, have a little party," long-beard offers.

Mark shakes his head once and long-beard steps back. *Oh, fuck, this guy is the one in charge*, I think as I am hauled off toward an office. I can feel the men behind me as well as their stares. It's as if a million needles are pricking my skin. Once we are inside the office, Mark looks right at me, his eyes cold, dead, and unfeeling.

It's terrifying.

"This has nothing to do with you. Don't take anything personally," he begins. My eyes widen.

How do I not take the fact that these assholes kidnapped me and want to fuck me like a blow up doll personally?

"Its business," he shrugs, not looking the least bit sorry.

"Fury isn't going to just give you what you want and be

done with it," I say. Mark cocks his head to the side before he speaks.

"Those men may be idiots, but I am not. We had a contract and we warned him that our competitors were fucking with us. Yet, they severed ties with us and went to the competitors. It's the principle of the thing now, Kentlee," he says, taking a step toward me. I freeze as his hand comes up and cups my cheek.

"He and his men are as good as dead, pretty girl. Mourn him quickly because come Monday, you will have a new place and a new life. Can you guess at what that is?" he asks as he dips his head lower and his lips brush against my ear.

"No," I croak.

"In my bed, as my *whore*. Every time I sink my cock inside of your pussy, it will be my victory against him. Killing him won't be enough. I need to disrespect him even in death, and I'll do it by owning you. *Then*, I'll do it again by being Bear's daddy," he says, releasing me and taking a step away.

My mouth drops open in full on shock as I stare at him, unable to speak.

"You didn't think I knew about that boy? I know everything, Kentlee. Your son will be raised to be a solider for me, and you'll breed more white children for me. They'll be beautiful," he grins before he leaves the room, locking me inside.

I sink to my knees and, for the first time since I was taken from my own home—I cry.

chapter twenty-six

Fury

"They wouldn't have taken her far if they want to draw you out," my Pops says as he lights up a cigarette next to me.

"Nope. Town ain't that big, but they could be at any one of the little ones around us," I say.

I'm tired as fuck.

My adrenaline has crashed and now I'm just fucking resigned to this being a complete cluster fuck.

"This isn't all about money. I know them, they want to make a point as well," Pops mutters. I nod.

Bear is safe at Tammy's, happy to be with his favorite grandmother type, and I've got fuck-all to go on to find Kentlee.

I can't help but wonder if we haven't already been through enough shit in our three years together. Right when we're happy, more comes raining down on us. It isn't fair to her, not in the slightest. Kentlee has never done a damn thing wrong, and here I go again, causing her pain. *I knew my life would fuck with hers if she was mine. I knew it, but I made her mine anyway, because I'm a selfish fucking prick.*

"You are a prick, but you did the right thing by claiming her," my dad says beside me.

I could kick myself for speaking my thoughts out loud.

"What's their point then?" I ask.

"To piss us off, to have the upper hand, to prove they can take what's ours and there's nothing that we can do about it. Mark is fucking sadistic. He'll do whatever it takes to get his point across," my dad informs me. It doesn't make me feel any better, at all.

"I know where they are," Bull says, stepping beside me. I turn to him as rage seeps through my veins.

"How?" I calmly ask. It's going against everything inside of me to be so goddamned calm right now.

"Kitty. I went to the club to check on the women and kids about ten minutes ago, and Kitty was running her mouth to another whore. She didn't see me; didn't know I was there. She's been feeding them information."

Red replaces the colors around me and I quickly walk to my bike. My Pops and Bull follow behind me, along with others, I'm sure—but I can't give a fuck.

My only mission is to get that whore and get some answers before I kill her.

The clubhouse is quiet. I walk inside to see women and children milling around. I don't care about them. My red, angry gaze is looking for just one person—*Kitty*. When I spot her, she's wearing a bikini top and cut offs, painting her toe-nails like she doesn't have a care in the world. I walk right up to her, my brothers at my back.

"Up," I grind out. She looks up at me and smiles—what she considers sexily—and slowly stands.

"Knew you'd get tired of that mommy pussy and come back," she says as she cups her breasts.

I almost roll my eyes, but I'm too fucking angry. I wrap my hand around her bicep and drag her behind me. I'm making a scene, I'm sure, but I don't give a fuck. I take her to our garage, where we house our bikes in the cold Idaho winters, and I throw her nasty ass on the concrete.

"Fury," she whines. I glare at her and she promptly shuts up.

"Where's my Old Lady?" I ask. She presses her lips together.

"How should I know?" she huffs.

I take my knife out of my side and bend down to her level. I watch her eyes widen and then she screams when I drag the top of the blade along her thigh. It's a good sized cut, but she'll survive.

"Wrong answer," I growl.

"Holy fuck, you're crazy," she whimpers. It doesn't affect me. She's a cold blooded, cold hearted *cunt*, and she deserves everything I'm going to give her.

I take the knife and slice her tit.

"Stupid bitch. I want my goddamned answers. I already know I'm fucking crazy," I roar in her face. She starts to cry.

"The Aryans and the *Bastards* are in it together," she blubbers.

"*Where is my Old Lady? Where's Kentlee?*" I scream in her face. I slice her other thigh and watch the blood drip down her leg.

"They told me they were taking her to a warehouse they rented just for this. They're going to get rid of your whole fucking club, you asshole. Then Kentlee's going to be Mark's whore. It's awesome. He even promised I could watch while he fucked her so hard he made her bleed. *I hate that dumb bitch*," Kitty screams. I can't hear another word. I wrap my fingers in her hair and I slice my blade across her neck. Blood goes fuckin' everywhere, but the bitch is quiet now, and fucking dead.

"Prez," Bull murmurs from behind me.

"She ain't gonna watch shit now, is she?" I say. He grins for a beat before he's on the phone with the brothers.

I turn around and lock eyes with Sniper. He's fucked this bitch more than once; he's also taken care of Kentlee when I couldn't.

"Good work, boss," he says with a wide smile. He looks fuckin' maniacal.

"I want to know where this warehouse is and I want to know now. If that crazy bastard thinks he's even going to lay a finger on my woman, or any member of my club, he's got another thing comin'."

"We find that fuckin' warehouse, I'm gonna pick off those motherfuckers one by one. Watch them drop like flies," he chuckles.

"Think Kitty knew where that warehouse was?" Bull asks looking down on Kitty as the blood drains from her lifeless body.

"She didn't know shit. No way those crazy fucks would

have told her any useful information. We need to find the rental contracts for those warehouses on the outskirts of town. Bet that's where they are," I order.

Finally, finally I see the light at the end of this long dark tunnel.

Kentlee

I sit in the little office waiting. I watch the men milling around through two large windows that give me the perfect view of these sick, *twisted* assholes. Bikers and skinheads alike. They seem to be separated by group, like they are in this *together*, but they aren't *working* together.

Nothing about this makes sense to me. Retribution, revenge, and money make sense, but killing Pierce and taking me doesn't make sense at all. I can't wrap my head around it.

"You look confused," Mark says as he walks back inside of the office, his cold gaze focused on me. He might be handsome, if he wasn't so fucking dead in the eyes and creepy.

"All of this is just because of that severed contract?" I ask, waving my hand around at the men who are talking and drinking.

"Pretty much. I'm a little dramatic, some might say." He grins, but it doesn't reach his eyes.

"Who told you about me?" I ask. He could have done this years ago; there's a reason this is happening now.

"A little whore named Kitty. *Man*, she really hates you," he laughs. My eyes widen—*that bitch.*

"And you promised her…" I let my words trail off and

Mark picks up where I left off.

"Oh, I didn't have to promise that bitch much. Just that I'd let her watch while I fucked you until you bled. She seemed happy enough with that, so she sang like a bird," he shrugs. I can't help the bile from rising in my mouth. *That nasty whore.*

"So what? You're partners with her?"

"Fuck no. I fucked her ass and sent her back to the *Notorious Devils* Club. She thinks she's helping me, but she'll die with the rest of them. I have no use for back stabbers. Women like that will sink ships," he mutters as he tucks some hair behind my ear.

The move is seemingly gentle, but I can see the depravity in his eyes.

The man is soulless.

"Yet, you're doing all this and you'll have a woman in your bed. What makes you think I'll be loyal?" I ask out of curiosity.

"You'll be loyal to me, don't you worry. If you aren't, I'll kill your son," he says with a shrug. I gasp as my hand flies over my mouth in shock.

"You wouldn't," I mutter, my lips trembling.

"What do I give a fuck about that kid? Of course, I'd kill him—so you better keep your ass in line, princess," he grunts before he slams the door, locking it again, leaving me alone with his words.

He'll kill him. He'd kill Bear. *Men like him are evil.* It's not enough to hurt me, but he would hold my innocent baby's life over my head? I close my eyes and I pray for Pierce to find me. Then I pray for something I never thought I would.

I pray that Pierce not only finds me, but also kills that sick son of a bitch.

303

I sit alone for what seems like hours, *happily*. I don't want to even *see* Mark, let alone talk to him again. He's a creep and he's scary.

I hear a loud bang and I stand up to look through the windows of the office. There is smoke everywhere, but then my eye catches something—or, rather, someone. A tall man with a messy man-bun and a black Notorious Devils cut—*Pierce*.

My heart literally skips a beat at the sight of him, but that is short lived. I feel a hand wrap around my throat from behind and then hot breath in my ear. I was so consumed with seeing him that I didn't hear the door being unlocked and opening again.

"You ain't home free yet, bitch," Mark says. His tone is so different from earlier, yet I recognize the voice as *his*.

I open my mouth to scream, but he squeezes my throat, blocking my oxygen until I relax my jaw. I am completely helpless as he drags me through the back of the warehouse. My ear is assaulted with the sounds of guns and screaming from where the men are fighting in front of us, but I can't see anything anymore.

Tears stream down my face because I know—I know that if he takes me out of this warehouse, that will be it for me. Pierce won't be able to track me down a second time, and there will be no breadcrumbs, no trails.

"That bitch betrayed me, just like I knew she would. I had hoped it would have been later, though," he murmurs as he continues to drag me away.

Once we are outside, I look around and see all of the bikes lined up, but no men.

This is it.

He's going to take me.

Rape me.

Torture me.

I close my eyes again and just accept my fate.

I wrap my hands around Mark's forearms and scratch as hard as I can while I simultaneously ram my heels into his shins. If I'm going down, I'm going down with a damn fight. If not for me, then for Bear.

"You bitch," he grunts. He turns me around and slaps me so hard that my body flies to the ground.

He then picks me up by my hair. It feels like it's being pulled out by the roots, and I try so hard not to scream, not to draw attention to myself. One man I could possibly overtake. More? No way.

"Fight me, you stupid bitch, and I won't be the only one fucking you when you get back to my club," he growls before he pulls me by my hair toward the unmarked vans in front of us.

I just hope that Pierce survives.

Those are my last thoughts before I feel myself falling and landing on Mark's body. His hold vanishes, and I quickly scramble to my feet. I look down to see a pool of blood forming underneath his head. There is a small round dot in the middle of his forehead, too.

I open my mouth to scream, but promptly close it. I can't draw attention to myself. I need to hide. I don't even want to think about who killed that asshole. I'm just glad he's dead. *Thank God for answered prayers*, I think as I look around for a place to hide.

I spot a stack of crates and make my way toward them as fast as I can. By the time I reach them, I've decided I need to take up running or something, because I am seriously out of shape. I huff and puff and try to catch my breath, but seriously, I need to start an exercise program. I huddle down and try to make myself as small as possible. I don't want anybody to find me.

"Where the fuck is she?" I hear Pierce roar.

I peek between the crates to see him holding a gun to the long-beard *Bastards* biker.

"Long gone, asshole," he grins.

I watch as Pierce presses the gun against his forehead and pulls the trigger. He doesn't even flinch. My eyes dart around, looking for anyone dangerous, but all I see are *Notorious Devils* cuts in the crowd. I let out a breath.

I stand from my hiding spot and step out, wiping my sweaty palms on my shorts before I begin to walk toward the group.

"That sick fuck was dragging her away. I shot him, but I didn't see where LeeLee went," Bates' voice rings out. I decide to just run.

I run toward Pierce.

He's standing with his hands on his hips, looking down, but Bates sees me and nudges him. When he looks up, my heart breaks. He looks devastated before complete surprise washes over his face. He opens his arms second before I leap into them. I wrap my legs around his waist and my arms around his neck as he takes a few steps back. Then I bury my face in his sweat soaked neck.

"Kentlee," he sighs, squeezing me tightly, his hands on my ass.

"I thought I was never going to see you again," I sob into his skin. He grunts as he holds me close.

"Let's get the fuck outta here," he murmurs to his men. I lift my head from his neck to look at Bates.

One night, about two years ago, Bates came home drunk off his ass and he admitted that he was a Sniper in the Marines. He killed so many people that he had lost count. He hated it. He hated the nightmares that came with it; hated the screams of the people who watched a man drop so suddenly. His nickname is Sniper, but he despises everything that was associated with it. He didn't want to pick people off from trees or rooftops anymore. He didn't want the nightmares. He wanted to be free. But he just killed a man. For me, he did it. He faced his demons—to save me.

I love him like I could love no other friend. He's my family, and now he's my savior and hero.

"*Thank you*," I mouth.

"*For you? Anything*," he mouths back before he smiles and walks off.

"Burn this place to the ground," Pierce calls out.

I hear a few people confirm before he sets me down and straddles his bike. Without a word, I crawl on behind him and wrap myself around his back. I hold onto his middle tightly as he takes me away from what could have been a deadly situation for us. Both of us and our love. I expect him to drive straight to the clubhouse, but he doesn't. Instead, he drives toward our home.

"We need showers before we get our boy," he mumbles. He turns the engine off on his bike and closes the garage door.

I follow him inside, in shock. I haven't stopped crying, but my tears are now silent ones that just steadily stream down my face. I'm not sad, I'm relieved; the tears are my adrenaline crashing and my relief taking over.

I follow Pierce into the house and into our bathroom. I watch him stoically as he strips his dirty, bloody clothes off and starts the shower. He turns to me and silently strips me of my own clothes before he takes my hands and leads me into the hot, steamy shower.

"I almost lost you," he says quietly as water streams over our bodies.

Neither of us are doing anything but staring at each other. It is as if we are frozen, afraid to move, afraid that one of us will suddenly disappear.

"I almost lost *you*," I repeat his words.

I almost lost him, but I was almost lost, as well.

"I was so scared," he admits. I watch tears fall from his eyes, now red-rimmed with his emotion.

"I was terrified," I admit before I throw my body against his.

"Never again. I'd kill them all again if I could, baby girl," he whispers into my neck. I feel his big hands on my thighs before he lifts my body up, pressing my back against the warm tiles.

"I need to feel you. I need to know you're here and you're safe," he murmurs as his lips brush mine.

"Take me, Pierce," I sigh, burying my hands in his long, wet hair.

Without a word, I feel his cock enter me in a slow, gentle move. His hands are on my hips and his eyes are focused on mine. He takes me slowly and carefully.

I can feel him, every single inch of him, as he glides in and out of my hot core.

We say nothing more, my gasps and his low grunts the only noises filling the room. When his lips touch mine, I sigh.

This isn't fucking to feel alive, this is cherishing each other because we survived. One wrong move and one of us, or both of us, could have died today.

I wrench my lips away from his when I feel my pussy begin to pulse, right before I come. I moan as my eyes flutter closed, but Pierce doesn't stop; he continues to slowly fuck me with precision and a rhythm that is perfectly wicked. His lips touch my neck as his fingers squeeze my ass even harder. I feel the vibration of his moan in my neck before I hear it; then he fills my body with his release.

"Thank fuck I got you back, baby girl. I would die without you," he mutters as his lips trail down my neck and then back up and over to my lips.

"I wouldn't have survived without you either, Pierce. Without you and without our Bear," I murmur. He grins for a split second before he releases me.

We spend the next few minutes washing all of the blood and dirt off of our bodies and out of our hair. Once we are finished, we dress and walk down to Tammy's house to get our boy. I can't wait another second to have him back in my arms.

"I know why you went with them quietly," Pierce says as we approach Tammy's.

"For Bear," I say, surely confirming his suspicions.

"Thank you, baby girl. Thank you for protecting him when I couldn't," he says. I see the pain clearly etched in his features.

"You cannot be with us twenty-four hours a day, Pierce. This shit happens. It could happen even if you weren't the *Notorious Devils'* president," I say, cupping his cheek.

"Yeah, but fact remains it happened *because* I'm the *Notorious Devils'* president. You'll always be a target," he says. I nod.

"I may always be a target, Pierce, but it's not worth being unhappy and lonely. I'll take whatever life hands me as long as you're at my side."

Fury

"I may always be a target, Pierce, but it's not worth being unhappy and lonely. I'll take whatever life hands me as long as you're at my side."

Kentlee's words ring in my head long after she says them. I'm lying in bed, hours after we've picked up Bear and spent time just loving each other, loving our family. I've sated my woman, hopefully exhausting her to the point where she won't have a nightmare about her fucking horrific day. Yet, I can't shut my brain off.

I slip out of bed, grabbing my phone and my jeans before I pull them on and go outside on the front porch.

"Can't sleep," the voice says on the other end.

"No, Pops, I can't," I admit.

I can hear a party in the background, but I don't care that I've interrupted him. There's some shuffling around and the music fades into the background.

"She's safe, they're safe." He confirms what my head knows, but I can't shake this feeling. This feeling that I've brought her into this shit and I should let her live a free life.

"How'd you do it?" I ask.

"Do what?" he sounds confused.

I forgot that he doesn't know what's been rattling around

in my head all night.

"Put mom in danger like you did by making her an Old Lady? How did you knowingly make her a target?"

"It's selfish of us, isn't it?" he asks. I grunt my agreement. "I did it partly because I'm a selfish prick and I wanted her; but that wasn't the only reason. I tried to keep her away from me when I knew she was going to be a target, when I knew I truly cared for her and she could be someone an enemy could hold over my head. She wouldn't accept it, though. She told me if I truly loved her, then I would do everything in my power to make her happy. Then she laid it on me, told me that she couldn't be happy unless she was mine. Fucked up, right?" he chuckles. I want to agree, but I could see Kentlee saying the same damn thing.

"You made her happy, though," I point out. He chuckles.

"Busted my ass to make her happy, son. Doesn't mean I didn't fuck up a lot – because I did. But I tried my damnedest to make sure she didn't regret one minute at my side. I already told you if I could do it all over again, I'd have given her more kids and been home more; but that doesn't mean that I didn't give her all that I had to give at the time. I did. I gave her everything—my heart included," he says.

"Okay," I whisper into the dark.

"Don't push all that beauty and love you have away, Pierce. Hold onto it with both hands," he says quietly before he ends the call. I set the phone down on the banister before I feel two slim arms wrap around my waist.

"What are you doin' up?" I ask, turning around and leaning my ass against the wood, pulling Kentlee into my arms. She's wearing one of my t-shirts and it looks sexy as fuck on her.

311

"Rolled over and the bed was empty," she shrugs. I place my finger beneath her chin, lifting her head so that our eyes can meet.

"Truth?" I ask, searching her pretty eyes.

"I felt you get up. I was sleeping, but restlessly. I followed you out a few minutes after you left the bed," she says. I know she heard my side of the conversation with my dad.

"I love you, baby girl, you know that?" I watch as she bites her bottom lip.

"But you're leaving us?" she asks.

It fucking kills me. I slide my hand around to cradle the back of her neck before I place a closed mouth kiss on her puffy lips.

"Never. I'm never leaving you, sugar. I love you *so* much," I admit as I press my forehead to hers.

"It sounded like you wanted to leave," she whispers. I hate that I have made her feel this way, this uncertain.

"I've shared how it scares me that you're my weakness, that people will use you to get to me. It happened, and it was terrifying. But neither of us would survive being separated. I couldn't imagine my life without you and Bear in it. I don't even want to think about it. So, no, I don't want to leave, and I'm not going to," I say. She wraps her arms around me a bit tighter, holding me before she whispers into the night.

"I was so lost when you were away and when I thought you didn't want us. I never want to feel like that again, Pierce. You're my rock. You're my heart. You're all rough and rowdy, and I love that about you. I love everything about you, but I want you to be as happy as I am."

"I'm happy. I'm so fuckin' happy, it aches inside, baby girl," I say before I bend down and take her mouth with mine.

I kiss her—my lover, my woman, my friend, and the woman who rests her heart in the palm of my hand.

The woman who's turned me into a complete pussy.

I can't give a fuck about it. There's absolutely nothing I would change about us.

I pick up my phone and then my girl and carry them both inside.

I spend the rest of the night telling and showing Kentlee how much I love and need her in my life. I wasn't living until she strutted that fine ass of hers in front of me on Main Street. I was going through the motions in life—*fucking, fighting and surviving*—but I wasn't living until I had something to fuckin' *live* for.

My woman.

My son.

My family.

epilogue

Six months later

Kentlee

"The zipper isn't going to go up," Rosie says from behind me as she tugs on the zipper of my wedding gown.

Today is my wedding day. I'm going to officially be *Mrs. Pierce Duhart;* though, I've been Fury's Old Lady for months now, a title that makes me as good as a wife with his brothers and other outlaw bikers.

My script tattoo of his name on my hip permanently marks me as his in his world. I want his name, though; and I want to easily change Bear's last name to Pierce's.

But I can't do any of that if my dress doesn't fit.

"I just tried it on last week and it was fine," I grind out as

I hold the sides of the dress back so that Rosie can pull the zipper up.

"Bitch, you're knocked up. How did you not give yourself some leeway?" she asks.

I grin, thinking about the baby Pierce and I are going to welcome into the world in another six months.

"I figured a week was fine. It fit like a glove last week," I grumble. She curses as she finally yanks the zipper up.

It's tight.

I let out a shaky breath and look at myself in the mirror. The dress is a blush color—because white was just ridiculous—and it has a sweetheart neckline, the bodice tight all the way to my knees, where it flares just a bit. It's mermaid style that hugs every single curve I have, which is more than I had six months ago.

Pierce has been feeding me, trying to get me to gain weight. Apparently, he missed the body I sported when we met. *Tits and ass* is what he missed, but he claims he just wants me to be healthy and I looked hungry. I smile as I slide my feet into my pale blue high heels.

My dreams come true today. Completely and totally fulfilled.

"Did your brother make it?" Rosie asks hesitantly. I shake my head.

My brother has been more and more distant lately. I don't know if it's because I accepted Pierce back into my life so easily, or if it's because he's tired of the family drama and the shit he gets from our parents by keeping our lines of communication open.

I asked him to walk me down the aisle about four months ago, and he told me he would let me know. I haven't heard from him since, and I am letting things lie. I love Connellee, but I'm not going to push him. If I did, then I would be no better than my parents. I'm not happy with him, though; in fact, I'm angry. I'm angry at him for being verbally supportive and then just disappearing.

"I'm sure he's busy being a fancy doctor," I say, trying to hold back my tears.

I'm an emotional mess with the pregnancy, not to mention my family and a wedding on top of it.

"You have all of us, though, so you're good," Rosie says with a grin before she wraps me in a hug.

Rosie and I have become extremely close since my abduction. We spend several days a week together with our children, just enjoy each other's company. She doesn't have contact with her family either, so it's a way for us to bond. We've become each other's support system.

"You ready?" she asks as she gathers her purse and slips on her own shoes.

"I am," I say with a nod. And I am. I am so ready. I am so excited to be Mrs. Pierce Duhart, I can hardly breathe.

Our wedding isn't a huge affair. The only guests are the club members and their Old Ladies or girlfriends. Pierce's father, Max, and his men came, as well. There are only about seventy guests, and the only people *I* invited were my neighbor, Tammy, and Candy from the club. That's okay, though. I don't mind. This group of men, and a few women, truly are my family now. Tammy knocks on the door to the bedroom, where I am getting dressed, and ushers Bear inside.

"You look lovely," she whispers as she wraps her arms around me.

I thank her before she leaves and then I look at my little

man. He's wearing a mini suit and he looks adorable.

"Are you ready?" I ask him. He nods, shifting from foot to foot.

When my brother didn't return my phone call, I decided that I would have Bear walk me down the aisle to his daddy. It seemed fitting. We are finally becoming a family, legally, and in the eyes of God.

When I said this to Pierce, he rolled his eyes and told me we were already a family. I know that we are, that we're a perfect family, but I want to be one in all aspects, not just in our hearts. So this wedding, it's important to me.

I let Pierce pick the venue, and I prayed that it wouldn't be a bar. I really did think that he would make it at the clubhouse, but he surprised me. *Shocked me, really*.

Our wedding is at an old barn out in the country. The barn is rustic and beautiful. Inside, there's a dance floor, along with a bar, and old lighting across the big beams that hold it together. Outside, there are chairs set up, making an aisle and tables off to the side for dinner. It's quiet and peaceful and breathtaking. I love that he truly thought of me while picking the venue.

I take Bear's hand and together we walk out of the old farm house and toward Pierce. I almost made Pierce wear a suit, and I'm sure he would have had I asked, but I wouldn't ask that of him. That's simply not his style.

He's standing at the end of the aisle, waiting for us; his hair in my favorite man-bun style, with his beard covered cheeks and chin. He's wearing dark black pants that I picked out, along with his black riding boots and a crisp, black, button up shirt. His cut is firmly in place and he looks so rugged and so tough, yet so incredibly gorgeous and handsome all rolled into one.

Once Bear and I make our way down the aisle, he runs over to Rosie, who is in the front row with her daughter.

I take Pierce's offered hands and we begin our ceremony.

Fury

Kentlee has been mine since the moment I saw her, but today, she's officially mine – *legally*.

I look around at all of our friends dancing, laughing, and drinking. *This is the life.* Our friends and family, celebrating our newest milestone. I watch as Kentlee kisses Bear good-night and Tammy takes him away.

It's getting late, and the kids are all leaving. I wish I were leaving too, so that I could start in on fucking my wife for the entire night; but it's a party, and she's having a good time, so I won't make her leave just yet.

I watch as she walks my way. Her dress is so fuckin' beautiful on her, showcasing those curves I've been working over-time to add to her small frame. Then of course, that sweet little baby bump she's suddenly sporting. I would be lying if I said that bump wasn't the best thing about her body right now. I never saw her grow with Bear, so I'm enjoying every-thing about it this time.

Honestly, I can't wait to knock her up again.

She's just so fuckin' breathtaking when she's pregnant.

"Hey, husband," she whispers as she sits down on my thigh.

"Baby girl," I murmur against her neck as I slide her hair

over to bare her shoulder.

"Today was perfect. Thank you so much," she sighs, leaning back against my chest. I wrap my palm around her stomach, feeling that life I created.

"You're perfect," I murmur. She giggles slightly before she turns her head and places a soft kiss against my jaw.

"Take me away and fuck me until I pass out," she whispers in my ear.

My cock goes rock hard in an instant. Kentlee's always enjoyed the way I fuck her, but *sweet Christ*, she's been unbelievably horny since getting knocked up. I fuckin' love the shit that flies out of her mouth.

"Yeah? I'm gonna eat that pussy until you scream," I mutter against her skin. I feel her squirm in my lap.

"Please, Pierce, I need you," she whimpers.

I know it's time to go.

I pick her up and yell goodbye to all of our guests, who hoot and holler as I carry my bride away.

I buckle her safely in the car and I *drive*. I wanted to take her somewhere nice for our honeymoon, but she refused. Said that she didn't want to go on vacation when she was pregnant and likely to get sick. So Tammy is watching Bear over the weekend while we hole up in a cabin, just twenty miles outside of town on a lake. I stocked everything this morning and it's waiting for us.

I'm on my way to make love to my wife.

Not my Old Lady or my woman, but my *wife*.

It's surreal and fantastic all at once.

"C'mon," I say as I lift her from the passenger seat of the car and carry her into the cabin.

"It's perfect, Pierce." She sighs when she sees the fire has been lit and the bed turned down in this little one-bedroom place away from the rest of the world. Our own little piece of solitude for a few days.

"You're perfect," I say, repeating my words from earlier. She is, and she will always be perfect *for* me and perfect *to* me.

"Fuck your wife, Pierce," she whispers.

I drop her to her feet and press my lips to hers.

I'm going to fuck her, *yeah*, but first I'm going to make love to her soft and gentle.

Then, I'm going to make her scream my name.

ROUGH & RAW
Notorious Devils MC Book 2

prologue

Brentlee

I made sure the bathroom door was locked.

Not that a lock would stop Scotty from breaking the door down. *He'd done it before.* For a man who was slim and worked behind a desk all day long, he had some serious strength.

I sat down on the closed toilet seat pressing my hands to my face. It had happened again. I had lost count of how many times Scotty had slapped me, punched me, kicked me, or raped me.

My entire relationship was a farce.

I hated him, but I had married him because my parents encouraged it. They loved that I had married a man with a fantastic career. My father scowled when he saw the yellowing bruises on my face but, never said a word. My mother pretended to be oblivious to the hell that I lived in.

I let my mind drift back in time, not for the first time, to the one and only man that I loved.

Bates Lukin.

I fell for Bates when I was just fourteen years old. He was the older bad boy and I loved everything about him—the thrill and the danger that surrounded him. I pursued him, *relentlessly,* and eventually he took notice. We spent one year together before he went away to Marine boot camp.

One beautiful year where I gave him everything—my love and my virginity.

"I won't ask you to wait for me, Brent. I know you're still enjoying high school and you deserve to have fun," Bates murmurs as he cups his hand around my cheek. I wrap my fingers around his wrist, holding onto him.

"But I love you," I say, my voice trembling with emotion.

"I don't doubt that, Brent. I love you, too; but I'm not coming back here. I have no clue where they'll send me, but I don't want to be anywhere near my father. You need to have fun in high school. Sitting around alone on Friday nights isn't your style. I wouldn't ask you to do that for me," he says as his dark eyes roam over my face, taking me in, memorizing me for quite possibly the last time – ever.

"I can stay faithful. Do you think you won't be able to?" I ask challengingly—angrily.

"For you, I could do anything, Brent. For you, I would do anything. But you're young and I can't hold you back like that," he sighs, pressing his forehead to mine.

"You're breaking my heart, Bates," I whisper, unable to hold the tears at bay.

"I know. At least you have a heart. I gave mine to you," he murmurs, running his nose along mine and pressing a closed mouth kiss against my lips.

"You can't have it back. I'll be waiting for you," I cry.

My fifteen-year-old heart was shattered the day Bates left for boot camp. *I would have waited for him.* I would have waited a lifetime. Months went by without news from him.

I would beg his sister, Mary-Anne, for any information she had.

At first, she obliged, sharing letters he sent to her. Then suddenly, she stopped. I knew he had told her to let me move on. He was *forcing* me to move on.

In my anger toward Bates, I turned into someone I didn't recognize.

I began drinking and became promiscuous. That lasted for about three years. Until my best friend's brother came back from law school. He saw me as a woman, and he wanted me.

Scotty and I were engaged mere months after we started dating, and our marriage was rushed. I was nineteen and he was just beginning his career. We were going to be the perfect couple. The *perfection* lasted until our honeymoon. The truth crashed through my little bubble with a vengeance. It was the first night he hit me. I had embarrassed him because I drank too much at our reception.

I was a stupid whore, a slut, and I was lucky he took pity on me and married me.

I *felt* stupid at that time. I *felt* stupid for falling for all of his shit. For not listening to my sister, Kentlee, when she tried to advise me to steer clear of the man. He didn't need to point out that I had been slutty. I owned that slut inside of me, but I wasn't that girl anymore. I was a wife, completely ready to devote my life to my new husband.

I had resigned myself to the hell I had made for myself. That was until I saw Kentlee with her new man in the grocery store three years later. I was eight months pregnant and had just survived another brutal attack by my *adoring* husband.

I didn't lie to myself; I didn't believe anything he said

when he apologized to me profusely every time he beat the shit out of me—but I was scared. Kentlee looked happy and her man, *looked* like a scary monster. Yet, when his eyes landed on my sister, I watched them soften before my own.

"Get your no good whore ass out here," my husband bellows from the other side of the bathroom door.

I suck in a breath and grasp the handle of the door, opening it to face my hell, my husband.

Bates - Sniper

I laid in the dark alone.

I hated sleeping alone.

The nightmares would always return.

Nightmares about the months I spent in the scorching dry desert while I was in the Marines, followed by my self-created nightmares about leaving the only girl I have ever loved – *Brentlee Johnson*.

Fifteen was too young for me to tie her down. She deserved to experience life, and by the time I found my way back to her, it was too late. She was engaged. I watched her from a distance, angry at the way her demeanor changed after her marriage, knowing exactly *why* it had changed. My father abused my mother my entire life. She refused to leave him and I watched as he hurt her, hurt me, and hurt my sister – *repeatedly*.

I kick the sheets off and find my pants, pulling them up my legs, not bothering to button them. I won't be wearing them long. Living in the clubhouse has its perks. *Pussy available twenty-four-seven.* I need something to exhaust me for a few hours. I won't fool myself into thinking I'll get a full night's sleep, but a couple hours would be nice, *at least.*

I walk into the room where the club whores hang out and sleep, noticing it's pretty empty, except for a sweet young thing that showed up a few weeks ago. I don't pretend to know her name. I'll never use it, and I'll never need it. She has long brown hair and brown eyes. Her body is thin, but curvy. She could look like Brentlee—*if I squinted, and was drunk and high.* I lift my chin toward her and hold out my hand. She quickly comes my way, wearing a bra and a pair of short shorts with platform flip flops.

"What do you want?" she asks in a little girl voice once we get inside of my room.

I hate that shit.

I guess it's supposed to make chicks sound sexy, but I can't stand it. Brentlee had a low rasp to her voice. With one word, my cock would be hard as nails – *every time.*

"You don't talk," I grit out through my clenched jaw. "Get on your knees and suck my cock," I order.

I smirk when she does as I say. I watch her sink to her knees before she shoves my jeans down with her little hands. Then she slides her hot mouth over me. She sucks me like a goddamned pro and it feels good.

I wrap my hands in her hair and hold her still before I start to fuck her mouth. I want to come, but not like this. I need to fuck, or I won't be able to sleep. I pull out of her mouth and order her to strip. She does it slowly and seductively, but I couldn't give a fuck. She's skinny with fake tits. I prefer long and lean.

I prefer Brentlee.

The girls doesn't even ask how I want her. She crawls to

the center of my bed – head down, ass up. I slide on a condom before I grab her bony as fuck hips and slam my cock inside of her. She's only a little wet and she cries out at first, but I don't stop. She's here to take my cock. I don't have to do fuck *for* her.

"You want to come, you'll have to make yourself," I say, sounding bored, because I am. This bitch is just taking it, making screeching noises that are fake as shit.

Once she starts touching her clit, her voice goes a bit deeper and I feel her shudder underneath me as her pussy starts to swell around my cock. *I close my eyes and imagine its Brentlee.* It's been almost eight years since I've been in her pussy, but I'll never forget the way it felt. Nothing else could compare. I start to pound her harder. I know I'm going to bruise her up, but I can't find a fuck to give as I feel my nuts tighten and then finally—*I come.*

I don't stay inside of her even a second after my release.

I pull out and yank the condom off of my cock, tying a knot in it and throwing it in the trash can.

"Gonna hit the can. Get gone," I bark as I wait for her to go.

I watch as she quickly dresses. Her face is bright red with embarrassment but she doesn't say a word. She slips past me and quickly heads down the hall. She knows her place and doesn't call me a dick, like she should. Some guys treat the bitches like queens here. Fuck them, eat them out, cuddle them and pretend they only have eyes for them for the night. I'm not one of those guys. They're here to offer a service. A service I fully intent to take advantage of. In exchange they get free food, a free place to live, and a little spending money. Fair trade for spreading their thighs. I'm not looking to make any of these whores my wife—ever.

I walk down the hall and use the can. After I wash my hands I take a look at myself in the mirror. I look fuckin' ancient. I've seen too much—done too much. I leave and go back to my room. Ignoring the clawing feeling I have inside of me, trying to get out, the one that wants me to go to *her*. I climb back into bed and I close my eyes. Sleep finally takes over, but it isn't dreamless.

It's full of Brentlee.

"I love you so much, Bates," she says, kissing my neck down my chest and just above my jeans.

Fuck, I feel like I'm going to blow my load right here and now.

"Love you too, baby," I whisper, trying and praying that I can hold it together for a few more minutes.

"I want to suck you," she murmurs as she begins to unzip my pants. I swear to Christ; my prayers are answered in this second.

I wake with a sweat, remembering the first time Brentlee took me in her mouth. I embarrassed myself, coming within seconds, but she took it all. Then she smiled as I wrapped her in my arms. Brentlee wasn't my first lay, but she was the best.

Even now, a *decade* later nobody can compare.

I told her once that I didn't have a heart because I gave it to her.

She still owns it all these years later.

Always has and always will.

also by
HAYLEY FAIMAN

MEN OF BASEBALL SERIES—
Pitching for Amalie
Catching Maggie
Forced Play for Libby
Sweet Spot for Victoria

RUSSIAN BRATVA SERIES—
Owned by the Badman
Seducing the Badman (April 2016)
Dancing for the Badman (Fall 2016)
Living for the Badman (2017)
Protected by the Badman (2017)

NOTORIOUS DEVILS MC—
Rough & Rowdy
Rough & Raw (Summer 2016)
Rough & Rugged (2017)
Rough & Real (2017)

Follow me on social media to stay current on the happenings in my little book world.

Facebook: www.facebook.com/authorhayleyfaiman

Goodreads: www.goodreads.com/author/show/10735805.
Hayley_Faiman

about the author

As an only child, Hayley Faiman had to entertain herself somehow. She started writing stories at the age of six and never really stopped.

Born in California, she met her now husband at the age of sixteen and married him at the age of twenty in 2004. After sixteen years together, he's still the love of her life. Hayley's husband joined the military and they lived in Oregon, where he was stationed with the US Coast Guard, before they moved back to California in 2006, where they had two little boys. Recently, the four of them moved out to Hill Country in Texas, where they adopted a new family member, a chocolate lab named Optimus Prime.

Most of Hayley's days are spent taking care of her two boys, going to the baseball fields for practice, or helping them with homework. Her evenings are spent with her husband and her nights - those are spent creating alpha book boyfriends.

acknowledgments

My Husband —My very own Rough & Rowdy man. The man whose endless support is unwavering. What would I do without you by my side and my biggest cheerleader and my best friend? Thank you babes. Always.

My mom— How do I thank the woman who is everything? The words THANK YOU are not enough. Ever. I appreciate the way you love me, and the support you've always given me.

Rosalyn—It's all been said before, and we'll say it again. God placed us in each other's path for a reason and what a beautiful thing it has become! What would I do without you? You keep me sane, talk me down from that ledge about a million times a day… and you made this book more than I could imagine it to be. THANK YOU!!

Nisha — My sister from another mister. Thank you for always being my friend. For always being around to chat when I need you. And for all those seriously inappropriate restaurant conversations and all the laughs!

Cassandra Searby— My boo! What would I do without our daily texts? I would probably go insane! Thank you for always being there, day in and day out! You're such an inspiration!

Cassy Roop— You always make my vision come to life, every time! Thank you for the gorgeous cover —AGAIN!

Stacey Blake— Your work is gorgeous from front to back. Thank you for always making my books so beautiful. I appreciate all of your hard work and dedication. You're truly a treasure and I'm lucky to have found you! You're seriously the best!!

Enticing Journey— Ena and Amanda— THANK YOU! Every single book that's released I have full faith that things will go swimmingly because of you two! I never feel apprehension leaving my babies in your capable hands. Thank you for all of your hard work. You are truly appreciated.